# The Horizontal Man

by HELEN EUSTIS

PENGUIN BOOKS

*To Jonah*

Penguin Books Ltd, Harmondsworth,
Middlesex, England
Penguin Books, 625 Madison Avenue,
New York, New York 10022, U.S.A.
Penguin Books Australia Ltd, Ringwood,
Victoria, Australia
Penguin Books Canada Limited, 2801 John Street,
Markham, Ontario, Canada L3R 1B4
Penguin Books (N.Z.) Ltd, 182–190 Wairau Road,
Auckland 10, New Zealand

First published in the United States of America by
Harper & Row, Publishers, Inc., 1946
First published in Great Britain by Hamish Hamilton 1947
Published in Penguin Books in Great Britain 1949
Published in Penguin Books in the United States of America 1982

LIBRARY OF CONGRESS CATALOGING IN PUBLICATION DATA
Eustis, Helen.
The horizontal man.
Reprint. Originally published: New York:
Harper & Row, 1946.
I. Title.
PS3509.U66H6 1982    813'.54    81-17933
ISBN 0 14 00.0718 0         AACR2

Printed in the United States of America by
George Banta Co., Inc., Harrisonburg, Virginia
Set in Baskerville

# THE HORIZONTAL MAN

## Chapter 1

THE firelight played over all the decent familiar objects of his everyday life; he viewed them desperately, looking for some symbol of succour. The firelight played on his rolling eyeballs, the careless tendrils of his black hair. 'Oh now,' he said, 'Oh now, I say, look here ...' trying to summon a tone of commonplace to breast the tide of nightmare that was rising in that room. But his voice came out of his throat piping with fear. Outside, the college clock tolled the half hour, measured, reassuring. He blessed the bells. After all, it was not nightmare. The telephone could ring, a knock could sound at the door, and the terror would be broken. He cleared his throat and began again. 'I say,' he said, almost tenderly, 'you're not well, you know. Do let me take you home.'

But it was no use. 'No!' she cried, loud and harsh – and it gave him hope that someone might hear that voice – 'I'm not sick! At last I am well, at last I can tell you, Kevin! My God, do you know that it is like water running down my dry throat to say that I love you?'

His hand gripped the mantel; slowly, and – he hoped – imperceptibly, he began to edge toward the door. But her eye saw everything; she took a step toward him. 'You can't stop me!' she triumphed. '*He* can't stop me! I'm free at last for once and all, and I tell you I will have you, Kevin; we can be together at last, rid of him!'

He was beginning to shake; another moment and he would be weeping with terror, he thought. No man was meant to witness this and live; it was a scene from hell; it was, of course, complete madness. It is madness, he said to himself, gripping the mantel to keep his hand from shaking, it is simply madness and insanity; it is foolish to fear it; you're behaving with the superstition of the Middle Ages. Be calm. Humour it. Outwit it. He took another cautious step toward the door. 'Look, my dear,' he said, trying firmness, essaying a smile which only, he was afraid, writhed on his face, 'truly you must go home and lie down. I'm going to run out and get you a cab now – there's sure to be one at the corner – and I'm going to take you home and put you to bed.'

But then he could bear it no longer, he turned his face from that figure, that indecent obscenity, he turned with the intention of walking calmly toward the door, but instead, met his death when the poker crashed, with a lightning upward blow, against the base of his skull.

## Chapter 2

THE dusk was coming down; the yellow lights filling the square windows around the quadrangle of dormitories. All day long she had knelt here on the window seat, her door locked, weeping, shaking, falling asleep of exhaustion, weeping again. Had a knock sounded on her door? It seemed many had, and many footsteps passed. How they would love to tear back the walls, expose her misery, point at her, stare at her wounds, secure in their smugness! She would let no one in. This was the moment of most terrible isolation of her life – to share it with anyone would be sacrilege. To whom could she speak here, to whom could she mourn? Only himself, and he was dead, her beautiful darling gone.

'Oh my dear!' she said, 'My darling!' and laying her head down on her forearms, wept again.

The quadrangle dripped and glistened under the sodden sky, the weeping, mourning sky. The trees shone wetly, the pavements reflected. There on the asphalt, four stories below, lay death – the short moment of terror, then peace. If only she had the courage to die! I hate you, Molly Morrison, she cried to herself, sobbing, I hate you!

If she had had courage – yesterday, the day before, last month – she would have run to him saying, I love you! I will black your boots, mend your clothes – anything! I love you! If yesterday were back again, how she would run to him, throw herself upon him, thrust herself between him and that bloody, importunate death! But there is no turning time; inexorably it moves from under you – what you were yesterday is fixed for always, making its mark on what you are today, what you will be to-morrow. What you are is a coward, Molly Morrison, she told herself in the deepest contempt of despair.

Good for words and weeping, that was all. How do you expect to be an artist, to speak your dearest thoughts in paint and line when you cannot even tell your love? Only the scribblings and scratchings, the horrible papers and note-books full of ... what could only disgust her now. Thank God it was gone and out of her sight, could no longer stare her in the face and confront her with that unbelievably infamous part of herself. The treachery of the written word!

All day, in spite of her grieving and moaning, a terrible

dreary sanity, like the dreary light of the November day, had held her in its grip; now, gratefully, she felt a gentle madness descending with the dusk. 'Do you remember,' she said conversationally, lifting her head from her arms, 'do you remember yesterday?'

'Yes, Molly,' he answered, in his sweet judicious voice, almost there before her, almost sitting in her own wicker chair with his long legs crossed before him. 'I remember.'

The black curls clenched on his forehead by the dampness, the pipe gripped in the corner of his mouth, he had sat in a booth in The Coffee Shoppe, a cup of cooling coffee before him, talking to Mrs Cramm. After its first leap at the sight of him, her heart had sunk to see those broad yet somehow ultimately female shoulders, that flaming, smoothly coiffed head in its molten braids, blocking him off from the rest of the world, precluding the possibility of herself, only a student, invading his grown-up faculty life; preventing her from approaching, asking breathlessly, Is this seat taken? May I sit there? The seat was taken – taken like a besieged city, to be sure, by Mrs Cramm's broad possessive buttocks. 'Darling!' said Mrs Cramm in her loud theatrical voice, meaning nothing by the endearment but her assertion of possession. Molly had sat in an empty booth where she could watch them, and had sunk her head over her books. 'Darling!' Mrs Cramm's voice rang out over the bleating of the juke box, over the chatter of the girls, turning the word like a knife in Molly's heart.

Bending her head over her *Outline of Modern European History*, she had envisaged a conversation with him. 'Do you think,' she would be saying to him, in a frank, curious sort of way (revealing nothing), 'do you think Mrs Cramm is –' not beautiful. Other people did not use that word as she had heard it used at home. Attractive. That was what they said – and perhaps it was more expressive after all. 'Do you think Mrs Cramm is *attractive*?' He cocked his head, maybe, and thought. 'I find her,' Molly pursued (but only in cowardice, only in imagination) 'rather *overwhelming*.' And then his head tipped back, he laughed and laughed, for overwhelming was surely the thing that Mrs Cramm was. She was like something blown up to twice its size. Like a child as big as an adult. Like a black cherry the size of an apple. Overwhelming. 'Darling!' rang out again, disrupting Molly's dream. How little that word must mean to her that she threw it out so lightly!

Then it was ten minutes to three, as she had known it must be at last, and time to leave the warm noisy coffee shop to go to her class. Sighing, she rose, gathered her books in her arm, and took her check to the cash register. But, like a miracle, suddenly he was beside her. 'Where are you going, Molly?' he said, laying his coin down beside hers. The cash register bell rang dizzily in her ears. 'To Raleigh,' she said faintly. 'Then I'll walk along with you,' he said, and held the door open for her, while Mrs Cramm sat deserted in the booth, swilling coffee.

He was a beautiful, sloppy, gaunt figure, standing up hatless in the mizzling rain, his lean black Modigliani head at the one end, his long, lean, shambling legs sticking too far out of his raincoat at the other. And she beside him, feeling half his size, clasping her books like their new baby to her breast, flushing and perspiring a little in the dampness. In silence they paced the walk beside the row of shops; when they came to the cross walk he looked down at her suddenly. 'Molly,' he said, 'you look pretty. What is it – a new sweater?'

9

She smiled at him, and blushed too, yet inside her spread a certain sadness. If he had thought of her as a woman he would never have spoken this way. It was only because he felt immune to her, because she was a student and no more, that he could speak so personally, with such ease. She shook her head no, still smiling, still blushing.

'No?' he said in mock surprise. 'Then where have my eyes been when you've worn it before? What colour would you say it was – a sort of actomaroon?'

Please don't talk baby talk to me, she wanted to say, it is positively insulting. For I am not a baby; I am very young, I am awkward, I know, but still I am a woman – don't you understand? What I want is to be your wife, your mistress, for all that I wear socks and sweaters like the rest of them; for all I talk of nothing but my midterm paper. Don't you see how it makes me feel to appear before you in this guise? It makes me feel like Cinderella, long, long before the ball. If I could say Darling as easily as Mrs Cramm ... But all she could say was, 'Well, some sort of a maroon, I guess.'

It was the hour when classes were changing, when students on foot and on bicycles streamed over the asphalt walks of the campus, and girls passing them spoke to him, said, 'Hello, Mr Boyle,' from time to time. They passed Mr Hungerford, who taught Shakespeare, wearing his white grieved face. 'Boyle,' he said, raising his hand in salute. 'See you later,' and walked on. Yet suddenly he turned to her as if they were in utter privacy, with his brows knitted, and said, 'Molly, have you a family?'

'Oh,' she said, surprised, 'why, yes.'

'Well,' he went on, 'do you like them?'

And all inside her, warm and good, she flushed, because this was a truly personal question, the kind you asked of someone you cared for. This meant – she must think it over in private, but already she could be almost sure – it meant he cared for her; even if never in the world could he be her lover, already he was her friend. 'No,' she said honestly, 'I can't say that I do. My father is a great man, but – '

'But you don't get along with your mother?' he laughed at her.

She frowned, wanting to say more, but it was he who spoke as they passed under the bare, dripping elms. 'Molly, I'm sorry to say that you're going to fail my course if something doesn't happen soon.'

She bowed her head; she should have known it would be this. Half the papers missing, and in the ones he had, only half what she meant said. How was she ever to say what she meant, when all she seemed to mean was, I love you, Kevin Boyle – meaning no disrespect, but it would sound so silly to say, I love you, Mr Boyle. And what she meant he must never see in any case, what she meant was to be secretly disposed of, reams and heaps of it, scribbled and scratched to her grinding shame, thrust from her sight lest it meet her eyes by accident, that evidence of her own madness ...

'I'm sorry,' she mumbled. 'I don't seem to be very bright.'

'That's nonsense,' he said sharply, 'and you know it, Molly. I don't know what's wrong with you, but I suspect you're upset about something.'

'Oh,' she said chokingly, lying in her teeth, 'oh, no!'

'Don't tell me no, like the little liar that you are,' he said, stopping by the walk that turned off to the Library. 'Come and see me one day and let us talk over the papers and whatever it is that's making you unhappy. When could you come? Tomorrow at four?'

Dumbly she nodded her head over and over until she could regain her voice; standing in the rain nodding and nodding like a foolish little Shetland pony with her bang falling into her eyes. 'Oh, yes,' she said finally, 'that would be fine, Mr Boyle.'

'Good,' he said; 'then to-morrow at four in my office. Good-bye, Molly.' He raised his hand and was off toward the Library, while she stumbled on toward Raleigh Hall, where her next class was. 'Good-bye, my darling!' she said, whispering it under her breath. If she had shouted it! If she had cried it to the housetops! Could it be that he might have turned, might have taken some different crossroad of his destiny which would have led him away from brutal, violent death? 'Good-bye, my darling,' she said now, aloud, to the blue November dusk, and flowed away on another torrent of tears.

Slowly, louder and louder in her ears, a sound made itself known beyond the sound of her own crying. Someone was knocking at the door. 'Molly,' a voice called, 'Molly, dear, please open the door! It's Miss Sanders.'

She did not, could not answer, but she held back her sobs and listened. Outside the door she could hear a colloquy carried on in low murmurs. She heard the words, ' ... all day ... ' and ' ... door's locked ... ' and ' ... doctor ...'

At this she caught her breath and went to her bureau. Feeling about in the darkness, she found a clean hand-kerchief, wiped her eyes and nose. 'Miss Sanders,' she called out in a harsh voice that did not sound like her own, 'I'll open the door for you if you'll make the rest of them go away.'

'Yes, dear, of course,' Miss Sanders' voice came back

eagerly. More colloquy; the sound of diminishing foot-steps. 'Let me in, Molly. Everyone's gone.'

She turned the key in the lock and opened the door. Miss Sanders stood in the bleak light of the corridor, twisting her hands and looking worried. 'Come in,' said Molly, in her new rough voice, and snapped on the over-head bulb. Miss Sanders stepped over the threshold, peering at Molly with her head cocked like a terribly worried hen's. She thrust her hand out toward Molly's face; Molly tossed her head and backed away.

'I only wanted to see if you were feverish,' said Miss Sanders meekly.

Molly laid her hand on her own cheek. 'No,' she said after a moment, as if she were a consulting doctor at her own case, 'I'm not. It's only,' she spoke very evenly, 'that I've been upset about the murder.'

As with a tremendous roll of tympani, the sky seemed to thunder, the room reeled, Miss Sanders swelled and diminished before her lightning-struck eyes. The body, the paper had said, was found lying on the hearth. If Mr Marks had not discovered it at 7 p.m., a severe fire might have resulted, as the dead man's coat was about to catch flame. The back of the head ... The back of the head was clotted with black curls and blood. Like a sleeping child he lay, his pale face pillowed peacefully on the bricks, his curved arm lying too close to the coals, so that the sleeve of his jacket was sending up a curl of smoke when they found him. Without so much as a Now-I-lay-me Kevin Boyle lay dead among his books and his private matters, the back of his head bashed in with a blunt instrument. Bashed – like an eggshell. Could the paper have said that? It sounded too graphic for a newspaper style. She must have made that up herself. The newspaper was here somewhere. She turned aside, forgetting Miss Sanders, to look for it.

'Why, Molly,' said Miss Sanders, calling her back – to the land of the living, you might say, 'did you *know* Mr Boyle?' Her round black chicken's eyes rolled in their rings of bare flesh.

'I had a class with him,' said Molly faintly.

'But, Molly – ' said Miss Sanders, working her hands, 'it's shocking, my dear, quite unreal and completely upsetting, but, Molly dear, you must pull yourself together! You haven't eaten all day. It isn't as if – I don't mean to sound heartless, but after all, you didn't know him *well*?' It began as a statement and ended as a question. Miss Sanders' pale, henlike face hung on her bones under the glare of the ceiling light, filled with a kind of inhuman birdlike kindness, but curious, too, wondering.

Now what shall I say, she thought, as she stood there facing it out with Miss Sanders. Oh no, I didn't know him; he was only my lover – I didn't know him – he was only my husband, I only thought about him every minute of my waking life ... Miss Sanders still stood before her, but dimmer, now; over her plump shoulder his saturnine, pipe-biting face grinned: Molly, my girl ... 'It was not,' she said vaguely, 'that he was my lover, *that* he was not ... ' and burst into a long low wail of anguish, her face hidden in her thin white hands.

Then Miss Sanders wheeled and flew down like an old rolling-eyed vulture, scenting scandal, scenting carrion, wheeling down on weeping Molly through layers of air, clutching her to her bosom, patting, half strangling. 'There, there, my dear,' she comforted hungrily, 'I'll tell you what we'll do – I'll just call a taxi and we'll go right over to the Infirmary. Dr Abby will give you a sedative and you'll have a good night's sleep. You'll see – everything will look quite different in the morning.'

Once she had been drunk, and it had been, in a way, like this. There had been a central theme – sometimes you lost the melody of it, then it returned again. You lost it because around it swirled mists and diffusions of sound, sometimes lulling, sometimes brazen. Like the putting on of the coat, the walking down the stairs, like the faces, eager, prying, looking up the stairs at her from where they clustered round the mail desk, and Miss Sanders bustling her back to the housemother's apartment while she put on her outdoor things; like the taxi, the steps. ...

In the hall of the Infirmary, the theme came back. There it was quiet and dark. She was glad she had come. One small lamp burned on a desk where a nurse sat writing, only her hand and the paper encircled in light. In the arches of darkness overhead the melody swelled out clear and purposeful, beautiful as a cadenza on a cello: Kevin Boyle is dead, was the theme; he was murdered yesterday, a bare three hours after you parted from him. Kevin Boyle is dead. You will never say to him, I love you, my darling.

Miss Sanders was murmuring to the nurse, leaving Molly standing swaying and alone in the vaults of darkness where the theme echoed. 'I love you, my darling,' Molly said, rather loudly and experimentally, as if she were drunk. In a bustle the nurse rose from her desk, making cooing, rustling noises like a flock of white pigeons.

'Come along, dear,' she said, 'we'll tuck you up in bed and give you a nice sleeping pill.'

## Chapter 3

MANY a time he had sat here with Kevin Boyle, slouched comfortably in the worn old armchairs, looking into the fire and talking of this and that – though mostly of that, mostly of Kevin. Oh, sometimes he would try to make a bold beginning, saying, Kevin, do you know what it is I want? I want to get married. But before the words were out of his mouth, Kevin would be roaring and shouting with laughter, slapping his knees and pulling his own hair. 'What in the name of God and the Devil does a man want to get married for?' he would say. 'Why, boy, you've nothing to gain but your chains!' Then it would be another tale of conquest – the shy, sly glance she had thrown at him, the note slipped under the door, the sweet warm wrestling in the strange bed ... Was ever a man so pursued of women? Could it be true that any man was so pursued? Or was it all a beautiful Irish fiction invented half to please that broth of a Kevin, half to torture poor, weak-chinned, bespectacled Leonard? Sometimes, after Kevin had crossed the hall to his own rooms and Leonard had brushed his teeth, put on his neat striped pyjamas, and folded himself between the tight-pulled sheets, he would lie there in a passion (for even a weak-chinned man with his glasses off is sometimes capable of passion) cursing the Irish who were born to outshine, with their wild romanticism, all the other, soberer, steadier, less noticeable races of mankind.

Yet if Kevin had been lying with his tales of conquest (not to say rape) it was his lies, at last, which had done him in. For last evening Leonard, sitting by the fire over his books, had heard Kevin's voice cry out 'No!' in protest, sounding through the two closed doors, had heard the thud, the slam, the footsteps, yet had never gone to investigate till more than an hour later, thinking this was one of *them*, the ladies who could not resist the melancholy Hibernian charm of him, who threw themselves upon him in the extremity of their passion (or so he had related it – many times) so that he had to disengage their clasping arms gently and let them know that no single woman would ever possess him for her own. It had been a long time before Leonard had got back to his books after that 'No,' that thud, that clacking latch. He had stared into the coals long and profitlessly, gritting his teeth, upper against lower, and cursing the Irish, without whom the rest of the world might have gone along its quiet way, flirting gently with librarians, and not wishing for what was beyond its means.

But two hours later, his notes prepared for the next day's classes, when he had knocked at Kevin's door to see if he was ready for supper, opened without waiting for an answer, Kevin had been lying dead, the back of his head smashed in with the poker.

What does a man think of when first he sees a corpse, and one done violently to death, at that? For Leonard had seen not so much as a dead grandmother, not so much as a dead dog, that he could remember, in all the days of his life, so that now ... now ... He was not sick at his stomach, although he would have expected himself to be. He stood there looking at Kevin's unmistakably dead body with a strange kind of excitement swelling inside him. Kevin is dead, he thought, somebody has murdered him. That is Kevin Boyle. He was alive and now he is dead. The thing to do is not to touch anything. The thing to do is call the police. Yet he stood there for minutes more, looking at the dead Kevin, lying there so peaceful (except for the bloody hole in his skull), peaceful as if in sleep, with his mouth a little open, and the smoke curling up from one sleeve that lay too close to the coals. The thing to do was not touch anything, but if he did not move that sleeve the corpse would catch fire. And at this thought the terrible thing had come over him that he was not shut of yet: he kept wanting to laugh. The corpse will catch fire, he thought, and giggled right out loud, nervously. Then he knew he would have to keep rein on himself for a long time to come, or every time he had to speak Kevin Boyle's name and tell how it was he had found him, he would begin to snicker helplessly, like a schoolboy who had perpetrated a hoax.

He had taken three cautious steps to the fireplace, leaned down and gingerly pinched up a piece of Kevin's sleeve in his fingers. The fabric was hot; the arm within it moved with a curious acquiescent limpness. Again he felt the horrible, shocking impulse to laugh. You would have to listen if I talked to you now, my boy! he crowed inwardly. And was deeply shocked at himself, and began to feel queasy, at last, at the sight and the faint smell of the blood.

He had gone through it all admirably; had shut the door carefully behind him, had called Miss Stone, the landlady, and broken the news, had telephoned the police, answered their questions, run to the corner for spirits of ammonia for Miss Stone, spoken to the reporter from the West Lyman *Star* – but cautiously, giving only the barest outline, avoiding all question of Kevin's character, his habits. He had not gone to bed until long after midnight, yet had risen as usual for an eight-thirty class. He had conducted himself well, and here was his reward. Across the hearth from him, in the worn leather chair where Kevin had so often lolled – indeed, he had had almost no callers *but* Kevin – the great George Hungerford now sat, hunched forward over his knees, prodding the coals with the short iron poker. It was not, Leonard observed in some wild and uncontrollable part of his mind, the day to be poking about with a poker, and he swallowed a nervous giggle as painfully as if it had been a retch. What was to become of him with this awful compulsion to laugh at the wrong moments? The charitable view of himself would be that he was simply hysterical with the events of the last day, but if he burst out laughing in George Hungerford's infinitely melancholy face, no such charitable view was likely to be taken. And what he felt at the sight of Hungerford, sitting there in his own chair, was far from laughter. Call it reverence. Call it incredulity. Call it a prayer of gratitude.

Suddenly Hungerford raised his head. 'Mix me a drink, will you, Marks?' he said, his face pale even in the firelight, and terribly worn. With a nervous jerk of eagerness Leonard was out of his chair and half across the room before the words had died on the quiet air. He pulled the light chain in the little closet where his refrigerator and sink stood. He took out an ice tray, letting water run over it. 'Marks!' Hungerford's voice came to him suddenly, sounding over the flowing water with a tortured, pleading note. 'Marks, who could have killed him? Why should *he*, of any of us, have to die?'

It was strange to Leonard that a man of Hungerford's intellect, Hungerford's sensitivity, his – why not say it? – genius, should question so naively a fate which, in the last analysis, Leonard could only feel as appropriate. Carefully he measured out the jiggers of whisky in each glass trying how to answer his innocence without sounding impertinent.

'He was,' he called at last, forcing open the soda bottle so that the warm effervescence ran down over his hand, 'a passionate man.'

'Passionate,' he heard Hungerford mumble, and the sound of a log breaking in two, with a snapping of sparks. He set the glasses on a tray, pulled the light chain again, and bore the drinks out into the dimly lighted room. He was gnawed by an enormous curiosity which he dared not indulge. Hungerford had visited Kevin two and three times a week. Leonard, coming home from the Library or crossing the hall to see if Kevin were free, would hear their voices behind the thin door, talking and talking. He did not dare to knock, Hungerford being Hungerford and Kevin being Kevin. But he had often wondered on what paths such conversation could have wandered. For himself, he had heard Kevin enlarge on only one subject – sex. Could it be that with Hungerford he had skirted the topic entirely?

He had just sat down with his drink when Hungerford said abruptly, as if clairvoyant, 'What makes you say that, Marks – that he was passionate? Was it something specific that led you to conclude ... Not to say, of course that it wasn't plain without any direct instance, but if there might be a clue –'

'Why,' said Leonard, giggling his nervous treble laugh, 'to tell you the truth, sir, we generally talked about women – that is to say, he did.'

Hungerford was afflicted by a severe tic which drew up the whole side of his face from time to time, like one of those rubber faces children play with and distort. Now the muscles of the left side of his serenely tragic mask drew together spasmodically, as if in agony. 'That was a side of him I never knew,' he said, leaning back in the chair and letting the poker drop. 'Our conversations were generally literary or professional. Possibly,' he added, his mouth sardonic, 'he regarded me as a creature whose passion was spent ... Did you know he was collecting poems for a book?'

Leonard shook his head, and a stab of bitter jealousy, the first since Kevin's murder, attacked him once more. So it was *not* done – his brutal eminence, their impossible, unequal rivalry. Ah, well ...

'But that's hardly relevant,' Hungerford frowned. 'As to women. It seemed to me he acted with utmost discretion with regard to the students.'

'Absolutely; he stayed absolutely clear of anything of that sort,' Leonard said quickly. He hesitated a moment, then risked it, with another snigger. 'To tell the truth, I often wondered how he avoided it so completely with the sort of – the sort of history he professed.'

Hungerford frowned deeper and chewed the inside of his cheek. 'Well,' he said, 'let us be open about it, Marks. What do you know of his relations with women?'

Have I, thought Leonard, in cautious anxiety, pushed too far? He made his face very serious and earnest. 'He was always most discreet and indirect, Mr Hungerford, in the sense that I never heard him mention a woman's name, and I was often puzzled as to whether a specific incident had occurred last week in West Lyman or ten years ago in Dublin. I even suspected sometimes that he was only indulging an aptitude for Rabelaisian invention. But as far as women coming to his rooms here, the only ones I have ever seen were Miss Stone and Mrs Cramm.'

'Oh, Freda ... ' said Hungerford, and waved his hand

in dismissal with a kind of exhausted humour. Inside Leonard flared a wave of rage; he knew he was about to say something unwise, unpolitic, but he could not help himself.

'Mrs Cramm,' he said carefully, 'was in and out a good deal. At all hours.'

'Freda has too much bark to be much of a biter,' said Hungerford and stared into the fire.

Hah! cried Leonard silently, if you only knew! The bite of her tongue! The bite of her indifference! The way she reduced a man to the place of poor relative with a glance and the ignoring of his joke. If he had a scar for every one of his sentences she had interrupted in English Department meetings, for the tête-à-têtes between himself and Kevin on which she had broken, sending him off to his rooms like a child who has out-stayed his bedtime ... She was the living negation of all that he counted his manhood. 'She always struck me as a rather violent woman,' he said quietly, 'but perhaps —'

'That's exactly it,' said Hungerford irritably, as if tired of the subject, 'if Freda had murdered Kevin she would now be enjoying her confession like an old courtesan writing her memoirs.'

'Of course, I don't know her,' Leonard mumbled. 'I've only seen her for minutes at Kevin's, and about the campus ...' He was desperately afraid he had said too much. He wanted so to remember this as perfect, to recollect in privacy that he had, for once, on this great occasion, said the right thing ...

Suddenly Hungerford took up his glass and drained off the whole drink at a gulp. He sat up in the chair, and it was plain that he was about to leave. Don't go, don't go! Leonard wanted to beg him. There are so many things we could have said ... 'I suppose there's no use indulging in amateur detection; the police will do what they can, and what they can't, we can't. I have no faith in the use of the academic intellect for practical purposes. We shall have to see. We shall simply have to see,' said Hungerford.

He set his hands in the arms of the chair, raised his elbows in the air preparatory to pushing himself to his feet. Suddenly the tic seized hold of his face; he sat frozen in the awkward position, staring into the fire, and to Leonard's horror two tears slipped over his eyelids, ran down his cheeks. Oh, Mr Hungerford! he wanted to cry, wanted to kneel at his feet, offering service. Oh Master! he would have cried, had he dared. But Hungerford's lips moved, drew together several times soundlessly before his voice issued. 'I loved that boy,' he said brokenly. 'With all the worn-out mechanics of my lost emotions I felt it in him for the first time in – how long? – Life,' he said finally, and rose like an old, old man. 'Life.'

Mutely Leonard rose too; took Hungerford's coat and hat from the closet, helped him into the sleeves. 'Goodnight, Marks,' said Hungerford, the great Hungerford – almost pitifully, looking into Leonard's eyes as they stood at the door.

It is over, mourned Leonard silently. He will never come again. I have lost my only, only opportunity. If only I could say something to hold him. But when he looked in Hungerford's ravaged face, the great wells of his mourning eyes, he was unable to speak in his own interest; the real emotion of his homage overcame him. Clumsily, he took hold of Hungerford's elbow and shook it a little. 'Get some sleep, sir,' he said rather chokingly. And that was the end.

## Chapter 4

THE brick faces of the neo-Gothic buildings showed bleakly in the night, illuminated by the cheerless street lamps. Hungerford walked slowly, draggingly, leaning on the crook of his umbrella, oblivious to the rain. The architecture of despair, he thought. The blood and bones of hopelessness. He hardly knew what he meant. Was he awake or asleep? Was this the landscape of some dream? Surely it was too awful to be real. The darkened Library, the buildings full of empty classrooms, the threatening olive-green shape of the mailbox under the lamp at the centre of the campus ... And then behind him, footsteps. Brisk, intended, rubber shod, and dull, yet plainly distinguishable. I know who that is, said his mind. That is Death. That is the old Reaper, gumshoeing behind you. He thought he would turn and shake Death's hand when Death came abreast of him. Hello, Death, said his mind, playing tricks, suddenly dancing foolishly in his head. The footsteps drew closer, gaining on him. Death would take his arm and they would walk together like the good friends they were. I have been your good friend for a long time, his mind said to Death, but you have turned your face away from me. Are we to be reunited now? Will you take me where you took Kevin Boyle, leave me safe from the pryings of hope and life? ... Death was at his side now, 'Good evening, Mr Hungerford,' said Death.

'Hello, Tom,' said George Hungerford wearily, leaning like a sick man on his umbrella.

'Wet night,' said the campus policeman.

'Very wet,' said George Hungerford, and hurrying his pace, passed on.

'Good-night, Mr Hungerford.'

'Good-night, Tom.'

Death, you bloody cheat, you humbug! The bare white bones of the auditorium grinned at him like a skull, white columned, barren. It was as if his whole life was a trial by torture to prove himself worthy of death. Ever since the grey morning when they waked him somehow, retching and vomiting, from the overdose of nembutal. Ever since then it had been one torture added to another, to last God knew how long, testing his readiness for death. The torture of breathing. The torture of doctors. The torture of the sanatorium, of learning to be quiet ... The torture of the note-books ... The torture of Kevin Boyle's murder. Yet since his attempted suicide he was aware that something had changed in him, grown hardier, more impervious to blows. When he held the razor to his wrist, debating whether he should cut the arteries, some new voice spoke in his head, small and far away, but indomitably authoritative, saying No! By its command he was compelled to go on and on, through the trials and agonies devised for him, never able to pass the examination that was to prove him ready to be graduated from life.

He walked through the iron gates of the college to the main street of the town. Across from the auditorium stood the house where he rented rooms, tall and Victorian, set back on its lawn behind its iron Saint Bernard. A lamp gleamed ruby, amber, and sapphire through the coloured panes of the hall door. He liked his tall old house. It had a bitter, friendly ugliness, like a hideous spinster who has learned the grim humour of the disappointments of life. He unlocked the door and climbed the stairs to his apartment. He was almost smiling at the friendly ugliness of the chocolate wallpaper, the dreary brown landscapes

in their gilt frames that hung over the stairs. He thought
he might sleep to-night. It was good for him to talk when
it touched at all on what was in his mind – even to so
colourless a figure as Leonard Marks. It was good to lay
aside however small a portion of the burden of silence in
something other than the addlepated chattering of the
faculty tea-room. He turned on the light in his living-
room, and inside his head the voice began to laugh, faint
and distant and vicious. For there on his desk lay the
notebook, opened wide; across the room the huge mad
handwriting screamed at him, commanding him to read,
commanding him to taste again the depths of human
vileness and despise ...

## Chapter 5

THE big hall filled slowly; the floor and then the balcony.
Finally the organ sounded out, the students rose, hymn-
books in hand.

> O God, our help in ages past,
> Our hope for years to come,
> Our shelter from the stormy blast
> And our eternal home.

They sat down again; from offstage President Bainbridge suddenly appeared, his face red, his gown billow-
ing, puffing on to the scene like a belated bridegroom.
Behind him the faculty sat in two rows, mute and blinking. A whisper passed over the rows of girls, audible as
the visibility of a little wind silvering a field of grass. The

president shuffled a handful of notes. 'The Athletic Association will hold trials for ... ' he read. 'Tryouts for *Antigone* will be held on ... ' At last he stopped, laid down the notes, and looked out at the field of faces upturned to him. Visibly he paused, braced himself, began.

'I believe all of you are aware of the subject on which I must speak this morning. Mr Kevin Boyle, a member of the English Department, was found murdered in his rooms on Monday evening. I find it purposeless to mention the horror and shock which has come to all of us in hearing this news. You may find it petty in me that I am going to speak of the matters of which I must speak this morning in the face of this kind of a catastrophe. Yet it is the unfortunate fate of a college president – ' there was the briefest murmur of amusement at the assumption that the fate of a college president might be conceived as unfortunate – 'always to be considering the matter of the reputation of the college. And it is of this I must speak this morning, philistine or even brutal as you may find it at the time of this tragedy.

'To be brief: we are beginning to be, and may expect to be even more in the future, besieged by newspapermen. Their business is to make of this event a story which will be as sensational as possible. Any one of you may be asked questions which by their very nature can elicit answers to be twisted to the damage of the college.' There was a pause for a presidential twinkle, then a parenthesis. 'I am talking to you like a trustees' meeting – I hope you will listen to me in kind.' A gentle shout of laughter went up. His round face drooped again to seriousness. 'I do not mean to imply that any of you will deliberately give out false or irresponsible information, or information which might more suitably be given to the police or myself. My only point is that newspapermen have a way with them – ' giggles – 'a way of putting matters in their most lurid light. I want to make a personal plea to every student in this college to abstain from conversation with any stranger who seems inclined to draw her out on the subject of Mr Boyle. I ask you this selfishly, because your behaviour will reflect on my position, and less selfishly, because in loyalty to this college which offers you so much, you must use your foresight and discretion to safeguard its reputation.'

The president withdrew to his armchair, the organist, observing him in her rear-view mirror, struck up once more; the audience rose for the closing hymn.

> *Once more the liberal year laughs out*
> *With richer stores than gems or gold ...*

When it was over, the organist began a recessional, the faculty filed off the stage in orderly fashion, the audience of girls rose and began struggling into their coats, pushing in a sluggish stream out the aisles.

'I think it's *silly*,' a clear voice rose out of an eddy of talk. 'You'd think we were children ... '

'He's thinking about that time those girls in Fairish House talked to the *Journal-American* reporter about drinking ... '

'God, what do you suppose *happened* to him, though? Do you suppose it's a *maniac* or something?'

'Miss Austen is going to take his classes ... '

'Oh, be honest and admit it's simply too fruity having a murder on the campus!'

They spilled out the doors and flowed between the white pillars of the Greek Revival front like sand flowing between the fingers of a hand. Outside was a brilliant blue Indian summer day, glorifying the bare November trees, the dingy grass. Around the steps of the auditorium there raged the usual pandemonium of chatter and movements, of disengaging bicycles from racks, of shouting across heads to distant friends.

'A girl in our house had such a mad crush on him that she went completely off her rocker. They sent her up to the Infirmary simply screaming with hysterics.'

'No! who?'

'Nobody you'd know. Some little creep of a freshman named Morrison. Very drippy.'

'Suppose *she* did it?'

'My dear, she doesn't have what it *takes*.'

Freda Cramm, looking enormous and golden in a very expensive russet tweed topcoat, wedged her way through the mass of girls and caught Miss Sanders by the elbow as she was turning down the brick wall toward the quadrangle. 'Maude!' she said commandingly. Miss Sanders turned and blinked her lashless eyes. 'Hello, Freda dear,' she said. 'Isn't it too horrible?'

'My dear,' said Freda ominously, 'you don't know *how* horrible!'

Miss Sanders simply blinked more violently, a mottling of nervous blotches beginning to discolour her neck.

'I want you to come to my house for coffee now,' said Freda. 'I have to talk to you. It's very important.'

'Now?' said Miss Sanders weakly. 'There's all the day's planning –'

'No, you must come,' Freda ordered, and steered her to the sleek black convertible, its top put back, which waited glossily at the curb.

Freda drove abominably. Miss Sanders sat in clenched

anxiety, pressing her feet against imaginary brakes as the car wound through the streets of the town. Twenty years ago Freda had been a pet student in Miss Sanders' house. Now that she was a member of the faculty (heaven knew why, for she had all the money she wanted and a good many opportunities for glamorous living) Miss Sanders found herself relegated (or elevated) to a position in Freda's life like that of a superannuated nanny in a noble English household, who, having dandled the young lady of the family in her infancy, now bends a deferential ear to her debutante confidences.

Freda lived on a hilltop back of the campus in a re-modelled mansion of the eighties, equipped with the most modern plumbing, the most baroque furniture. She extracted Miss Sanders rather forcibly from her wraps, ordered the maid to bring coffee, and led the way to the anachronistic solarium, where the Indian-summer sun poured its splendour on to the comfortable bamboo furniture. She would allow no questions until the coffee was poured, the sugar and cream measured, the maid retired to the bowels of the house. Then she sighed deep, and reclined in her chair. 'Maude darling,' she said, 'I talk too much.'

Miss Sanders, sitting up toward the edge of her seat, holding her cup and saucer in mid-air, blinked her eyes and didn't know what to say. This was incontrovertibly true.

Freda sighed again and closed her eyes a moment. Since her divorce, she had become quite stout; it always startled Miss Sanders to recall the picture of her as a long, gawky girl in the chemise dresses of the 1920's. Her small, delicate, deceptively gentle features were strangely im-bedded in the new flesh, yet they had managed to retain much of the force of their old seductiveness. 'I've been seeing too much of Kevin Boyle,' Freda went on. 'It's bound to come out.'

For a moment a little smile flickered in the corner of Miss Sanders' lips. She was certainly having her share of Kevin Boyle's 'girl friends,' as they said. The little Morrison girl – well, think of that later. 'Come on, Freda,' she said in a timidly teasing way, 'out with it!'

Freda opened her heavy-lidded eyes and stared through the plate glass down to the valley below the house, where the river meandered through the flat, frost-burnt meadows. Was she going to be practical or dramatic, Miss Sanders wondered. 'Darling, it isn't that I've been sleeping with him,' Freda said practically. 'It's just that I've been talking too much again.'

Somewhere, buried deep under Maude Sanders' hen-like exterior, her fluttering manner, her kindly ineffectuality, was a little spear of ridicule which responded irresistibly to the stimulus of Freda's flamboyant egocentricity. 'After all these years,' she essayed, 'how could that make any difference?'

'Well,' said Freda, 'it could make a lot of difference, it seems to me, if he had been loose-mouthed about some of the things we talked about. Because if some of the things I said in perfect innocence and frankness – The fact is he had a letter that belonged to me. We had a quarrel about it.'

'What sort of letter?'

Freda stamped out her cigarette and rose to pace the brick floor like an overfed cat. 'Oh, it's too maddening!' she said. Miss Sanders sat blinking, waiting for her to go on. 'It was just an ordinary begging letter,' said Freda overprotestingly, at last.

'Then I can't see –'

'Oh, you don't understand!' cried Freda. 'We had this horrible fight about it. Kevin was perfectly brutal. And I went off in a rage, leaving the thing behind, and I can't be sure he destroyed it.'

'Suppose he didn't? If it was just an ordinary sort of begging letter, how could it reflect on you, Freda?'

Freda stood in front of the windows with her hands clasped behind her back. 'Well, it wasn't *just* an ordinary begging letter. It was rather horrible. Oh, Maude, you don't know how utterly nasty people can be!'

'Who was it from?'

'Oh, one of my lame-duck relatives.'

Miss Sanders went on quietly blinking, but an internal smile illuminated her eyes. The story was growing plainer to her with each scrap that Freda tossed out. A poor relative had asked her (with signal lack of insight) for money. Freda had refused, but had felt uncomfortable about it, so she had gone to Mr Boyle with the story, hoping for outside justification of her behaviour. Mr Boyle, a young man with a good deal of charm, but little tact, from what Maude Sanders had been able to observe of him at faculty dinners, had told Freda she had been wrong in refusing. And Freda, who could bear to be wrong almost less than she could bear to give away money, had got in a fight with him in order to discredit his opinion. It was not difficult to piece this together from her remembrance of Freda's impoverished college days, when she had cultivated the wealthier girls on the campus, choosing her friends as carefully and by the same standards as a bond salesman chooses his customers, and when politic or possible, borrowing their fur coats, their ready cash, their young men. She had acquired

Michael Cramm by this means – borrowing him from a drab little heiress – who, as she later justly pointed out, had much less need for him than she. She had parted from him later only under the pressure of his willingness to settle a large piece of property on her in return for being freed to marry the showgirl of his choice. Freda had many public vices; parsimony was the one she tried to keep secret, even from herself. 'It does seem to me,' Miss Sanders said finally, 'that you're making something out of nothing. Suppose a letter belonging to you is found in Mr Boyle's effects. Even suppose that the police question you about it. I hardly see –'

'Maude,' said Freda, sitting down and clasping her hands in her lap, 'you know how I *yell*?'

In silence, Miss Sanders agreed that in moments of emotional stress, Freda had been known to raise her voice.

'Well, there I was in this rattletrap house Kevin lives in – lived in – screaming like a banshee because he practically accused me of stealing bread out of starving mouths – I mean, Maude, he was practically a *Communist*, you know – and when I was finally leaving in a rage, there was that slimy Leonard Marks, just putting his key in the lock across the hall. Now, goodness knows how long he had been listening.'

'Mr Marks?' said Miss Sanders. 'Oh, Freda, I hardly think – I mean, he's such a –'

'Pipsqueak,' supplied Freda. 'That's just the point. I can't stand the man; I've been abominably rude to him, and he's just the one to hate me like poison and make a point of bringing it up that I was heard behaving like a fishwife in Kevin's apartment last week. Furthermore Kevin may have talked to him.'

'About you? Oh, Freda, I *do* have the impression that Mr Boyle was above all things a *gentleman*!'

Freda snorted. 'I did a lot of talking to Kevin because – well, he was one of the few people around here you *could* talk to without having him blanch at your language. But I never laboured under the impression that he was a sealed vault. A man like Kevin Boyle needs a man like Leonard Marks to show off to. He needed the good opinion of the world – otherwise why would he have been an assistant professor in an expensive women's college instead of a wild Irish poet in a Greenwich Village attic? Leonard Marks would have provided an excellent listener – a man with no life of his own would drink up Kevin's tales of roistering and hobnobbing with the great, without competing or condemning, or even doubting the veraciousness.'

Miss Sanders, who was not always the fool she made herself out to be, thought, Yes, Freda dear, like you and me, while remarking aloud, 'I doubt that Mr Marks could feel that anything Mr Boyle might have repeated would have bearing on the murder.'

'The point is, he might put odds and ends together and motivate them with his own dislike for me. I was in and out of Kevin's place a good deal. Everybody in the neighbourhood must know it from seeing the car outside.'

Miss Sanders frowned and tapped her finger on her imitation alligator bag. 'Couldn't you go to Mr Marks?' she wondered.

Freda sighed and poured more coffee for both of them. 'I've positively antagonized him,' she said. 'Couldn't stand the sight of him. I've insulted him several times. Now, how will it look if after the murder I go to him and say, Look here, Marks, don't repeat anything Kevin may have said I said to the police?'

Miss Sanders knit her brows. The cook at Birnham House had already threatened to leave several times. Miss Sanders had been expected back a half-hour ago to do the ordering and plan to-morrow's meals. An immediate conclusion of some kind must be made, but she allowed a silence to elapse while she tried to think of one that would would be foolproof. Finally she began tentatively, 'What if ... what if you gave a large party – quite large. Asked all the members of the English Department, say, so that it would seem natural to have Mr Marks. Then, rather unostentatiously, pay him a good deal of attention – win him over to your side?'

Freda frowned, pinched her lower lip between her fingers. 'Not bad,' she muttered. 'Not bad at all. In fact, very good. Could I make it some sort of memorial thing for Kevin – otherwise wouldn't it look funny to be giving a party? I'll think about it. I really think that's very good. If it's a memorial, I can have it soon, too, so that I can get to Marks before ... unless he's already ... '

Miss Sanders gathered up her bag decisively. 'Freda, I positively *must* ... ' Freda rose abruptly. 'Oh, darling, I've been keeping you! You're an angel, Maude, and I love you dearly!'

Making small murmurs of deprecation, Miss Sanders made her way to the door, retrieved her coat and hat. 'I'll drive you back to the house,' said Freda. 'I have to go to my office anyway.'

Back in the autumn sunlight, the spicy air, Miss Sanders felt a sudden surge of gaiety and liberation, such as a visit with Freda was always likely to give her. 'Freda,' she said in a spurt of indiscretion, 'the most appalling thing has happened at Birnham. A little freshman has collapsed over the murder. She's a neurotic little

35

thing in any case and seems to have had one of those violent crushes on Mr Boyle. It looks like a nervous breakdown to me. I think we'll have to send her home.'

'*Really?*' cried Freda, turning her attention dangerously from the road in her ever-ready prurience. 'You don't suppose she *did* it?'

'Oh, pooh,' said Miss Sanders, laughing as they recklessly rounded the corner into the quadrangle, 'she didn't do it any more than you did!'

## Chapter 6

'I GOTTA get an angle,' crooned the young man, rocking his face between his hands. 'I simply gotta get an angle.'

The bartender slammed his beer down in front of him unsympathetically, and began mixing an Alexander for an order from the back room.

'Who drinks that stuff?' said the young man, looking nauseated.

'College girls,' said the bartender, pouring the liquid into a glass.

'Makes me want to puke to think of it,' said the young man. The bartender said nothing, but signalled to a waitress, who carried the glass away.

'Listen, Joe, whattaya know?' the young man pursued. 'Honestly, somebody's gotta know something. Haven't you heard anybody talking? Can't you even make something up? I'm supposed to get a story.'

A pleased look came over the bartender's craggy, embittered face. 'See no evil, hear no evil, speak no evil,' he said. It was a joke.·

'Listen, Joe,' the young man pleaded, 'didn't the guy ever come in here?'

'Name's Stanislas,' said the bartender, relapsing into moroseness.

'Oh, all *right*!' said the young man; 'but look, didn't you ever see the fellow?'

'Yep,' said the bartender.

'Well, what kind of a guy was he? Did he come here with women?'

'Nope,' said Stanislas, swiping the bar with a damp cloth.

'Did he flirt with the waitresses? Was he mixed up with the local strong-arm boys? Was he a pansy? A lot of these college professors are.'

Stanislas went on wiping the bar, his eyes lowered. 'Used to come here about every other night,' he said at last. 'Always some bunch of girls – students – would ask him to come sit at their booth in the back room. He'd go and sit with 'em. Ten o'clock they'd leave – have to be back at the college at ten-fifteen. Then he'd come out here and have another beer. Maybe he'd meet Mr Marks. Maybe he'd meet Mr Hungerford. Him and Mr Hungerford would talk poetry like. Him and Mr Marks'd talk about women. He'd tell some mighty hot stories all right about all the dames couldn't stay away from him, but the truth of it is, I never seen him with no woman. Used to go down to one of the local houses and get himself laid once in a while, that I know for a fact. Used to go down to New York ever so often. Tell you the truth,' said Stanislas, warming at last and leaning on the bar with the cloth in his hand. 'I think he was a kind of timid fellow, for all his big talk.'

'Oh hell,' said the reporter disgustedly, 'that's no story.'

Stanislas' brow lowered. 'If you don't like it you know what you can do with it. Now you know as much as I do.'

'Gimme another beer,' said the reporter.

'Listen, mister,' said the bartender, 'why'n't you go in the back room and strike up a conversation with some of them students. They're always full of a pack of lies.'

'Try anything,' muttered the young man, climbing down from his stool, his beer in his hand.

The back room had two rows of fumed-oak booths running the length of the walls. The reporter carried his beer to an empty booth opposite one where two girls sat. He could have passed for a college boy, with his crew cut and his horn-rimmed glasses, his sloppy tweeds. He sat down discreetly, not giving the girls any kind of obvious eye. One of them was quite a tomato – what is referred to as a long-stemmed American beauty. This was going to be what you call mixing business with pleasure. The other was on the dumpy side, with a frowsy feather cut and horn-rimmed glasses like the young man's own. She was wearing dungarees and a sweatshirt; the first had on a pale-pink sweater and skirt – good enough to eat. The reporter sat regarding them out of the corner of his eye as he sipped his beer, thinking about the best approach. Casing the joint, you might say. The pink one was not so bright – she was the one to work on. The fat cookie looked like an intellectual. She was the one to watch out for at first, but if you get her on your side, she could help you more. O.K., now he had it straight. He raised his head and looked straight into the fat one's eyes. 'Can I sit with you?'

Fatty looked him up and down very coolly and turned to the beauty. 'Do we want to talk to him?' she said in a cold voice. 'I think he's a reporter.'

She was smart and no mistake. In a way it made things easier.

The one in the pink sweater ran her hand under the fine blond hair that fell to her shoulders like gentle plumes. She giggled. 'I think reporters are *cute*,' she said in a severe southern accent.

He had crossed the aisle and sat down beside the pink sweater before any discussion could go on. 'My name is Jack Donelly,' he said, pursuing the frank line.

'Mine is Kate Innes,' said Fatty, 'and this is Honey Sacheveral.'

'Well, you have to have a drink with me now,' he said, 'now that I'm *in*,' and laughed. 'What'll it be?'

'Scotch and soda,' said Kate promptly.

'Alexayunduh,' said Honey, and giggled.

He beckoned to the waitress and ordered, changing to Scotch himself.

'Well,' said Kate, leaning against the back of the booth and folding her short arms across her sweatshirt, 'the president told us not to talk to reporters this morning. Naturally we have to try it. Like sticking beans up your nose.'

'*What?*' said Donelly, slightly alarmed.

'Skip it,' said Kate. 'What do you want to worm out of us?'

He did not look at her, but brought out a handful of change from his pocket and selected some nickels. 'I'm tired of worming things out of people,' he said. 'All day I go around worming, and what do I get – not even an early bird. What'll I play on the juke machine?'

'Stah-dust,' said Honey immediately, and giggled.

'Let's see how *your* taste runs,' said Kate, rather menacingly.

While he was gone the waitress brought the drinks and mixed the highballs.

*Sometimes I WON-der why I spend my lonely ni-i-ghts –\** whined the record. Honey hummed and leaned back against the seat. A delicate line of cream collected on her upper lip; she ran out her tongue and removed it neatly, leaving the fuchsia lipstick intact.

'What paper are you on?' said Kate.

'*Messenger*,' he said glumly.

'Scandal sheet,' said Kate.

'A person has to eat,' said Donelly. 'Anyway, I'm a good Guild member.'

'*Mah* daddy says,' Honey remarked suddenly, speaking from what seemed to be a trance, 'don't quarrel with your bread and butter.'

'Practical puss, aren't you?' said Donelly, in some surprise.

'Will you buy me another Alexayunduh, Mistuh Donelly?' she said, looking at him slant-eyed.

'A pleasure, my dear,' he replied benignly, summoning the waitress.

'Don't act so regal,' said Kate. 'You should know I know it's on the expense account.'

'You should remember what Honey's daddy says,' cracked Donelly, and drew a grin for the first time.

'So what have you picked up about the murder?' Kate said, looking down at her drink.

'Isn't it just aw-ful?' said Honey dreamily. 'Isn't it simply terrible? He was so dar-lin'.'

'He was darlin' as all get out,' said Kate, and finished off the last of her Scotch. Jack ordered her another without asking.

'I haven't found out a damn thing,' he said disgustedly. 'All I know is what I read in the papers. Not a

\*By permission of the copyright proprietor Mills, Music, Inc.

single soul who has ever been to his rooms has an alibi for the time of the murder, and nobody seems to care. Leonard Marks was sitting across the hall in his room – could have come over and slugged him as easy as not. George Hungerford was sleeping off a sick headache. That's a fine alibi. A dame named Freda Cramm was out for a drive to see the hunter's moon rise. Nobody remembers seeing her. The landlady in the place where he lives was at the movies – nobody saw her there. Nobody saw anybody. I personally think that either the guy slipped and fell on the poker, thereby busting in his own head, or else everybody in town bumped him off in a group. No out-of-town connections known. A showgirl named Bubbles Merryweather has turned up in New York with a poem which he dedicated to her after a warm evening in the local bistros, but that was the only time she ever saw him, and could be her press agent wrote the thing anyhow – for my money it stinks. It's what you call a mystery.'

'There's a girl at our house,' said Honey dreamily, 'who had an aw-ful crush on him.'

Kate set her drink down abruptly and glared at her, 'Shut up!' she snapped. 'Nobody asked you anything!'

Honey ran her hand under her hair, unmoved. 'It does not make any difference,' she said. 'She's an awful drip.'

'She's a nice enough kid,' said Kate fiercely. 'She's just miserable. Keep your trap shut when you don't know what you're talking about, which is usually.'

'Ah-ah-ah!' said Donelly. 'Birds in their little nests agree! What drew you two turtle-doves together is something I've been asking myself all evening.'

'I'm making a study of remnants of feudalism in the United States for a sociology course,' said Kate coldly.

'Are you ready for another Alexander, honey-chile?' said the reporter tenderly, and she was.

He thought he wouldn't push it just now; he put some more nickels in the machine and came back to the table. 'Dance?' he said to Kate. She turned scarlet. 'In these?' she said, looking down at her dungarees. Then she tightened her mouth. 'Sure.' Honey sipped indifferently at her Alexander, mildly surprised at this turn of events, but as he had predicted to himself, not unduly disturbed. If he had danced with Honey, Kate would have sulked the rest of the evening. Surprisingly, she was not a bad dancer. She floated along like a firm little balloon in her dirty tennis shoes. When it seemed a possible moment, he said, 'Did Honey have a crush on this guy?'

'That narcissist?' said Kate scornfully. 'Two loves has she and both of them are herself.'

'Then what's she got against the kid that had a crush on Boyle?'

'You wouldn't try to pump me, would you, mister?' said Kate. 'Ask her.'

'O.K., I will,' he said, getting a little sore.

They danced for a while in silence, and when the record was over, went back to the table. Honey's drink was gone again; she was beginning to look glassy-eyed.

'What about the kid that had the crush on Boyle?' said Donelly abruptly, sitting down beside her.

'Huh?' she said, coming out of her fog. 'I beg your pardon? Oh – Mister – I forget your name. She has an awful crush on him. Juss tanawfulcrush. *She* got *so* hys-*ter*-ical *they* had to send her to the In-*fir*-mary. Mr I-forgetchername, will you buy me another Alexayunduh?'

'You mean so you can go to the Infirmary too?' said Kate. 'You're plastered, Sacheveral.'

Honey raised her hand in a gracious but too sweeping gesture, then ran it under her hair. 'The Sacheverals *always* hold their liquor like gentlemen. I mean, ladies too. I mean.'

'Pull yourself together, chum,' said Kate rising abruptly. 'It's five of ten and I'm going to walk you home.'

Jack rose too. 'Look, I've got a car, let me drive you.'

'Nuh-uh,' Kate refused, thrusting Honey's limp arms into the sleeves of her polo coat. 'Not that I think you're wolf enough for the two of us, but she needs the walk if she's going to face Miss Sanders.'

She was propelling the giggling Honey out into the bar when he caught at her elbow desperately. 'Look,' he said, 'give me a break. What's the name of the cookie with the crush?'

'Morrison,' said Honey, before Kate could stop her, 'Molly Morrison. And is she a *goon*!'

Kate let go of Honey, who reeled slightly, then sat down on a bar stool, smiling amiably. 'I think you're a heel,' she said to Donelly fiercely. 'You leave that kid alone! If this sees the light of print I'll – I'll rend you limb from limb! I'll bash *your* head with a poker!'

Donelly smirked. 'Business is business,' he said, 'but I do love spirit in a woman. Tell you what, Chubby, if I thought you could look other than as if you'd just crawled out from under a car, I'd ask you to take in a flick with me Friday night.'

'You!' spluttered Kate. 'You yellow journalist!' But he saw the rust of pink come into her face as she grabbed Honey roughly and hauled her out of the bar.

## Chapter 7

THE light in the room was a pale diffused whiteness coming through the neat sterile curtains. The blankets were white, the iron bed was white, the absurd nightshirt they had put her into was white. Her brain too was white – she saw it lying inside her skull like some strange, beautiful, convoluted white coral. She thought what a fine painting her brain would make. She began composing a letter to her father. Dear Daddy, she would say, I would like you to paint a picture of my brain. It is to be very white and pure, with pure grey-white shadows in the crevices. It is to be lying on a thick white plate, which is decorated with an olive-green band. ... Then, as she imagined this, she suddenly saw that in the centre of the white, white brain, which had somehow, magically, been cleft, a little red heart lay, like the Sacred Heart in the engraving on the wall of her Catholic nurse's room when she was a little girl. 'Oh, this is very silly!' she said out loud, and giggled, and the tears ran down her cheeks into the pillow.

She was just dropping off to sleep again when Miss Justin stuck her white-capped head around the door. 'Molly,' she said in a blasting whisper, 'are you awake?'

She opened her eyes wide and tried to keep the room from tilting. They kept giving her pills – sedatives. 'Yes,' she said thickly, 'I'm awake – I think.'

'Your brother is here,' Miss Justin said, and withdrew her head before Molly could answer.

Now this is really very strange, she thought. Because, *surely* I have no brother. I *couldn't* be as mixed up as *that*. But Miss Justin had said so. 'Lord have mercy, can this be I?' Molly said aloud, giggling, the tears running out of her eyes once more.

She heard their voices outside her door – Miss Justin's and a man's. In a moment Miss Justin stuck her head round again. 'Here he is!' she cried. Then a young tweedy-looking man with a crew cut and horn-rimmed glasses edged through the door. 'Molly!' he said, in what sounded to her like a very loud voice. He shut the door behind him.

'Why,' she said, 'I don't know you at all.' And began to cry.

'Sh-sh-sh!' he said nervously, tiptoeing to her bedside. 'There's nothing to cry about.'

'Nothing to cry about!' she repeated in bitter hopelessness, the tears pouring and pouring out from under her closed eyelids. She felt something being pushed into her hand; she opened her eyes and saw it was the young man's handkerchief. She was grateful, but could not speak. She blew her nose.

'Molly,' he said, 'I want to help you.'

'Help me?' she said violently. 'Help me? No one can help me. They all hate me, and now he is dead.'

'Why,' he said, 'I'm sure nobody hates you, Molly. Who do you think could hate you?'

'They all do,' she said. 'All of them. I sit at the tables with them, looking at their cold faces, and I think that if by magic I disappeared, no one would know the difference. And if I say, Pass the butter, Pass the cream, nobody hears me until I say it too loud. Then they all look at me and laugh at me and hate me. They laugh at my clothes and my ... ' Now she was sobbing uncontrollably in great convulsive hiccoughs.

'Molly!' he tried to stop her, 'Molly!'

Gradually the sobbing slowed. 'Molly, do you know what happened to Mr Boyle?'

'Oh,' she moaned, twisting away on the pillow, 'he was murdered, most cruelly murdered. Do you think it was my fault he was murdered?'

'Your fault – how could it have been your fault, Molly?'

'Do you think I could have turned him from it if I'd been brave? Suppose I had said to him, I love you. That would have changed his whole life, you know, however much or little, for better or for worse. If I had said to him, I love you, my darling, I will black your boots, mend your clothes ... Kevin Boyle!'

'Did you ever go to his house, Molly?'

'Go to his house? It's as if I had lain in his bed by his heart every night that I lay down to sleep. You close your eyes, and there you are, nestled and cradled in warmth .. '

'Molly,' the voice broke in, 'where were you when the murder took place?'

Her hands were over her upturned face, hiding it, her words came out muffled from under her palms. 'I feel sometimes that it might have been myself that killed him, that broke his darling head. For if I had had the courage ... '

'Was he in love with you, Molly?'

At that she laughed out loud between her hands, in the midst of her tears. 'In love with me? Why, he hardly knew I was on the earth, and yet ... '

Miss Justin's bright voice broke in as she opened the door. 'Time's up, Mr Morrison!' she cried. 'Can't have our little girl all tired out!'

'Good-bye, Molly,' said the man's voice. 'I'll be back.'

She was broken and sunk with the disappointment of

not being able to finish what she had to say ... 'Why?' she almost shouted at him. 'Why should you?'

'Oh, Molly,' soothed Miss Justin, 'your brother wants to see you cheer up, just as we all do!'

'My brother!' said Molly sardonically, and began to sob again as the door closed.

## Chapter 8

### SCHOOLGIRL CRUSH KEY TO CAMPUS MURDER?

*

### 'MY FAULT HE DIED' — MOLLY MORRISON TELLS 'MESSENGER REPORTER'

*

### NEWSMAN DISCOVERS NEW SUSPECT IN BOYLE KILLING

*

West Lyman, Conn., November 17th (*Messenger Exclusive*). 'Was it my fault he was murdered?' moaned Molly Morrison, prostrate in her shaded room at the vine-clad Infirmary of exclusive Hollymount College. When queried, she lapsed into one of the fits of weeping which have characterized her state since she has been a patient in the Hollymount Infirmary, where she was taken last Tuesday when she collapsed after the murder of Kevin Boyle. Molly, a wan but pretty girl of eighteen, described Boyle as her lover and spoke of frequent visits to his home. Her whereabouts at the time of the murder are as yet undetermined, but fellow students knew of her 'crush' on the handsome young professor of English, and described her frequent walks in the direction of the house where he lodged.

Boyle, a twenty-nine-year-old professor of English literature and author of some published verse, was killed last Monday, November 13, in his rooms, at 145 West Street, West Lyman, Connecticut. Police have as yet made no arrests in connection with the murder.

Miss Morrison, a student at Hollymount, in her freshman year, is a native of Cincinnati, Ohio, and daughter of the well-known portrait and landscape painter, Miles Morrison, and Mrs. Dorothea Morrison.'

The bleak light came through the long windows and refracted pallidly from Bainbridge's bald head. He sat at his large desk between large studio portraits of his large wife and three children, and looked down at the newspaper, slowly shaking his head. 'Just what I was afraid of,' he said with mournful finality.

His secretary was pacing up and down the room, her face scarlet. It was one of her numerous (always well-performed) duties to get angry for Mr Bainbridge. 'It's – it's unconscionable!' she spluttered. 'It's yellow journalism! Why, Mr Bainbridge, it isn't even a Hearst paper!'

The president laughed shortly. He laid the paper down and began tapping it with his forefinger. 'What's to be done, what's to be done ... '

'Make them retract!' said Miss Seltzer fiercely.

'How do I know it isn't true?'

'Oh dear,' she moaned, 'I should have called the Infirmary at *once*. How they could have let him *in* ... '

'Good,' said Bainbridge, rising from his chair and

slapping his hand down on the paper. 'Call Miss Wellaby or Dr Abby or somebody. I'll call Alex Brill. He'll have some suggestion.'

Miss Seltzer disappeared to the reception desk to use her phone; Bainbridge took up the instrument on his desk to call Alexander Brill, the consulting lawyer for the college. Miss Seltzer was back by the time he was finished; they looked at each other hopelessly.

'What are lawyers for, anyhow, Seltz?' said the president miserably. 'When it isn't in the law books they're no more use than anybody else.'

'You pays your money and they makes your choice,' said Miss Seltzer. 'What did he say?'

'Oh, he was sensible, but no more than you or I could have been. The real point is that the milk is spilt, as we both knew, I suppose. He suggested that I inform myself as thoroughly as possible as to the facts about the girl so that I would be able to meet the questions that are bound to come up. Damn it, Seltz, when I talked to Hungerford, he told me he had it on good authority that Boyle was pretty careful about students.'

'Oh, Mr Bainbridge, you know how Mr Hungerford is! He wouldn't know about a thing like that. Even before his breakdown last year he was a regular as – ascetic – or do I mean aesthetic?' said Miss Seltzer, who affected malapropisms as a contrast to her academic surroundings.

'What about the Infirmary?'

'I talked to Miss Justin. She says the only person who has been to see the girl is her brother. He asked to see her alone.'

'That doesn't make sense. Probably – oh, I'll have to go up there and have a talk with them.' He was rising from his swivel chair when the phone rang. He started to lift it out of its cradle, then motioned to Miss Seltzer. 'I don't want to talk to anybody until I've got just what has been going on straight in my mind.'

She picked up the phone. 'Hello? Who's calling? Oh ... Will you hold the wire a moment?' She pressed her palm over the speaking end of the phone. 'The Chief of Police,' she said, with a half-comical look of woe.

'O God,' said Bainbridge. 'Damn, damn ... Yes, I guess I'd better speak to him.' He took the phone. 'Hello, Captain Flaherty. Yes, yes, I have. Yes, I just did. I can't imagine ... You WHAT? ... Oh, look here, Flaherty! The least you could have done was to call me first ... Town and gown be damned, there a lot of taxpayers in this town wouldn't have property to tax if it weren't for the business they do with this college ... ' Miss Seltzer was nodding her head and clapping her hands in silent approval.

'Give him what-for!' she mouthed without sound.

'Don't apologize; I see no excuse for it. Look here, Flaherty –' Bainbridge was passing his free hand rapidly over his bald spot and looking at the ceiling. 'Why do you suppose we have that girl in the Infirmary? Because the college doctors suspect and have suspected that she is seriously mentally unbalanced ... You didn't give me a chance. If you'd called me first ... I certainly did ... We've called in a psychiatrist who is to see her to-day ... Dr Julian Forstmann from Springfield. We should have a report to-morrow. He's coming to examine her ... If you let out a word of that confession ... '

Miss Seltzer's jaw dropped, her eyes grew round as the lenses of her Oxford glasses, and she clasped her hands in pantomimed prayer.

'I should think so ... ' said Bainbridge. 'Hold everything until you hear from him. All right. I'll call you. Good-bye.'

He hung up the phone and immediately gestured wildly to Miss Seltzer. 'Get Forstmann on the phone! Get him right away!'

She ran to the outer office, got her special address book, and rang Dr Forstmann. She had to wait while Dr Forstmann finished on another wire. Bainbridge looked up at her rather helplessly, sunk in his tilted chair. 'My God, Seltz,' he said softly, 'how do I know I'm not aiding and abetting a criminal? What do I know about the girl? The old save-the-surface instinct ... '

'Now, Mr Bainbridge,' she soothed, the telephone still at her ear, 'there's a ninety-nine and forty-four hundredths per cent. chance ... Hello? Dr Forstmann? Here's Mr Bainbridge to speak to you.

'Julian?' said Bainbridge, and relaxed visibly at the sound of the professional voice at his ear. 'You saw it? How soon can you look her over? My dear man, *I* don't know why you weren't called before ... I wish to God you had been ... I know, I know ... How soon could you look her over? I have to talk to you, too – she's signed a confession. Yes ... God, I don't know ... If you could see her first ... Can you make it in three-quarters of an hour? ... Not till one-thirty? ... Oh, all right, I'll meet you at my office at one-thirty ... Yes, of course I am. What did you expect, a state of coma? ... Don't tell me to be calm, you – you psychoanalyst!' He hung up and sighed. To Miss Seltzer's raised eyebrows he replied, 'Be here at one-thirty.' Once more he raised himself from his chair, this time somewhat wearily. 'Well, I'm going to the Infirmary to find out what they have on the girl. Have the Registrar's office send up her records. Put off all engagements for to-day, and phone Mrs Bainbridge that I won't be home to lunch. I'll be back in about an hour, I guess. Try to hold everything at arm's length until then.'

'You said –' breathed Miss Seltzer, 'you said – *confession*?'

'I did,' said Bainbridge, taking his coat and hat from the old-fashioned hat tree in the corner. 'Signed confession that she killed him.'

## Chapter 9

DR JULIAN FORSTMANN arrived at one-thirty sharp. 'Hello Seltz,' he said to Miss Seltzer hurriedly, and knocked on the president's door. Bainbridge opened it with his hat and coat in hand. 'Don't come in and sit down,' he said. 'I'll tell you what I know on the way to the Infirmary. I want to be able to tell the police as soon as I can that you've examined her.'

Forstmann nodded his Lincoln-like forelock into his eyes, and the two men left the building together. 'Take my car,' said Forstmann.

'All right.'

Indian summer was holding. The bare vaults of the trees spread black against the brilliant sky. Dr Forstmann drove in silence, and for a few moments Bainbridge said nothing either. 'How's Hungerford?' said Dr Forstmann suddenly.

The president turned. 'Hungerford? Oh, he seems very well. Doesn't go out much, but handles his classes all right.'

Forstmann grunted and turned the car down a side street. 'Tell me about the girl,' he said. 'We're almost there.'

'It's hard,' said Bainbridge. 'When I come right down to it, I don't know very much. I know nothing at all of the child personally. I didn't try to see her.'

'What about her family?' said Forstmann. They drew up in front of the white clapboard Infirmary – vine-clad, as the *Messenger* had described it. 'How about her academic record and so forth?'

'I looked up what we had on her,' said Bainbridge, settling back in his corner of the seat. Forstmann pulled the brake and switched off the ignition. 'Comes from Cincinnati, father is an artist, mother is a – housewife. Went to public school, showed a marked talent for drawing. Fair enough marks in high school, passed her college boards easily. Won a small scholarship, in fact. Since she's been here she's been failing four out of five courses, the fifth being an art course – drawing. I am told by the housemother in her dormitory that she has been rather unpopular and antisocial. Since she's been in the Infirmary, some of the girls have told Miss Sanders – that's the housemother – that she was always writing in journals, or something of the sort, but frankly, I haven't felt justified in having the girl's room searched for private papers as yet. I'm probably overdelicate.'

'Yes,' said Forstmann gravely. 'It would probably be best to have such matters in a safe place, in any case.'

'Good,' said Bainbridge; 'I'll have Miss Sanders look through her things. Then there has been this so-called crush on Boyle. She's been pretty obviously in love with him, I gather, and when he was killed, she went completely haywire. Miss Sanders thought it best to send her to the Infirmary. She wrote to the girl's mother, but hasn't had an answer. Let me see. Am I telling you anything you want to know?'

'Go ahead,' Forstmann nodded.

'Yesterday, a young man turned up who announced himself at the Infirmary as her brother. The head nurse had no reason to suspect he was anything else, and let him in to see her. That, apparently, was the *Messenger* reporter,' said Bainbridge, pulling his ear.

'So?' said the doctor, raising his eyebrows and hooking his long arm over the steering wheel.

'The next thing was that Flaherty, the chief of police, got hold of the *Messenger* story first thing this morning, and came high-tailing it up here, blustered his way into the girl's room, and got a confession from her – by what means I don't like to think, knowing Flaherty's attitude about his duty to the tax-payers.'

'Have you seen – or have you got the confession?'

'Oh, Lord,' groaned Bainbridge. 'What a fool! Of course you would want to see that first of all. I had so little inclination to see Flaherty that I never even thought of it.'

'Never mind. I'll see it later. What else?'

'I guess that's about all. No, I can't think of anything. Shall we go in, then?'

They got out of the car and hurried up the brick walk, looking like Mutt and Jeff, the psychiatrist tall and lanky, the president short and rotund. 'Will you see the girl at once?' said Bainbridge.

'First the nurse and the charts,' said Forstmann. 'I thought that if it was at all possible I'd give her a Rorschach test to-day.'

'That's the ink-blot thing?'

Forstmann nodded.

'You witch-doctors!' said Bainbridge, and rang the door-bell. A nurse opened the door, a red-headed, hatchet-faced woman who had been weeping. 'Oh, Miss – ah –'

'Justin, Mr Bainbridge,' said the nurse, and looked as if she were going to begin to cry again.

'Miss Justin is putting herself through the torments of the damned for having let the reporter in,' said Bainbridge wearily to his companion. 'It is with difficulty that I have restrained her from turning in her uniform. Maybe you can convince her, Dr Forstmann, that it could, as they say, have happened to anyone.'

'Are you Molly Morrison's nurse?' asked Forstmann. 'Have you her charts?'

'Oh yes, Dr Forstmann,' cried Miss Justin in relief, and disappeared starchily down the hall. Bainbridge shook his head in admiration. 'All morning she wept on my shoulder. You present her with a titbit of occupational therapy and she's off as happily as a beagle after a rabbit. It's as my wife used to say when the children were in nursery school – child psychology doesn't work for parents.'

'I think you'd better go away, Lucien,' said Forstmann amiably. 'You communicate your state of nerves to everyone but me.'

'What's the matter with you?' said Bainbridge. 'I've always meant to ask.

'Psychiatrists are meant to be nonconductors – that's all. Now go away and balance the budget or something.'

'Oh, Julian, be charitable and let me wait! You know I'll want to have the verdict as soon as you've seen her.'

'You won't have anything like a *verdict*, Lucien,' said

Dr Forstmann. 'You'll have my opinion, which in this case is as fallible as yours or Flaherty's. The girl is undoubtedly neurotic from what has been said of her, but so are most of the people you know; I can probably tell you whether or not she is psychotic, but that still won't prove her a murderess. As for the Rorschach test, there isn't nearly enough statistical material to support its absolute validity – I use it because I have found it helpful as a short cut to diagnosis. In any case, I can't have the test scored before to-morrow at the earliest, assuming that I find the girl in a state to take it. My advice to you – which I render gratis – is to go and take a long walk in the country, come home and take a nap, wake up and have a drink ready for me at five o'clock.'

'Five o'clock!' said Bainbridge reproachfully. 'Oh, Julian!'

'I may have to go back to town,' said the doctor, 'and in any case I want some time to think how I can best advise you. Now go on, go on home, get out before you send Miss Justin into her act again – go on, I hear her coming.'

Woebegone, the president let himself out the door as Dr Forstmann took off his coat and hat and set down his brief case just as Miss Justin arrived with the charts in her hand. She gave them to him and stood sniffing as he looked them over. 'Had a good deal of seconal, hasn't she?'

'Oh, Dr Forstmann,' Miss Justin exploded, 'Dr Abby gave me permission to give it to her at my discretion because the girl just never would have slept – just lay there crying and crying to herself.'

'I'm surprised I haven't heard about her from Dr Abby before now.'

'Oh,' said Miss Justin, making her red-rimmed eyes wide, 'she's not what you'd call crazy, you know. That is, you would never have thought so until – oh, Dr Forst-mann,' cried Miss Justin, an incipient howl in her voice, 'I'll just never forgive myself! I mean, even if she did it! I mean –'

'Suppose you let me see her now,' said Forstmann quickly.

'Oh yes, Doctor!' sniffed Miss Justin, and led him off foward the end of the hall. She opened the last door and said through it in a bright voice, 'Here's Dr Forstmann to see you, Molly!' She led him into a dim white room. Through the curious sterile light he made out a white, bloated face on the pillow, a pointed face under an auburn bang, distorted by weeping – almost like the face of a drowned girl. 'How do you do?' the face said faintly, politely.

'How's our girl, now?' said Miss Justin, half to the doctor.

'Suppose you let me speak with Molly alone for a few moments,' said the psychiatrist.

'Of course, of course,' agreed Miss Justin, and dis-appeared in a rustle.

Forstmann pulled the low wicker chair up to the bed-side, sat down and crossed his long legs, then rose again. 'Mind if I raise the shade?' he said.

'Oh no,' said the face, and something came over it which was almost recognizable as a smile; 'I feel just like a corpse all laid out here.' But immediately the tears began to pour from the swollen slits of eyes, down the temples to the pillow.

Forstmann raised the shade and sat down again. 'That better?' he said, but the face only rolled away from him.

'Why like a corpse, Molly?' he said. 'What makes you say that?'

'Oh, I don't know,' she said, so faintly that he could hardly hear her. 'It's like white flowers – waxy – and white skin, and – everything is so white. I keep thinking about my brain.'

'What about your brain?'

'I keep thinking what a fine painting it would make. I couldn't paint it, but my father could.'

'Why couldn't you paint it yourself? You thought of it.'

The face turned back to him now, he thought he could see something like indignation on it. 'Oh, this is a really *fine* painting that I have in mind.'

'Is your father Miles Morrison?'

'Yes,' she said, almost eagerly, 'do you know his work?'

'There's a painting – a landscape – in the Springfield Museum.'

'Yes!' she said excitedly. 'I know it, I know it! You're the first one who's known about it!'

'Molly,' he said, 'I'm a psychiatrist. I'm here to find out why it is you're so unhappy.' At this she sobbed out loud, once, then caught her breath. 'And to see if you can't find the source of your unhappiness and be rid of it.'

'That's impossible,' she said flatly.

'I don't think so,' he said.

'It is incontrovertible,' she said with dignity. 'He is dead. I killed him.'

Forstmann sat forward in his chair. 'How did you kill him, Molly?'

'I killed him because I had no courage. I killed him.'

'Why did you kill him, Molly?'

She opened her swollen eyes a little wider and stared at him. 'Why? Why, because I had no courage.'

'Listen, Molly,' he said, 'do you mean literally that

you killed Kevin Boyle, or do you mean that you feel you
are responsible for his death?'

She began to sob aloud and roll her head back and
forth on the pillow. 'I killed him!' she said. 'I killed him,
I killed him! I murdered him! He is dead, murdered, and
I killed him! He was all I had in the world and I killed
him!'

'If you killed him, Molly, you must have had a great
deal of hostility against him – you must have wanted to
do him an injury,' said Forstmann deliberately.

Suddenly she propped herself up on her elbows, her
head rolling weakly on her neck. 'If you think that,' she
whispered, 'you are very wrong, and I will never speak
to you again.' She fell back on the pillow and tears welled
up in her eyes again. 'And I should be sorry for that,' she
went on, whispering, 'because you look like him.'

'Like Kevin Boyle, Molly?'

'Of course,' she whispered harshly, 'of course, like
him.'


## Chapter 10

WHEN Bainbridge returned to his office in spite of Dr
Forstman's advice, sneaking in at the back door of
College Hall in order to avoid possible lurking reporters,
he found Miss Seltzer alone in the outer office except for
a bedraggled figure sitting in a pose of utter dejection on
one of the straight chairs. When he walked in, Miss
Seltzer raised her head from the typing, and her eyebrows flew up her forehead as she indicated the visitor.

'I managed to stall everybody except Miss Innes here,'

she said. 'She says she must speak to you about the story in the *Messenger*.'

Bainbridge removed his hat. 'Very well, very well,' he said, in weary irritation. 'Come inside, Miss – whatever you said your name was.'

'Innes,' said Kate drearily, 'Kate Innes.' She followed Bainbridge into his office.

'Sit down,' he said, as he removed his coat and hat, hung them on the hat tree. She obeyed. Then he sat down behind his desk and looked at her pointedly. 'Well?'

'Mr Bainbridge,' she said, 'I feel terrible.'

The president looked her over from top to toe. She was clad in a smudgy polo coat, blue jeans and sweatshirt, and a pair of elderly tennis shoes. Her short hair bent weakly upward from her face. Her horn-rimmed glasses were sliding down her gleaming nose. For once in a way he let himself go. 'You *look* terrible,' he snapped back at her. 'You girls are a blot on the institution of womanhood. I sometimes feel that the students at Hollymount have created a third sex – and please don't misunderstand me – which bears little resemblance to the male and none to the female.'

'It's just an affectation,' said Kate meekly.

'For God's sake, when are you going to grow out of it?' said Bainbridge, his temper almost spent. 'Well, get on with it. You didn't come here for a lecture on apparel. I'll save that for a general assembly. What's on your mind?'

'Mr Bainbridge,' said Kate miserably, 'that story in the *Messenger* is all my fault, in a way.'

'It doesn't matter whose fault it is any more,' Bainbridge said resignedly. 'The damage is done now. But I suppose you want to make your confession and that's what I'm here for. You seem to have good sense, girl. What in the world possessed you to talk to a reporter instead of coming to me or to the police if you had some kind of information you felt to be important?'

'I *didn't* have anything at all – I – we – it was all my damned curiosity. Like sticking beans up your nose,' said Kate. 'I don't know what good it will do, really, but if I tell you how it was, I'm pretty sure we can get hold of the reporter who wrote the piece, and when we do – ' her brows drew together, 'if nothing else comes of it, *you* can put a scare into him, and I know *I* can make him feel so low he'll be able to sit on a dime and swing his feet. He is,' she added more complacently, 'a rather malleable young man, I should judge.'

'Oh, you should, should you?' said Bainbridge, and rose from behind his desk. 'If I don't eat now, I'm not going to get any lunch to-day. Have you had yours, Miss – don't tell me now – Innes?'

Kate shook her head No.

'Then you'll join me; otherwise I'll have to eat while you watch me with your mouth watering.' Bainbridge stuck his head out the door and said to Miss Seltzer, 'Have The Coffee Shoppe send me a liverwurst sandwich on rye bread and a black coffee. What'll you have, Miss Innes?'

'The same,' said Kate.

He went back to his desk and sat down again. 'Now, what's the story?'

Kate looked down at her lap for a moment, then pushed her glasses up her nose. 'Mr Bainbridge, there is another person involved in this story, but I am morally responsible. If I bring this other person in just to keep myself from getting involved in a pack of white lies, will you believe me when I say I'm the one who really deserves the blame? I mean, are you willing to assume that I have better than average intelligence and this other person is a high-grade moron – which is no insult, Mr Bainbridge: she's just an average student.'

'I don't know,' said Bainbridge. 'I'll have to see.'

Kate looked at him suspiciously for a moment. 'Well, I'll just not mention the other person's name, then. Here's how it happened: I was sitting in the Harlow Taproom with this other person when a young man came in whom I spotted at once for a reporter.'

'How?' said Bainbridge.

'Well, he looked like a Harvard boy except for the rings around his eyes and a certain indefinable something.'

'I guess I'll have to take your word for it.'

'I *deliberately lured* him to come and sit with us, Mr Bainbridge, because you had asked us not to talk to reporters!'

'Oh, fine, fine!' snorted Bainbridge. 'This leads me to regard my position of mentor in an entirely new light.'

'I can't help it, Mr Bainbridge,' said Kate solemnly; 'when anybody talks to me as if I hadn't good sense, I'm immediately tempted to act as if I hadn't. Like sticking beans up your nose.'

'That's a very suggestive phrase; would you elucidate its meaning?'

'Why, you don't know the story about the mother who said to her children the last thing before she went out, Now be sure not to stick beans up your nose? Naturally, they would never have thought of it if she hadn't put the idea into their heads.'

Bainbridge nodded sadly, and at that moment Miss Seltzer appeared with the paper bag of lunch. Bainbridge removed the sandwiches and cartons from the bag to his blotter, Kate wrestled out of her coat, and for a moment they were silent while they arranged themselves to eat.

'Well,' said Kate, around a partially consumed mouthful, 'I guess my motivations are sort of irrelevant. The point is, he came and sat with us, and we had a couple of drinks, and one thing led to another until this person I was with got a little tight.' She laid down her sandwiches on the paper napkin that lay on the arm of her chair and gazed at him steadfastly over the rim of her glasses. 'If I were noble, Mr Bainbridge, I'd say I was the one who let the cat out of the bag, but anybody can see I'm not the kind of girl a man gets drunk and worms things out of.'

'Anybody,' said Bainbridge, as drily as he could with his mouth full.

'So this person began responding to his little insinuations about what did we know about the murder by talking about Molly Morrison, because her crush on Mr Boyle had gotten to be the house joke, only when she went to the Infirmary after he was killed, it was more the house scandal.'

'What do you think of Molly Morrison?' said Bainbridge, with sudden sharpness.

'What do I think of her?'

'I mean, how do you size her up? How did she seem among the other girls? I've talked to Miss Sanders, but I'm glad to have a chance to hear how she appeared to other students.'

Kate paused a moment and pushed her glasses up. 'Well,' she began slowly, 'I didn't see an awful lot of her because I'm a Senior and she's a Freshman, and besides we're on different floors. But I noticed her, because I could see she was miserable, only I'm not the type to be helpful with lame-ducks, even when I want to – I just go crashing in where angels fear to tread. Nobody liked her much, because she was too quiet and scared and obviously a misfit. She was a little too intellectual for her own good, too.'

'She was failing four out of five subjects, although I don't know why I should be telling you,' said Bainbridge.

'You know that doesn't mean a thing as well as I do,' said Kate, who was warming up with the coffee. 'My guess is that she came from some sort of artistic or intellectual family where she heard real adults talking most of the time.'

'Her father is a painter – Miles Morrison.'

'Gee, I'm getting good!'

'Don't let it go to your head,' said Bainbridge, who had been forgetting he was a college president under the stresses of the day. 'What were the girls saying about her – ah – attachment to Mr Boyle?'

'Well, it was very obvious that she had a terrible crush on him – she was always seeing to it that she sat in his booth at The Coffee Shoppe and when she couldn't, she would moon at him from near by. She was in his section of freshman English, and the girls in the class with her said she would always have something cooked up to talk to him about after class. Then there were some of us in the house who were kind of nauseated by the girlish response to all the wild Irish charm he passed around. Not Molly's – she had a kind of dignity about it, in a way I couldn't explain – maybe just because she was so hard hit. But the ones who didn't really care about him, but who were always shooting off their mouths about wasn't he *dar-ling*. One day she spoke up at the table – which was unusual in itself – and gave me the devil after I'd taken a crack at Our Kevin, and after that she got a certain amount of attention and riding about her great love. It always made me squirm when they went after her – it seemed to mean so much more to her than an ordinary crush – as if it were the only thing she had in life.'

'Miss Innes,' said Bainbridge, who had been staring gravely into his carton of coffee while Kate talked, 'what would you say if I told you that Molly Morrison signed a confession of having murdered Kevin Boyle for the police this morning?'

Kate went white, then flushed bright red. 'Oh no!' she said, wadding her paper napkin in her hand. 'That's impossible! It's all that *Messenger* thing – that damned distorted –'

Bainbridge was watching her steadily. 'You mean you think she is incapable of such an act?'

'As murder? Absolutely! I'll – I'll stake my reputation on it!'

Bainbridge raised his eyebrows. 'Well, I hope you're right. We're going to have a professional opinion on it this afternoon – Dr Forstmann, our consulting psychiatrist, is examining the girl. But I would like to show how you, knowing Molly Morrison, would explain that confession.'

Without hesitation Kate said, 'Pure hysteria. She's thought about the murder until somehow she's twisted it around so she thinks she could have saved him, or something. And probably when the police questioned her, she took some kind of pleasure in accusing herself.'

Bainbridge pulled his ear and shook his head. 'The

things you children say!' he remarked insultingly. 'Where do you borrow your wisdom?'

But now that she had confessed and eaten, Kate refused to be baited. 'I'm a psychology major,' she said composedly. 'A little Freud and a little Horney combined with a certain amount of common sense go a long way. Have you ever read a book called *The Criminal, the Judge and the Public*, by Alexander and Staub, Mr Bainbridge? It suffers from a strictly Freudian viewpoint, but it makes certain sound conclusions about the desire for love and the fear of punishment which seem relevant to the case in hand. The authors say –'

Bainbridge raised his hand and cried, 'Please, Miss Innes, I'm having a hard enough day; don't begin educating me! What I wanted to say was that if you honestly feel that it's impossible for Molly Morrison to have committed this murder, you won't feel you're acting as my – ah – stooge if I ask you to make a definite effort to scotch some of the wild rumours that are bound to crop up – probably have already. So far we've been able to keep this thing relatively quiet and to restrain conjecture. With the *Messenger* article, I imagine that all hell – if you'll pardon the expression – will break loose.'

Kate began working her way into her coat as if ready for immediate action. 'What about the reporter, Mr Bainbridge? Do you want to level him? Sa-ay! I'll bet you that between us we could enlist him in an *anti*-smear campaign! I mean,' she said, blushing, 'he seemed a *relatively* decent guy.'

'I don't imagine we could persuade him to focus attention *away* from the college, which is my objective at the moment, so I can't see much point in bothering with him.'

'No, wait a moment,' said Kate, excitedly flapping the empty end of her coat-sleeve. 'It never does to antagonize the press. I'll bet that if you talked to him and scared him witless first – threatened a libel suit or something – and then relented, you could get yourself some publicity of the kind you'd really like to have.'

'The only kind of publicity I want at this juncture is an honorary obituary some forty years hence,' said Bainbridge, 'although ... '

'See him, Mr Bainbridge!' pleaded Kate. 'I'm *sure* there'd be something in it – besides my seeing him beaten down to his socks – and if I could just feel I'd done something to vindicate myself for being such a ninny –'

'All right,' said Bainbridge doubtfully. 'I suppose I'm going to have to see some reporter some time. When can you bring him round?'

'Well,' said Kate, 'he said something about a movie to-night ... '

Bainbridge cocked an eyebrow, but said nothing except, 'Very well, you can bring him round to my house, if you like, between eight and nine.'

'Good,' cried Kate, rising and pulling her coat all the way on. 'If I have to manacle him.' She paused in the half-open door with a worried look. 'Mr Bainbridge, don't you think you ought to give me a demerit or something? I kind of defamed the good name of the college, you know.'

'A demerit won't help me,' said the president. 'From now on you're a public relations woman working for me behind the lines of the student body. Just keep that in mind and we'll neglect the demerit.'

'A very sound disciplinary measure,' said Kate, nodding approvingly until her glasses slid to the end of her nose. Bainbridge could hear her rubber soles thudding helter-skelter down the staircase outside the office door.

## Chapter 11

HUNGERFORD lay on the day bed, clutching the mattress as if the couch were rocking and he feared to fall off. His eyes were strained open in self-torture, focused on the row of volumes on the top shelf of his bookcase. *The Round Earth's Corners*, by George Hungerford. *The Psychology of Chance*, by George Hungerford. *Where No Man Pursueth*, by George Hungerford. *Henry James, an Anatomy of Anxiety*, by George Hungerford, *Edgar Allan Poe, the Great Neurotic*, by George Hungerford.

'Where there is no vision the people perish,' he said aloud. The room was blue with early winter twilight. Outside, the bare branches rattled against the window-panes, the windows rattled in their frames. He began to shiver, although the apartment was overheated – the steam was knocking and sizzling in the radiator.

He had perished, for he had lost his vision. In his mind the corpse of his imagination lay dead and rotting, poisoning his being with its remains. He could no more set pen to paper with words of his own creating than he could ... give birth to a child ... No ... Fly ... Than he could ... Sometimes he looked in the mirror and thought it was the face of his own corpse he saw there. His vision had perished. On the table, within reach of his hand, lay the single capsule, resplendent on a saucer, and a tumbler of water, jewelled with bubbles all around the sides. The thing to do now was clutch the mattress until it became

68

quite unbearable, until strange things began to happen
in your brain and you were terrified, you sat up with a
jerk, you swallowed the capsule and gratefully found unconsciousness, as one day, one sweet day, you would find
death.

Twilight was the worst hour, because it was the hour of
indecision. The day had its own tone: grey, or resplendent
with sun, full of the grinding efforts of talking to students,
chattering with imbecile colleagues, lecturing to classes;
the more private burdens of shaving one's face, keeping
one's shoes shined, paring one's fingernails, preventing
one's flesh from stinking of putrefaction. (Too bitter.
These things he should not think for a half hour or so. It
was the poem had done it. Kevin Boyle's poem. No. Not
Kevin. Get on with the train of the thought.)

The nights too had their tone. Sometimes a student
asked him to a dormitory to a faculty dinner, and when
he could bear it at all, he went. More often he called at
the last minute, saying he was ill. But when the shades
were drawn, the lamps lighted, one could write one's
letters, move about among one's books, mark one's
papers. And if the crippled mind found itself capable of
moving from the house after the efforts of the day, one
could – once – have gone to call on Kevin Boyle. Why
Kevin? (He was asking this coolly – he had not allowed
his emotions to outstrip his time schedule – truly he had
not.) For Kevin understood so little the agonies which
had become his daily fare, and in general he found it
more and more his custom to keep clear of those in whom
he could not detect the symptoms of infection by his own
disease. Perhaps it was that Kevin was his only hold on
health; Kevin was youth and strength; might become the
poet and the man George Hungerford had once hoped to

be. Now his mind threw up Kevin Boyle's poem, complete, intact, on an uncontrollable wave of nausea:

> *He who has eaten ambition, accepted it into his person*
> *Cannot un-eat or reject it : it is not part of his essence.*
> *Once a man has devoured hope and desire for power*
> *He must accept his exclusion out of the ranks of humility.*
> *He must declare for devotion, renouncing renunciation,*
> *Abstaining from his abstentions, asserting against denial.*
> *For he is as much committed to commission and to deed*
> *As to Pluto, Persephone, who ate pomegranate seed.*

'You must get away from here,' Hungerford had said to him in most deadly earnestness. 'If you want to be a poet, you must not stay. You will be wrung dry – and I know how foolish it sounds to you that I should assume one place more than another could injure a writer – but because human nature is flawed and cracks under certain pressures, I know this to be *true*!'

But Kevin had laughed his high awkward laugh, the only crevice in his smooth Irish exterior through which you might detect a little core of uncertainty in him, even in him. 'I'll stay yet awhile,' he had said overconfidently, in a way which made Hungerford know that he doubted himself. 'I've nothing to lose, and three square meals a day plus a pleasant life to gain.'

'You've a great, great deal to lose,' Hungerford had said to him sadly. Though he had not meant that Kevin would lose his life. No, not that. In life, in strife, without friend, without wife ...

His mind was getting ahead of the schedule. There were many ways he could tell, and this was one of them – the rhymes. He could not take the capsule until the hand had reached six o'clock. Then he could sleep like death for an hour, and be able to go down to his supper. Now he must check, backtrack a bit, for the hand said only ten minutes of the hour. Like a woman in labour, he gripped the mattress, pulling hard at the muscles of his neck, gritting his teeth.

Last year at this time the lot of them would have been collected in the sitting-room for tomato juice or some other bland apéritif. Among them the doctors, the nurses would be wandering like policemen through a crowd of strikers, dispensing cheerful little warnings of normality. Perhaps if he had gone to one of the really expensive sanatoria instead of to the obscure establishment he had found within his means, he would have despised it less. Yet he doubted it ... He had hated those doctors and nurses with the blind rage of a wise man in minority for the fools in power. The sickening good sense of them! Keep yourself occupied, keep your body fit, learn to mouth the proper clichés and you will solve all problems. They were one step removed, one short step only, from the self-improvement quacks, the philistine executioners of the spirit who said kindly but firmly, Pull yourself together, man, it's all in your mind, as if the mind were the most dispensable part of the man.

Bainbridge had sent him there when he began to crack. The quarrel with Freda Cramm when he had told her at last what a bloody bitch he thought she was; the attempted suicide (the bitterness of failing even at your own death!); and the foul, unutterable kindness of them all, hovering over him, sucking the beautiful gossip from his wounds. 'You'll be much happier ... ' they said. 'You're worn out ... It's an occupational disease. You need a rest.' Bainbridge was more sensible, cooler than the others. He had made the arrangements and sent him off to the sanatorium, had given him a year's leave of absence. And when he came back, having learned to dissemble – something – he found himself honorary chairman of the English Department, smothered in kindness, in understanding. Sometimes he would close his eyes and devise tortures for the kindest of them. It was doing battle with smoke ... In smoke, my head broke; I thought you spoke, but I awoke ... The room was almost completely dark; he could see the illuminated hand on the clock. Still five minutes to six. He drew up his knees and twisted on the bed. All was not kindness. All was not understanding. There was malice and torture and brutality too. Someone hated him, deeply and bitterly. Someone wished to drive him mad. And, not impossibly, it was the same someone who had murdered Kevin Boyle ...

He had sometimes thought it was a college girl, perpetrating a diabolical hoax. Yet he could not imagine what warped mind could have chosen such a means, or him for an object. It had begun last month, just as college was getting into its yearly rhythm. He had returned from supper one evening to find an open notebook lying on his desk. It was a common sort of notebook – he had a number of the same sort himself – brown cardboard covers which turned back on a spiral spring so that the pages lay flat when you opened it. He had gone to examine it, and found the pages covered with enormous, backhand, yet somehow warped schoolgirl writing. There was a date at the top; what followed was an entry in a journal, an entry devoted to a description of himself. It was in part obscene, in part exaggeratedly cruel, in part brutally true. Most of all there was the impression of a mind which was cunning, sensitive to evil only, and brutal beyond words. All that George Hungerford had feared in another human being in his life – the ferreting out of another's doubts of self, the use of them to flay the other's spirit with a merciless hand. It was of such a devilishness that he could not remember a word of it, only the terrible shock of first reading, the impact of the hatred someone bore for him. Carefully, he had laid the tablet away, meaning to examine it at some time when the shock of its vileness had diminished, but he had never found the courage, until one day it lay open again on his desk, a new entry, a new page of vitriolic animosity and obscenity. There had been several now – five or six. They came when he was at his weakest, his most vulnerable, his weariest. He would have stumbled out to dinner, bleary from his drugged sleep; when he returned, almost revived with food and lights and the companionship of the restaurant, it would be there waiting to destroy him: the white pages, the lunatic calligraphy. It was diabolical – obviously the work of a madwoman (for it became plain that the writer was a woman or girl). And he did not know where to turn for a solution, now that Kevin Boyle was dead. For in the last entry it had become clear that the creature was someone known to both of them – or at least someone who knew them both – someone, in fact, who had been in love with Kevin.

The hand of the clock reached the top; it was six. He closed his eyes. Could he – was it possible that he could sleep without the capsule? For a moment his muscles relaxed. Then suddenly his entire body contracted in a spasm; the telephone bell drilled mercilessly; Hungerford started like a man pierced by a bullet. Shaking all over, he rose unsteadily and lifted the phone from its cradle. 'Hello,' he said tremulously.

'George,' said the miniature voice at his ear, 'It's Freda Cramm.'

'He-hello,' he stammered, trying to keep his jaws from clacking together, 'Hello, Freda.'

'George, I want to ask a favour of you.'

He closed his eyes wearily, swaying as he stood. 'Yes.'

'I want to get the English Department together for some sort of memorial gathering for Kevin Boyle.'

'The funeral baked meats,' said Hungerford, almost inaudibly.

'What?'

'Nothing.'

'It was something nasty, I can tell.'

'Quite innocent, I assure you.'

'Kevin told me you had the manuscript of his book of poems,' said Freda. 'Have you it still?'

'Yes, I have.'

'I wondered if you would be willing to read a group of them to us on Friday evening, and maybe say something about them? What do you think?'

I think it is a maudlin, disgusting, self-advertising notion, and quite typical of your very vulgar mind, he thought. 'Very well; at what time?'

'Oh, George, that's wonderful! You see, Philip Frisbee, one of the editors from Cornish House, is passing through, and there might be a possibility of their doing the book.'

'What difference does it make,' said Hungerford, 'now he's dead?' But he knew he was being unreasonable – he only wanted to end the conversation and sleep; he must not bicker this way.

'Why,' Freda bridled audibly, 'I should think you'd be glad ... ' Then, just as audibly, he could hear her recollecting that he had had a nervous breakdown, that he had been in a sanatorium last year, that she must humour him ... 'If you won't mind doing it, I think it will be a fine memorial for Kevin,' she said, 'If you come at eight on Saturday, and plan on reading at eight-thirty.'

'Very well,' he said shortly, and hung up.

The room was quite dark now, the furniture looming in black blotches. His hands were shaking; suddenly the side of his face drew together in the distorting tic, and the thing in his mind began to happen. He flung himself on the table by the day bed, but he upset the water. No matter; he took the capsule and swallowed it dry, the gelatinous sides melting and sticking in his throat. He lay down and clutched the mattress again. Now he was safe from it, sleep would come; he could even think of it, because it could not happen to him now. It was that a terrible thing happened in his head. There was a mountain – that was his brain. He was on the plain, looking up at it. Suddenly he saw a crevice begin to open down its side, a terrible wound from which the bowels of the earth in all their foulness came spilling out ... the mountain was splitting apart, and at the same time something was happening to him. His face contorted into the tic because it was changing, slowly, slowly changing, his hands were changing, his feet were changing – but it was never really accomplished, thank God. He would, when it happened, get up, turn on the light, pace the floor, recite poems, have a drink, run out into the street to where the lights of town shone, or, as to-day, take the capsule and sleep.

## Chapter 12

A GIRL came through the swinging doors and stood in the middle of the corridor. 'Kate In-nes! Tel-e-phone!' she shouted. Down the corridor a door burst open and a grotesque figure scuttled out. The hair was pinned in flat snails over the head, the face was white with grease, a red flannel bathrobe partly covered complete nudity, and one foot was in a white-fur scuff while the other was bare.

'Innes!' gasped the girl as the figure dashed around her as if she were second base. 'Are you sick?'

'Don't bother me!' muttered Kate. 'Is it an outside call?'

'Yes,' said the girl weakly. 'Yes it is. A man, come to think of it.'

But Kate was gone. 'My God!' screamed the girl faintly. 'Bring my smelling salts, Maude – Innes has a man!'

In the phone booth at the head of the stairs Kate shut the door carefully and tried to find an ungreased portion of her cheek against which to lay the receiver.

'Hello,' she said silkily.

'Hello, gorgeous,' said the voice at her ear, 'still the cutest tomato on the vine?'

'Just a little love apple waiting to be plucked,' she said, blushed, stuck out her tongue at the telephone, and drew her brows together.

'Think you can get out of your overalls long enough to take in a flicker to-night?'

'Why, Mr Donelly,' she said, like honey out of a comb, 'at least I assume from the southern Bronx accent that it is Mr Donelly, I think that would be *lovely*.' She scowled horribly and stuck out her tongue again, as if to reassure herself.

'Hey, are you sick or something?' said the voice. 'You don't sound like yourself.'

'Oh, Mr Donelly,' she breathed, this time crossing her eyes at the telephone because she couldn't talk and stick her tongue out at the same time, 'since the other night I don't *feel* like myself.'

'Hey, cut that stuff out, baby! I don't trust you.'

'I have my moods,' said Kate, crossing her legs as well as she could in the limited space. 'You remember me as – ah – crustier?'

'It was the crust that got me. Could you get a little of it back before to-night?'

'I'll work on it, Mr Donelly, I sho'ly will work on it.'

'I'll pick you up at seven-thirty or so. I'd ask you to dinner, but I have to see a man.'

'That's so kind of you, so terribly kind. Make it eight,' said Kate, and hung up. 'That rat,' she whispered to herself fiercely. 'That snake in the grass! That – that traitor to his class!'

She swept out of the phone booth and back down the hall, exposing wide reaches of her ample anatomy as she walked.

At eight o'clock she sat resplendent in the smoking-room of Birnham House, kibitzing on a bridge game. Her hair was clean and curled, she had forgone her glasses and had, as she put it, painted herself like a Third Avenue harlot, although the effect was not so glaring as she pretended. A black dress did its best for her girdled curves; she wore sheer stockings and black pumps. At five minutes after eight the maid came to the door and said, 'Miss Innes, you have a caller.' Gathering up her

77

purse and squinting in order to avoid the furniture, she made her way into the foyer where Donelly stood, digging his hands into the pockets of his reversible and reading a post-card that lay writing-side-up on the mail desk. Observing his activity she forgot herself for the moment and remarked savagely, 'Once a bloodhound, always a son of a bitch.'

He winced and put his hand up as if to ward off a blow. 'Crusty is the word, all right,' he said in a hurt voice. 'Say, you look just as cute as a little red wagon!'

'I please you? Good. You may help me with my coat.' In a queenly manner she picked up her borrowed Persian lamb and held it out to him. He helped her into it and they set off. In the doorway she paused and looked up at him through the mascara. 'I forgot to tell you, I have to stop at a friend's house to pick up a book. Will you go by Eden Street?'

'Sure, sure,' he said innocently. They got into an elderly Plymouth coupe with labels stuck on the windshield saying *Press* and *Messenger*.

At Kate's direction they wound through the dark streets of the town and in a few moments pulled up in front of Bainbridge's house.

'Quite a little shack your friend has,' Donelly remarked, pulling on the brake.

'Just a fourteen-room bungalow,' Kate answered abstractedly. 'Come on in; I won't be a minute.'

'Hey,' said Donelly suspiciously, 'what gives here?'

She turned on him viciously. 'I'm a white slaver – didn't you know? What have you got to lose?'

'O.K., O.K.,' he pacified meekly, and piled out of the car.

Kate rang the bell and Bainbridge himself opened the

door. 'Hello, Mr Bainbridge,' she said. 'May I present that Galahad of the newspaper world, Mr Jack Donelly?'

'Oh-oh,' said Donelly, and regarded the tips of his shoes.

'How do you do, Mr Donelly?' said the president. 'Will you permit me to observe that it is a somewhat mixed pleasure to meet you?'

'I'll permit you,' said Donelly resignedly.

'Won't you come in?'

'As Miss Innes so aptly puts it, what have I got to lose?'

Bainbridge ushered them into the living-room, where a fire crackled and the lamps shone dimly against the dark cherry panelling. When they were out of their coats and seated, a silence fell. Finally Bainbridge, staring into the fire with his plump hands resting on his knees, spoke, 'So you're in the newspaper business, Mr Donelly.'

'Racket is what they generally say,' said Jack.

'I suppose it was in the line of business that you misrepresented yourself to gain admission to a sick girl's room and led her to say things which might twist into an admission of having committed murder?'

'I was sent here to get a story; I got one.'

'Oh, you did, you did indeed,' said Bainbridge. Kate snorted. Another silence fell in which the fire popped, and someone walked across the floor of the room overhead.

Suddenly Bainbridge looked up. 'Is it your impression that Molly Morrison murdered Kevin Boyle?' he said to Donelly.

The reporter raised his head and stared back at him a moment. 'How should I know?' he said defensively. 'I'm sent here to find out what I can – I take what I find and make it into a story to help raise circulation. That's what

I'm paid for – not to have an expert opinion on who murdered who.'

'*Whom*,' muttered Kate.

'I didn't ask you what you knew,' Bainbridge pointed out gently; 'I asked you for your impression. I asked if it was your impression that Molly Morrison murdered Boyle. I'm not baiting you, Donelly. I'll leave that to Miss Innes. Frankly, I'm scared of your paper – it's known as a scandal sheet, and I'd much prefer to have you working with me than to have you against me.'

'I don't see just how that will work out,' said Jack sulkily.

'Neither do I, neither do I,' said Bainbridge. 'But I thought we might talk it over. Will you answer my question?'

'No,' said Jack finally, 'it is not my impression that that kid murdered Boyle – whatever good my impression is to anybody; but it is also my impression that any district attorney who had nobody better to pick on could work up a pretty enough case against her. Nobody knows where she was at the time of the murder – somebody thought she saw her in the Library, but she wasn't sure; somebody thought she might have been at The Coffee Shoppe; another person was positive she saw her at the movies. So much for her alibi. As for her own account of herself, it's my opinion that the kid is a little off her rocker – as you might gather from the story. And I'm not too proud of it, if you're waiting for me to say so.'

Kate sniffed.

Bainbridge shook his head. 'Then she has too many alibis, and every other person at all personally connected with Boyle has none at all.' He paused, beating his knees with his fingers. 'Mr Donelly, the police have co-operated with me in hushing up the fact that Molly Morrison signed a confession for them this morning –'

'Holy smoke!' breathed Jack.

'Since then,' Bainbridge continued, 'I have had her examined by Dr Forstmann, our consulting psychiatrist. Unfortunately, he gave me just the same answer that you did a moment ago – that he could give an impression, but not a verdict. That was before he saw the girl. Since he has seen her, he won't even give his impression as to whether she could or could not possibly have been the killer – says she was too much disturbed when he saw her and he can't surmise as to what she could or could not have committed in the way of violence. Her perturbation, he says, may actually result from the emotional expenditure of committing the murder, or may be pure reaction to the news of Boyle's violent death, since she seems to have placed an importance on Boyle far beyond any actual relation she had with him. Unless she had some secret connection with him of which we know nothing ... Oh, Lord,' Bainbridge groaned finally, 'it's such a mess.'

'It certainly is,' said Jack, scratching his crew cut impolitely, 'and I don't get it. Why are you spilling all this to me?'

'I don't exactly know,' said Bainbridge frankly. 'Mainly, I think, because I'm getting tired of regarding the press as a large party of ambushed Indians whom I have to look for behind every tree. One always fears the known less than the unknown. I haven't much hope of your co-operation, but I thought I could have a look at you at least.'

'What's *your* impression?' said Donelly sniffily.

'You *seem* human,' said the president.

'Yeah, but what's the angle – what's in it for you?' said Jack. 'What do you want me to do?'

'Oh,' said Bainbridge, 'I guess I had something in mind of this sort – I give you first call on what information I get – and I've already given you the confession story ahead of the other papers – if you'll help me tone the *Messenger's* view of the lurid side of college life a bit. After all, I'm a sort of duenna to five hundred young women, Mr Donelly. Put yourself in my place and have a heart.'

'Unfortunately my paper has a policy to the effect that if a story stinks, we make it stink worse.'

'I somehow felt I was speaking to you rather than to your paper, Mr Donelly.'

'Oh, that line,' said Jack, hunching his shoulders and staring into the fire.

'I rather imagined that Miss Innes might help me to enforce my persuasion – she gave me what may have been an over-optimistic view of your conscience.'

Donelly got up and thrust his hands in his pockets as he glared at Kate over Bainbridge's head. 'What do you want me to do? Play detective?'

'Oh, that's a great deal more than I expect. I somehow have a profound conviction that this murder will be traced to some simple person with simple motivations, if it is traced at all – someone who entered the house with the intention of robbery, and was frightened by Boyle, or something of the sort. More than anything now, I should like to prevent this Morrison child's reputation from being ruined, until it seems there is a good deal more evidence against her than now exists.'

'More than a confession?' said Jack.

Bainbridge stood up suddenly and faced him. 'Yes,' he said hotly, 'more than a confession obtained by as big a moron of a police chief as one could hope to find, from a drugged and hysterical girl, who has already had her words twisted into lies – in effect if not in fact – in a scurrilous newspaper piece written by you, Mr Donelly. Molly Morrison may be a murderess, but you doubt it, I doubt it, Miss Innes doubts it. Does it make you happy to think of the kind of scandal that will surround her after this thing, even if she comes out legally clear?'

'Honestly, Mr Bainbridge,' said Jack, 'I can't drop that story, big a heel as I may be. I'm not in the business for my health, and the story's too hot. It's the only hot lead of the murder.'

'How about this – ah – Bubbles Merryweather?'

'She's been cleared and double-checked,' said Jack impatiently; 'don't you read the papers?'

Kate rose too. 'I guess I'll have to work on him, Mr Bainbridge. I still have faith in the re-education of criminals, but there's no use wasting more of *your* time. I'll have to dream up something to enforce his motivation toward reform.'

Jack glanced at her unresponsively, Bainbridge forced a smile. 'Thanks, Miss Innes.'

'Good-night, sir,' said Jack uncomfortably.

They moved from the living-room to the hall.

'Good-night, Mr Bainbridge; I'm sorry,' said Kate.

'Good-night.'

Outside a wind had sprung up and was whipping dry leaves down the sidewalks and across the lawns. In silence Kate and Jack got into the car. Jack stepped on the starter. 'It's too late for the movies,' he said expressionlessly; 'want a drink?'

'You can take me home,' said Kate.

'I thought you wanted to reform me.'

'You can take me home.'

'All right,' said Jack, and swung the car angrily in a U-turn. They drove in silence for five minutes.

'This isn't the way to the quad,' Kate said indignantly at last.

'Oh, hell,' said Jack, 'I just wasn't paying attention. I'm driving past the scene of the crime out of sheer habit. You'll get home all right, picklepuss. What's the matter – want to be a virgin all your life?'

'There's a difference between abstention and discrimination,' said Kate huffily, and turned her gaze out the window. Suddenly she sat forward in the seat and yelled, 'Hey, stop!'

'Want to neck?' said her companion acidly.

'Oh, Donelly, you bore me,' she brushed him off. 'There's a light in Kevin Boyle's apartment!'

'No doubt the murderer has come back to check on clues,' said Jack with fatigued sarcasm. He stopped in front of an ugly, rambling, grey frame house. Across the front of it ran a series of small-paned windows, behind which a light was flickering, though uncertainly. 'Like a flashlight!' said Kate breathlessly.

'All right, all right, I'll go look,' said Jack. 'You stay there.'

'The hell I'll stay here!' whispered Kate, opening the door.

'If you make those steps creak,' hissed Jack irately, 'I'll make you sign a pledge to lose ten pounds before I take you out again.'

She glared at him in silence as they mounted the porch steps with exaggerated stealth. The light was out on the porch; the corner of the house covered them in shadow. They crossed on tiptoe to where a single window of Kevin Boyle's apartment looked out on the porch. 'Can't see a damn thing,' whispered Jack.

'Shut up,' said Kate. They made cups of their hands and peered through the glass. Behind them the house door opened quietly, a step sounded in the porch, and a woman gave a short scream. They whirled around and found themselves confronted by the massive figure of Freda Cramm.

'Mrs Cramm!' said Kate quaveringly.

For a long moment Freda glared at them, then Jack recovered himself and went into his spiel, like a barber at a side-show: 'Hello, Mrs Cramm, care to make a statement for the *Messenger* as to why you were visiting the apartment of the deceased at – ah – ' he looked at his watch – '9.14 on the evening of the seventeenth?'

'I wasn't –' began Freda Cramm.

'Ah-ah-ah, Mrs Cramm!' cautioned Jack. 'We've been peeking.'

'Oh, Jack, we didn't –' mumbled Kate, who had suddenly lost her *savoir faire*.

'*I* did,' growled Jack.

Freda was looking at Kate with a threatening eye. 'This is Miss Innes, editor of the *The Holly*, I believe,' she remarked in a voice of doom.

'Yes,' blithered Kate, 'I mean –'

'I assume, Miss Innes, that since Wednesday morning chapel was required, you heard Mr Bainbridge's remarks about students associating with reporters?'

'Yes, Mrs Cramm, we just came from Mr Bainbridge's house, as you can easily find out if you call him,' put in Jack smoothly. 'If you don't care to make a statement, I'm wondering just how to word this. "Leaving the house of the murdered man, flashlight in hand, Mrs Cramm refuses to –" '

'My dear man,' said Freda, suddenly urbane, 'it's

quite simple. It's just that it irritates me to be jumped at from dark corners. Certainly I was in Kevin Boyle's apartment. I'm getting a collection of Mr Boyle's poems together to show to a publisher – Philip Frisbee at Cornish House to make it *quite* authentic. I have most of the manuscripts from Mr Boyle's book, but one of my favourite poems was missing, I found, so I went to look for it.'

'Did you find it?' said Jack.

'As a matter of fact, I didn't.'

'Maybe it would have been easier if you'd turned on the light.'

Freda threw back her head and suddenly laughed her full, stagy laugh. It rang out startlingly, making them all aware that they had been talking in hushed tones. 'I *love* it!' she cried. 'Oh, I *love* it! Oh, *do* suspect me of the murder – nothing so gay has happened to me in years! If you'll notice, my dear, darling *Messenger* reporter, this porch light is out?'

Jack nodded dubiously.

'It's quite as simple as a blown fuse – evidently Kevin's apartment is on the same circuit. Run in and try it – I do assure you you'll find every lamp in the place dead!'

'Lucky you had a flashlight,' said Jack sourly.

'Isn't it?' agreed Freda brightly. 'Why don't you children run me up to my house and I'll give you some cocoa or something. The reason I have a flashlight is that I happened to walk. My driveway is always black as the ace of spades. Do come along and have something hot.'

'Miss Innes here is on a diet,' said Jack, 'but get in and I'll drive you home.'

'Now, in that case, I can see I mustn't spoil your twosome,' said Freda with elephantine coyness. 'And if it comes to diets, of course I'd *much* better walk.'

'Just as you please,' said Jack. Together they descended the porch steps.

'Good-ni-eet!' cried Freda, waving to them as she turned down the sidewalk.

'Good-night,' said Kate and Jack in unison.

They got into the car before she was out of sight.

'Short circuit!' snorted Jack.

'Diet!' snarled Kate. 'Aren't you even going to check on whether there was one?'

'I'll give dollars for doughnuts there was one all right. They aren't hard to produce, and she must have known I'd check.'

'Which you aren't doing.'

'Oh, *all right*.' He climbed out of the car again and back up the porch steps. Kate left her door open to watch him. Just as he reached the front door, the porch light winked on, the front door opened and a tall gaunt woman was silhouetted in it. 'Yes,' she said to Jack nervously, 'did you want something?'

'Oh,' said Jack ' – ah – Miss Stone, isn't it? Have you – I mean *had* you blown a fuse?'

'Yes,' said Miss Stone, with her nervously interrogative inflection, 'yes, we had, I just put a new one in.'

'Well, I'm from the electric shop. Mrs Cramm phoned for me.'

'Phoned for you? There's no Mrs Cramm here. You must have the wrong house, young man.'

'Oh no,' said Jack easily. 'She said she was phoning from Mr Boyle's apartment. I just met her on the way out. She said she'd been looking for a manuscript in his place. Didn't you let her in?'

Miss Stone's hands flew to her topknot and fluttered there like two distracted birds, playing with her hairpins.

'Oh, dear me!' she cried. 'Oh, dear me, no! And how could she have got in otherwise, for the door was tight locked?'

## Chapter 13

HE laid his tuxedo tenderly on the bed. It was new – the first he had ever owned. His black oxfords, carefully polished, were set beneath it, and a pair of black silk socks. The shirt, collar studs, and tie. His hands trembled a little as he assembled them all on the bed. He had bought them, all at once, except the shoes, in a medium-priced New York haberdashery, where they had cost just a bit more than he could afford. They represented his homage to himself after the letter had come assuring him the job. He had the habit of giving himself presents on special occasions, because no one else did. His father was dead, he supported his mother, and there was no other soul in the world who sufficiently cared for him to make such gestures. Suddenly, in the midst of arranging his shaving things in careful preparation, he stopped and stared at himself in the paint-flecked bathroom mirror. That was a thing that he and Kevin had in common. He remembered a night last month when Boyle had burst into his room without knocking, a bottle of Scotch under his arm. 'Let's get drunk, Leonard, old boy,' he had cried, 'for it's the day of my coming into the world, and not a soul to present me with a gift but my own sweet self. Get out the mixings, lad, and let's become roaring boys!' ... Then he shook his head and went on arranging his shaving implements, taking old-maidish care, selecting a new blade, screwing it into the razor. Not comparable, really. Probably it was only that no one had known it was Kevin's birthday. If Freda Cramm, for instance ...

Suddenly Leonard set up a tuneless little hum, wetted his shaving brush, and swiped it around the jar of soap. Briskly he lathered his face, avoiding with care the tuft of moustache on his upper lip, and began to shave. When he had cleared the suds off one side of his face, he stopped shaving, leaned his hands on the bowl, looked his reflection straight in the eye, and, for once in a way, laughed out loud his odd womanish cackle. He had not yet recovered from the strange ailment that had overtaken him after the murder – he was still likely to giggle at the name of Kevin Boyle, and he thought it best to get the laughter as thoroughly out of his system as possible before to-night, since to-night the name of Kevin Boyle was likely to be bandied about a good deal.

It is, he remarked to himself, an ill wind that blows nobody good. Best to face it finally and frankly, perhaps: he, Leonard Marks, had gained a good deal by Kevin's death, and he could not, for the life of him, be anything but glad. And why not? he argued with his middlewestern, churchy background. Shall I pretend overwhelming grief at the death of a man whom I knew for two months? Shall I ignore the fact that for me his murder has become an invaluable social and professional asset? Yet he gasped a little and cut his cheek with the razor as he thought this, for he had been brought up in a stuffy world of piety and hypocrisy; to mourn the dead was the convention, and the convention was the law. What would Freda Cramm make of such shilly-shallyings with the past? To-night he was invited to Freda Cramm's house; now was the time to let the past bury its dead, and look bravely to the future.

He had come to Hollymount as an instructor in English with high hopes, as the saying went. With a brand new Ph.D. from Columbia, a reputation as a serious scholar among his fellow graduate students, and a number of A's and other encomiums from his professors, he came prepared to sweep all before him, to rise from honour to honour. But already, in November of his first year, it had been made plain that it was not to be that way – not that way at all.

Nothing in New York had prepared him for the reception he had received here. His meagre room on 114th Street had often been a centre for scholarly debates on the Elizabethan poets. His professors had not taken him to their bosoms socially, to be sure, but they had loaded him with academic praise. Yet from the moment he had taken lodgings in West Lyman, settled his few belongings and set about his work, nothing had been as he had hoped. Had he dreamed of scholarly discussions of the varying editions of *Hamlet* with George Hungerford, the great scholar, critic, and novelist? He remembered his first conversation often and bitterly. He had approached him in the faculty tea room, brightly, intelligently, with a question on his lips. 'Do you think, sir – ' Leonard had begun. But Hungerford, who had been staring out the window with his strange fixed gaze, whirled about suddenly and said, 'Young man, I make it a practice never to think these days unless I am paid for it,' and had walked away, leaving Leonard almost weeping with humiliation. Yet he had forgiven Hungerford. Afterwards he had learned of his nervous breakdown and his consequent eccentricities, and even if there had been no such excuse, his love of the man's work would have forced him to overlook the rudeness. No, it was the ones like Freda Cramm, the big, overbearing, husbandless women who peopled the faculty of Hollymount, who peered at him, leered at him, and set him running off with his tail between his legs after their acid thrusts, who rankled. The same who purred and fawned on Kevin Boyle – they had convinced him at last that whatever his successes in the past, here he was regarded as – what? Not even on trial. Already condemned as something they thought of as a hopeless bore. The students too – whispering and muttering through his lectures; giggling at him before his back was turned. He was invited nowhere but to the most general gatherings – the President's reception; only once to a faculty dinner in a dormitory. If he had said that he knew Kevin little, he must also say that it was only Kevin whom he had known at all here. The only talk he had, finally, was the hours of Kevin's boasting by the fire, the recitals of Kevin's successes ground like salt in his wounds. He had spent two months of miserable loneliness with the sense of being not disliked, but un-liked. In the last week he had had more attention than in the eight that preceded it, and all because Kevin Boyle, who had lived across the hall from him, was murdered, and with his own ears he had heard the footsteps of the murderer outside his door. He had talked to the president of the college privately three or four times, George Hungerford had called on him, the ladies in the tea room had condescended to ply him with questions, and now he had been specifically invited to the house of Freda Cramm for a memorial reading of the poems of Kevin Boyle.

He dusted his face with talcum and dampening a nail-white pencil drew it meticulously under each of his fingernails. Then he put away his toilet articles and cleaned the bowl, whistling softly through his teeth. He looked at his watch. Seven-fifteen. He had allowed himself a little too much time. He sat down on the bed, drew on his socks, and clasped the garters around his skinny, heavily furred legs. Suddenly, thrillingly, his telephone – that symbol of unfulfilled hope, since no one ever called him – rang loudly. In his shorts, oblivious of neighbours in his excitement, he strode into the unshaded living-room. 'Hullo?' he said anxiously.

'Mr Marks?' said a commanding, female voice at his ear.

'Ye-yes?'

'Oh, Mr Marks. I'm in a devil of a hole, and I'm counting on you to help me out. It's Freda Cramm.'

Of course, of course it was Freda Cramm! 'Of course, of course, Mrs Cramm, anything I can –'

'George Hungerford was to read Kevin's poems and now he's begged off with some excuse about being sick. You knew Kevin's work – Mr Marks, *could* you read them instead?'

'R-read Kevin's poems?' he quavered.

'Yes, I mean, I thought you could dash over a bit early and look through them – I'll show you the ones George had selected.'

'Oh, Mrs Cramm, I –' Suddenly the picture of all their hostile faces rose before him, and himself the child who has forgotten his piece at the recital, the eight-year-old orator urinating in his trouser leg. 'Oh, Mrs Cramm –'

'Oh, now, dear, darling Mr Marks, there simply isn't anything you can say but yes, so say it! Really, I *will* be in such a devil of a hole, and frankly, it will be awfully good for you, as you should see yourself.'

'For me?'

'Of course, with all the English Department and Bainbridge there, and you really have an awfully good voice – I know you'll read them well – I mean, people will *remember* you.'

It was as if she had noticed, and cared. Even though she had taken part in harrying him, she still had noticed that he was in the predicament of rabbit pursued by hounds. Could it be – could it be that everything *would* change? 'Well, if you think –' he faltered.

'I do, I do really think! Now, get your trousers on' – he started, as if she could see through the telephone – 'and come right over. You *are* being an angel and saving my life, Mr Marks.'

She had hung up. 'Goodbye,' he said to the air. His hands were trembling and sweating. He ran back to the bedroom, jerked on his clothes clumsily, brushed his hair, polished his glasses. His tie would not tie. It simply would not tie.

'Oh, blast!' he whispered. 'Oh, damn and blast!' At last he got it straight. At the last moment he called a taxi regally, and was wafted off to Freda Cramm's house as if he were Lohengrin being transported to Elsa by special swan.

## Chapter 14

THEY had parted rather gruffly, and she wasn't sure whether they were supposed to be sore or not. She supposed that according to Hoyle she should have waited until he called her, but this was business – anyway, that *was* what her *conscious* mind had to say about it. She regarded herself in the mirror with some dissatisfaction. 'You are not what they call a man's woman, toots,' she remarked, and fishing a nickel out of her dungarees pocket, went to the phone booth. It was five-thirty, when people should be taking baths or getting ready to have a drink, or should be home for some reason; it seemed the most likely time to catch him. She got the Harlow, and they rang his room for her. 'Hello,' he said, hard and fast. He sounded cross, and she blushed. 'Hello,' she said, trying to sound cross too, 'this is Kate Innes.'

'Why, cookie!' he said in a pleased voice, and she relaxed.

'Listen, my erring Lincoln Steffens,' she sneered, 'I have for you what is known in the Grade B's as a hot tip.'

'Gee,' he said irresponsibly, 'isn't this cute – you calling me.'

'It is solely in the interests of justice,' she snarled, 'so don't get overheated about it.'

'Well, shoot the snoop to me, droop,' he requested amiably.

'Did you know Freda Cramm is throwing a memorial gathering for Kevin Boyle this evening?'

'No. Is that the customary gesture when a colleague gets bumped off? Me, I never had an education.'

'For my money,' said Kate seriously, 'something smells. I don't know what, exactly – maybe I'm just turning melodramatic in my old age, but first we meet the lady coming out of his apartment; now she's giving a memorial party or something – in my right mind I'd say that was just typical of her; give that woman a chance to exhibit herself and right away she starts a strip tease – only I keep wondering if it's more. How well did she know Boyle? – she certainly admitted she went to his place a lot. Could she have been in love with him, or vice versa?'

'Not vice versa, unless my unfailing eye for femininity is dimmed, but go on.'

'Well, stop me if I sound like Hercule Poirot, but I do find murders rather heady for my blood, and I have the feeling you ought to take a look-in at this gathering.'

'You mean put on my blue lace and go as Elsa Maxwell?'

'You can find a way to get in, stupid. After all, you're supposed to be a yellow journalist from a pink tabloid.'

'Oh, sure, I can get in all right. But you have before you a man in whom duty wars with inclination. I had dreams of getting out my pipe and slippers and pulling up to a big open bar with you to-night.'

'Not with me will you be bending the elbow, friend – I have a lab report due Monday.'

'All right, honey,' he said wistfully. 'Where's the dame's house?'

'It's behind the campus, way the hell and gone out Eden Street. Could you find Bainbridge's house again?

'Yeah, I think so.'

'Well, just keep going to the top of the hill,' she directed. 'As a matter of fact, I seem to remember there is some sort of sun porch on the house you might get in. She was talking about it at a faculty dinner here once – about how the architect had designed it to be warm even in the dead of winter if the sun was shining, but you couldn't use it if it wasn't.'

'What if I catch a cold?' he said plaintively.

'Drink a hot lemonade.'

'You're as hard-boiled as a city editor, but I love it ' he sighed. 'All right. Can I call you to-night and let you know how it comes out?'

'No outside calls to the dormitories after ten-fifteen,' she said, 'and you'll be there later than that if you have any luck. Call me to-morrow,' She blushed.

'O.K., honey. Good-bye, now.'

She left the booth, noting her pulse rate scientifically. Out of some compulsion which she did not examine, she changed from dungarees to a sweater and skirt, and devoted some time to brushing her hair. At supper she sat abstractedly, chewing a hangnail instead of eating. There was chocolate pudding for dessert, and when she gave hers away to the girl sitting next to her, her table mates made gestures of fainting. 'Innes,' said the girl who had taken Jack's call yesterday, 'is irrefutably in love.'

'I am not!' she said hotly, coming out of a brown study with all her armour down, and then blushed radiantly. A great hoot went up so that the other girls in the dining-room turned to look at their table. She pulled herself together and organized a strong defence of attack which kept them in line until the end of the meal. Then, making noises about her lab report, she ran upstairs immediately, and locked herself in her room, first tacking a DO NOT DISTURB sign to the door.

From 7.15 to 8.15 she typed diligently. From 8.15 to 8.34 she made graphs. From 8.34 to 8.50 she chewed the hangnail. At 8.50 she got her nail scissors and cut it off. At 9.03 she said to herself, aloud, and in a very reasonable tone, 'O.K., so suppose I am?' got her coat from the closet, put it on, started out of the door, came back, rooted in a dresser drawer and found a lipstick, which she used. Then she hurtled down the stairs and out into the night.

## Chapter 15

ALL the lamps in the room were lighted, illuminating the
turquoise walls with a gentle yet festive brilliance. The
doorbell rang at odd intervals, the maid would open the
door, Freda would make a little rush toward the hall, and
the volume of the talk would rise a bit, though always
restrained, memorial in tone. Faces shimmered with two
emotions: embarrassment and excitement. It was embarrassing to feel excited at a gathering in honour of the
dead – practically a funeral service, in fact, Kevin Boyle
had left directions in a will that his body be cremated
without ceremony – yet such a lovely party: all the
English Department in evening-dress (however variant
the vintage), the chrysanthemums radiant as van Gogh
suns in the lamplight, the excellent whisky. ... The doorbell sounded a final peal, and Bainbridge entered after a
moment, his wife on his arm, chatting with Freda. Some
crossed the room to greet him, some merely eyed him and
returned to their talk. When the two of them were seated,
Freda raised her hands and her voice and commanded
the room to silence. 'Will you all sit down and make
yourselves comfortable?' she said. There was a rustle, a
redistribution of guests. When everyone had found places,
Freda went on, 'George Hungerford was to read Kevin
Boyle's poems to us this evening, but he has phoned to
say he is ill and unable to do so. Mr Marks has very
kindly consented to read in his place.' There was a tiny
murmur and turning of heads in the room, whether at the
absence of Hungerford or the presence of Marks it would
have been difficult to say. Freda nodded to Leonard,
who sat in the farthest corner of the room, shuffling and

reshuffling typescript, moistening his lips with his tongue, and whispering the poems over to himself. 'Will you?' she said.

Leonard cleared his throat, and hunched his chair out around the end of the table behind which he had hidden. But he was not to be let off. 'Sit over here by the fireplace, Mr Marks,' Freda commanded. So he had to rise, to pick his way among them, to plant himself at the side of Bainbridge himself. When he had resettled, an expectant hush fell. 'I thought – ' he began desperately, but his voice came out a dry squeak. He cleared his throat and began again. 'I thought I would say something about Kevin Boyle's poems, but then I decided that I might better let them speak for themselves.' His face turned bright scarlet, and he ducked his head agonizedly, once more reshuffling the sheets. 'Mrs Cramm and Mr Hungerford have made this selection in chronological order. The first poem is called – ' he looked at it, drew out his handkerchief and loosed into a strangled cough – '*Timor Mortis Conturbat Me*.' ... He began to read, sounding as if invisible hands were at his throat. The room was tense with response to his tension. But the words and meaning took hold at last; even Leonard seemed to forget that it was he who was on exhibit in listening to the sense of Kevin Boyle's poems.

Halfway through the reading, a slight disturbance sounded from the closed door to the sun porch, and a few heads turned momentarily. Jack Donelly, lying shivering on the brick solarium floor, somewhat camouflaged by the bamboo coffee table under which he reclined, rose to his knees as abruptly as he dared and whirled round on all fours like an angry Newfoundland, the coffee table dangling like a saddle from his back. 'What the hell!' he said in an enraged whisper.

'Down, Fido!' came a whisper in return, and the sound of the latch being half closed. In a moment Kate joined him in his prone indignity and they lay regarding each other blinkingly, their faces dimly lit by the glow that shone through the thin curtains on the glass-paned door to the living-room.

'You're a damned nuisance,' hissed Jack. 'Go away!'

For answer, Kate propped her chin on her hands and waved her feet airily behind her.

'Listen, baby, chivalry is as dead as an old T. S. Eliot geranium as far as I'm concerned, and if we get sent up for housebreaking, we'll split the sentence evenly, believe me.'

'I can take care of myself,' said Kate, looking at him rather absently. 'What's been going on?'

'Not a damn thing except that I'm getting a severe sinus attack,' Jack whispered back disgustedly, 'and Marks has been spouting that *merde* for the last three hours, at a rough guess.'

'Your judgment is fair but your time discrimination is poor,' said Kate, edging forward a little on her stomach. 'Where's la Cramm?'

'Somewhere off around the corner so you can't see her.'

'Let's get closer to the door, and I'll tell you who's who.'

'Our faces will catch the light.'

'Nobody could see us with the light shining on the other side of that curtain.'

'Look,' whispered Jack irritably, rising on one elbow, 'if you get caught, this will be a schoolgirl prank. If I get caught, it's a misdemeanour or something. You annoy me, brat, and I wish you'd go away.'

Kate looked at him with her round face shining dimly

in the curtained glow from the door. It turned a barely perceptible shade pinker and two large shimmering tears unexpectedly rolled out of her eyes and formed little canals around the inside rims of her glasses. Her mouth opened in a silent Oh. She rose to her hands and knees and the tears fell to the floor in two quiet little splats.

'Why, cookie!' said Jack in amazement. He made a move toward her, and the coffee table rose irately on two legs. For a moment they juggled it between them like a football in a complicated pass.

'Get down!' whispered Kate suddenly, and they flattened themselves just as an unseen hand opened the door between the porch and the living-room. Without their noticing it, the reading was over, and the stream of conversation was babbling on again. ' ... Terribly hot in here ... ' they heard Freda Cramm's voice trailing away from them. For a moment they lay still and flat, afraid of catching the light if they rose. Snatches of conversation reached them: ' ... what perfect little jewels of verse ... ' a female voice. ' ... reminiscent of the earlier Yeats ... ' a male. 'Don't you find them a little *difficult*?' ... 'Of course, I realize that nowadays you young people scorn the pre-Raphaelites ... '

Jack performed a difficult disengaging movement without raising himself from the floor, and worked his way clear of the coffee table. He gave Kate's ankle a gentle yank. 'Let's get behind the sofa here,' he whispered urgently.

'Why?' she whispered back. 'Then we can't see anything.' But he was already disappearing behind the piece of furniture in question, so she rose to her hands and knees and followed, grumbling breathily.

'Now,' he said, when she had collected herself in the

dark shadow, and planting his lips on hers, maintained this position with her full consent until interrupted by the startling sound of a step on the brick floor of the porch.

They sprang apart as guiltily as a Victorian couple on the parlour sofa, quickly collected themselves, and peered cautiously around opposite ends of the porch. Whoever had come out of the door had closed it after him again: once more the light was dimmer. A man's figure was silhouetted against the lighted door. For a moment he seemed to be looking about the floor for something, his face still dark against the light, so that they could make out nothing but a pair of protruding ears. At last his glance stopped, and he moved toward where a large brass maple-syrup kettle, which was intended for a waste-basket, stood by a chair. Out of his pocket he drew a piece of paper, and tearing it into tiny bits, he let them shiver down through the air into the kettle. He looked down at them indecisively for a moment, then, with an indistinguishable exclamation, stooped down and carefully collected them again out of the receptacle, and holding his pocket open with one hand, dropped the bits into it with the other. Suddenly the door was snatched wide open, and Kate and Jack popped back behind the sofa.

'Why, Mr Marks,' said Freda Cramm's voice coyly, 'are you hiding from the idiocy of our adulation? You know how well you read, don't you?'

'Oh,' came Leonard Marks' voice in a hoarse croak, 'ah – Mrs Cramm – ah – not at all – just – ah – getting a breath of cool air.'

'Well, come in, come in!' pleaded Freda warmly; drew him back into the living-room and closed the door.

'Get *that*!' breathed Kate dazedly, but was masterfully

recalled to dalliance, and spent the time until the breaking up of the party in what can only be described as necking on the icy brick floor of Freda Cramm's solarium.

## Chapter 16

THE guests withdrew from the warm turquoise room in a serpentine body, the last stragglers chatting among the chrysanthemums as the first departures extracted their coats from the hall closet by the door. Standing beside Freda, Leonard made feeble motions toward retrieving his wraps, but was detained by her firm hand on his arm. She kept him standing beside her as she said good-byes, he noted, with amazement, quite as if he were the host or the guest of honour. Perhaps he was the guest of honour. A substitute, but nevertheless – was that going too far? His head was humming pleasantly with the drinks he had consumed; he was incapable of such weighty decisions.

In twos and threes the English Department passed through the door, each saying some congratulatory word to Leonard on the way out. At last they were all gone – the last was standing on the doorstep mouthing politeness when Leonard made a final effort toward his own departure. But this time Freda firmly and distinctly closed the front door and turned to him with a warm smile. 'Ah,' she sighed. 'Now we can have a drink in peace.'

He was seized with a sense of unreality; he thought his head might suddenly grow wings and take off from his neck. 'Oh,' he said, 'oh, ah, yes, that would be nice.'

But no matter how much he made an ass of himself, no

matter how he stammered and bungled, still she kept smiling and being pleasant to him. It was like a dream – a good dream. He stuffed his hands in his pockets, twitched his moustache, and followed her back into the empty room – beautiful, yet slightly *en déshabille* with empty glasses and full ash-trays, like a lovely woman after love. This was a thought worthy of Kevin Boyle, who would have spoken it aloud and collected the kudos due on it, but Leonard could only redden and walk to the fireplace, where he kicked the andiron and stood frowning into the fire.

Freda stood at the table where the decanters, the siphons, the silver thermos bowl of ice were, and mixed their drinks. He studied her broad, fleshy back, solid under mauve chiffon, her big haunches, her cushioned elbows, the netted chignon of red hair low on her neck. In her pierced ears little old-fashioned diamond pendants dangled and swung briskly as she moved. She turned and came toward him, carrying glasses filled with whisky and soda. Her face was weary, mischievous, sardonic, and utterly frank all at once, and for the first time, by God for the very first time, she seemed to be looking at him as if he were a human being, not some kind of a – some kind of a worm or example of a lower biological order. His hands began to tremble and he stuffed them deeper in his pockets, then was obliged to remove one to accept the drink. Facing him, Freda lifted her glass to eye level. 'Skoal,' she said, looking him full in his eyes as if they both knew the same secret. 'Skoal,' he imitated, and drank too. Then she set her drink on the coffee table in front of the sofa, and with a swift gesture, gathered up her skirts and lay down. 'Ah,' she breathed, kicked her shoes to the floor, and raising her quivering arms, began removing the tortoise-shell pins from her knot of hair. The ice in Leonard's glass began to tinkle uncontrollably. What was she – was it possible that – oh, how could he think such things? He took a big swallow of his drink.

'Leonard darling,' she said, 'you read beautifully.' And at this he was obliged to set his glass on the mantel, for this was the first time that anyone at Hollymount – even Kevin Boyle, who had addressed him as Marks, or Boy, or Lad – had called him by his first name.

'Thank you,' he said weakly.

'But,' she went on, 'I am so tired of faculty gatherings that I retch at the thought.'

His mind burgeoned with questions. Then why did she live here? Why did she teach at Hollymount? Surely she could afford not to – that was plain. Why had she given this party to-night? 'They seem a bit stuffy, don't they?' he essayed timidly.

She wiggled round on the sofa, passed her hand across her eyes, and sighed. 'Well, we've said Amen over Kevin, and that relieves me, because it seems uncivilized to me to do without a funeral – it leaves you with such an unfinished feeling about the dead. When some kind of last rites have been said you can put them from your mind and go on to the living.'

'I should have thought,' he ventured, 'that you would find funerals barbarian.'

She threw back her head and laughed so that he could see the roof of her mouth and several gold fillings in her teeth. 'Now, darling, I can see you think of me as one of the conventionally unconventional. You must get that notion out of your head if we're to be friends at all – ' his heart leaped – 'because I'm the firmest of believers in form and ritual. I'll tell you a secret. I gave out to all of them that the occasion of the reading was to interest Philip Frisbee in Kevin's poems, but the fact is that I knew from the beginning he couldn't come. Oh, I'll give him the poems to read, right enough. But the truth is that I couldn't bear not to have some sort of farewell made to Kevin – I felt that his poor ghost was wandering among us crying and moaning for its last good-bye. You think that's foolishly sentimental?' She paused, and cocked her head.

'No,' he said. 'Oh no. The whole thing was such a shock. I mean the violence. It's hard to get out of your head. You know, I never saw a dead man before. Not even one I didn't know.'

She nodded, her long eyes lustrous with understanding. 'Violence that strikes in our midst shakes us in a strange way,' she said mysteriously. 'Personally, I think there are not enough murders. They feed us in some way. See how avidly we devour all accounts of crime, or detective stories! And after all, the responsibility of giving death is a small one which we regard so seriously in comparison to the responsibility of giving life, which we take so lightly.'

'Oh, goodness!' said Leonard incautiously, and blushed. He backed up a little along the mantel, and took another quick swallow of his drink.

'There are two separate pleasures,' she went on, not noticing his shock. She removed the last pin from the knot of hair, leaving it to uncoil like a fiery snake down her shoulder. 'The pleasure of vicarious violence, and the pleasure at the detection and punishment of the crime of another. In the first we can enjoy the emotional outlet without undertaking the penalty, and in the second we can shiver deliciously with the knowledge that we cannot be found out, since our share in the business was secret, and of the mind. Don't you feel, Leonard darling, that you're just a *little* bit guilty of every crime you've ever heard of?'

Liquor was overtaking Leonard, buzzing in his head, throwing down barriers that the mind had set up against the blood. The polish of spurious worldliness was rubbing thin, as the traditions of his pious middle-western forefathers shouldered their way to the surface of his conscious mind. The whore that sitteth upon the waters! his grandfather's voice thundered in his ear, and he admitted freely that he was alarmed. 'You seem to have a low opinion of humanity,' he remarked with courageous primness.

Freda threw her head back again and laughed her big laugh while she ran her fingers through her twist of hair, spreading it around her shoulders like a copper serape. 'Oh, Leonard Marks, Leonard Marks!' was all the answer she had to give him. She took her glass from where she had set it on the table, and sipped. Then she went on, 'I very much doubt that there'll be any pleasure of detection in this case, unless some fictional detective plants himself fortuitously in our midst.'

'Who do you think could have done it?' said Leonard, reeling a little against the mantel.

She shook her head. 'I do wish it were some eminent colleague – oh, I do wish it! But that's asking too much of fate, and it doesn't sound very reasonable. Kevin hadn't been here long enough to make any good enemies. And some more damning bit of evidence would already have turned up, I imagine – unless the police are holding out on us, of course – a probability which I regard as quite beyond their mental capacity.'

'What about the little girl – the student who was interviewed by the *Messenger*?'

'Oh, of course it's a possibility – quite a possibility,' considered Freda. 'But I rather think that if it's ever solved it will turn out that some sneak thief came in and was surprised by Kevin or something of the sort.'

'I don't know,' said Leonard. 'I don't know. It seems awfully unlikely any sneak thief would choose Miss Stone's to break into. It's not very – very *prosperous* looking. If only I'd come out when I heard the thud. But boarding-houses are full of thuds, you know – or perhaps you don't.' He heard his voice coming back to him through a slight buzzing in his blood. He tried to recollect how many drinks he had had, but wavered between three and four. It seemed to him that Freda Cramm was looking at him rather sharply, and he grinned back at her. 'He had a rather extensive love life, you know,' he said, and positively leered.

'How do you know?' she demanded.

'He was quite a raconteur,' said Leonard happily, shaking his head and enjoying his own sophisticated vocabulary. 'Quite a raconteur.'

It seemed to him that at this Freda sat up a little straighter on the sofa, but he could not be sure if this were actually the case or if it was only a part of the general tendency to defy the law of gravity that all objects seemed suddenly to have acquired. At any rate, she did raise her hand to rearrange her heavy veil of hair. 'Where do you think *I* might have fitted into his love life, Leonard?' he heard her say with a peculiarly steely coyness. Did she feel that ... Could she be concerned about ... He pulled himself to attention and straightened his tuxedo jacket, tilting slightly to the left and staring at her

astigmatically in what he intended for a reassuring gaze.
'Oh, Mrs Cramm!' he said seriously (for, after all, she
had never asked him to call her Freda), 'Kevin was a
*gentleman*! He never mentioned your name!'

'Now, confess, Leonard,' she pursued in a pseudo-
jocular tone (but he could hear the anxiety behind it),
'surely you must have noticed I was rather a frequent
visitor to Kevin's apartment.'

In his bosom the springs of chivalry welled warmly.
She was, he told himself, a good, a delicate woman. Poor
thing, for all her brave talk and pretended brazenness,
she was as concerned for her reputation as his own
mother. He looked at her long and lovingly. 'I knew you
were one of Kevin's *very good friends*, Mrs Cramm,' he
said in deep, tender, pastor-like tones.

'For all my yelling at him like a banshee and giving
Miss Stone's house a bad name?' she pushed on – jovially,
she would have had him think, but now, with the new
supersensitive vision that had been granted him, he could
see through this pretence, straight to her worried,
womanly heart.

'I'm sure you are accusing yourself unjustly, Mrs
Cramm,' he intoned expressively. 'I *know* you for the lady
that you are.' He would have liked to restate this more
definitely, but vague as it was, it caused her to relax, to
lie back, though still chewing her lip nervously. Don't
worry, *dear* Mrs Cramm! his chivalrous heart cried out
to her. 'So, so,' she said, her voice coming from a great
distance. 'You regarded it as a platonic relation. And the
great joke of it is, Leonard, that it's true – never touched
the hem of my gown, as the saying goes.'

'Of course not, of course not, Mrs Cramm,' agreed
Leonard earnestly. 'Always had the greatest respect for

you.' He took a swallow of his drink, toasting her in silence.

'He never,' she said, 'mentioned quarrelling with me?'

'Oh, Mrs Cramm,' assured Leonard, 'we never discussed you at all!'

Suddenly he saw her sit forward with a rapid movement of which he knew he would be incapable at this moment. 'Are you lying?' she said sharply.

'Lying?' he repeated in reproachful bewilderment. 'Why should I lie?'

They were silent for a moment while Leonard thought he would like to sit down. Yet he couldn't see where he was to sit and still converse comfortably with Mrs Cramm except on the sofa beside her feet. Suddenly it was absolutely imperative that he sit down before he fall down. With wavering step he made his way to plump down beside her gold-stockinged extremities. They lay like two gracefully fashioned caramels on the rosy velour cushion. Attached to them were two not ill-favoured ankles, and beyond, disappearing into clouds of mauve chiffon like the members of some Tiepolo goddess, there must unquestionably follow legs. At the termination of this thought stood Leonard's Baptist grandfather, raising a prohibitive hand. Freda lay with her delicately violet-ringed eyes closed like some sleeping Venus, or Brünhilde. Leonard began to tremble. Why not – after all, why not – but before his mind had by any means completed the sentence, a monstrous thing occurred. By a will quite outside his own, his hand was on her ankle and sliding timorously up her calf. He looked down at it in horror. 'Oh, Mrs Cramm!' he cried, and looked at her face for sympathetic amazement at the shocking thing that was taking place. But her features were quite impassive, her eyes slightly open, slumbrous yet piercing. As he stared at her, she opened her mouth and thrust her flat creamy arms straight up into the air. 'A-ah!' she yawned frankly. 'Suddenly I'm completely done in. Leonard, I'm going to send you packing.' And she swung her desecrated limbs to the floor, fished for her shoes, and squeezed her feet into them. Together they rose, he swaying. 'Yes,' he said in relief. 'Oh, yes, Mrs Cramm!'

Out into the hall they swam, his mind reeling with liquor and the impudicity of what he had nearly done. Freda opened the coat closet and removed the one masculine garment that remained there from its hanger. 'This must be yours,' she said without expression, and handed it to him. He struggled into it silently, while she held his new grey felt hat. His head spun and floated with his exertions. He stared at Freda, standing there in her graceful robes, on the floor, or perhaps on the air a foot or so above. How beautiful she appeared, how calm and madonna-like, golden, full bosomed, impassive. Suddenly the devil took hold of him – how else could one explain such an atrocity? – he threw his arms around her and implanted his wet lips on hers. 'Oh, Mrs Cramm!' he breathed reverently, between embraces, 'Oh, Mrs Cramm!'

She suffered him to hold her, crushing his own hat where she held it between them. Then she disengaged herself forcibly and handed him his mashed hat. 'You're drunk,' she said, 'you – you pipsqueak!' And almost pushed him out into the chilly night.

## Chapter 17

HE rose abruptly, went to the bathroom and threw up. He tottered back to the bedroom, sat down on the edge of the bed for a moment, his head in his hands. He looked at the clock. Nine-forty-five. He struggled into his bath-robe, rose gingerly, and made his way to the kitchenette with the aid of several pieces of furniture. By great concentration he managed to measure water and coffee into the percolator and set it on the gas plate. With this hope in view he was able to withdraw a jar of tomato juice from the refrigerator and pour out a glass, which he drank in small sips. The coffee began to bubble into the little glass dome. He waited as long as he could, then poured out a cupful. He staggered into the living-room, slopping the coffee into the saucer. It was a terrible day – the sky was black, the rain pouring. Also, he couldn't see things very well – ah, no wonder, he had forgotten to put on his glasses. He debated the possibility of going into the bed-room to get them, then leaned his head against the back of the chair and closed his eyes. But then the floor began to rock; he was obliged to open them again and drink a large swallow of coffee, which burned his tongue and throat. In response to this attack, his stomach gave a heave, but then subsided. He was able to turn his attention to less tangible effects of debauchery – guilt, shame, and mocking laughter.

He had made a fool of himself, an awful fool. He who hesitates is lost, his mind regurgitated. Faint heart never won fair maiden. Opportunity knocks but once. Fools rush in where angels fear to ... How happy he had been last evening before going out ... how miserably, idiotically happy. It seemed life was conspiring to teach him that happiness for him was only a prelude to ... Pride goeth before a fall. Was it pride? No, it seemed to him he had always been reasonably humble. What he had been proud of were real, tangible accomplishments – a Phi Beta Kappa key, a Ph. D. ... His father had always said his mother spoiled him. Praise to the face sure disgrace. All the adages of his childhood were coming back to him in gusts, like reminders of an undigested meal. He should never have drunk so much – oh, he knew a great deal better than to drink so much, with the kind of stomach *he* had!

Pipsqueak! He had never heard the expression before, but he knew at once what it meant. A creature beneath contempt. A sort of larva. The kind of person you ask to serve on the committees that do the most dirty work, the sort of person whom you always interrupt. That was what she really meant. It had all come out.

Because he tried to kiss her? That was odd. Because she had been so – so kind up to then. Was she really a puritan, for all her ribald talk? Plainly she did not want *him* to kiss her, that was plain, but why be so – so brutal about it? She had behaved as if ... behaved as if ... His thought stream was muddied and boiling with misery and poisonous secretions ... And *everyone* had been so kind. Praising him for his reading – saying good-night to him as if he were guest of honour. Could it all be a gigantic hoax designed to dash him to earth after first elevating him to a great height? It hardly seemed they would have bothered – *she* would have bothered. Oh dear, it was all so confusing! He took a large swallow of coffee.

He must think it out in orderly fashion. It seemed to him that something was afoot, whatever he meant by that, and he wasn't sure. It all began with Kevin Boyle's murder. Now, what could such a thing have to do with him, Leonard Marks? Well, he lived across the hall. He had, as a matter of fact, heard the murderer leave after the crime. If he had been a little more curious, in fact, he might have caught the murderer. As it happened, he heard nothing but the most unidentifiable of noises, beyond Kevin's loud No. He did not even know if the footsteps sounding in the hall were those of a man or of a woman. Of a woman? What did that remind him of? ...

*The pleasure of violence*, she had said. *There are not enough murders. But the criminal will not be caught this time.* ... He took his spinning head between his hands. Had she really said those things, or had he invented them for her in his cups? But he heard her voice, remembered his own shock. By God, he even remembered thinking of his grandfather preaching about the whore that sitteth upon the waters! He stood up abruptly, pounded one fist on the other palm, and then sat down again, clutching at his forehead. And he had thought she was concerned for her virtue! Ha! His heart had warmed to her, he had thought of her in the same breath with his own mother. Oh, sacrilege! But was it really possible that *she* ... ?

'*Somebody* has to commit murders,' he assured himself aloud, and got up, more cautiously this time, taking his empty cup to the kitchenette for more coffee. He felt a little better, he noticed, but his feet were cold. He looked down at them. No wonder. He had forgotten his slippers. Carrying the coffee back to the living-room, he touched a match to the already laid fire, the newspaper caught, and the kindling began to crackle. Why not, why not? He felt very excited. He extended his long, bluish toes toward the blaze. Think of her character. She was a woman of self-advertised violence. This in itself, of course, warned caution. Barking dogs never bite. And yet ... and yet he wouldn't like to have her after *him* with a poker. Not, of course, that she had shown signs of being after him with anything ... His spirits sank again; he swallowed more coffee and lit a tentative cigarette. Suddenly he sat forward.

*What was all that business about quarrelling?* Yelling like a banshee, she said – wait! It was coming back! He saw her mauve chiffon skirts spilling down from the seat of the sofa like the mist from a waterfall. He saw the enormous creamy orbs of her bosom bursting up from the decolletage of her dress. He saw her leaning forward a little, the snake of hair down one shoulder ... *He never*, she said, *mentioned quarrelling with me!* 'Oh, boy!' said Leonard aloud, inadvertently, and rose to pace the draughty floor, regardless of his bare feet. Was he rushing to a conclusion? It all seemed so pat. How had he begun this train of thought? Think back ... By wondering ... by wondering why Freda had made all the fuss over him. Wondering why she had ... and then she hadn't. It all could *fit* so neatly, if you accepted the premise. The premise that Freda had murdered Kevin Boyle ... He stopped dead in the middle of the floor, his feet purple, his mouth agape. And at that moment a knock sounded on his door, as fatefully as if this were the second act of *Macbeth*.

He paused a moment, listening, then girded up his bathrobe and opened the door. There, on his doorsill, stood a sharp-looking young man with horn-rimmed glasses, and his hat on the back of his head. 'Mr Marks?' he said, somehow injecting breeziness into those two words. 'I'm from the *Messenger*. Wondered if you'd care to tell me a little something about Mr Boyle's poetry.'

'Oh,' said Leonard, aware of his bare feet, his un-shaven face, his heavy breath, and his uncertain vision, 'uh – all right. Come in.'

The young man entered, looking round Leonard's apartment with exaggerated appraisal. 'Won't you take off your coat?' said Leonard. 'Won't you sit down?' And wondered why he was being so bloody polite, because he had hated this young man on sight.

'Thank you, thank you,' said the reporter, and remov-ing his coat, sat down, looking much too much at home in Leonard's own chair.

'Some coffee?' said Leonard, caught inexorably in the compulsion of his manners.

But the young man said he had already breakfasted. 'I understand there was a reading of Mr Boyle's poetry last night.'

Leonard sat down in the chair that he thought of as being for visitors and tucked his naked feet under it. 'Yes,' he affirmed. 'Ah, yes, at Mrs Cramm's house. A sort of memorial gathering, I believe.'

'You believe?' said the young man rudely. 'I thought you were the one who read the stuff.'

'Oh,' said Leonard, 'ah – yes, of course.'

'Well,' demanded the questioner, 'what do you think of it?'

'Think of it?' echoed Leonard.

'Yeah – what do you think of the poetry?' The young man looked at him inquisitively. 'You look a little under the weather,' he remarked. 'Hung?'

'I beg your pardon?' said Leonard.

'I said,' said the young man, raising his voice as if Leonard were deaf, 'have you a hangover?'

'Oh,' said Leonard. 'Oh, ah, that. Ah, yes, I daresay I

have.' Ever since this young man had come on the scene, things had seemed very strange in a distant way – like a Kafka novel. Somebody walks into your room, and you have a dim feeling that he doesn't belong there, yet it seems altogether too out of order to say, What are you doing here? or Get the hell out ... and besides, you are not too sure he would go. It might turn out that you were the one who was ... A wave of nausea came sweeping down on Leonard like a rip tide. He had only time to say 'Excuse me,' in a strangled voice, and dash for the bathroom.

When he came back he felt very weak, yet somehow stronger. He had washed his face, combed his hair, put on his glasses and his slippers. He had tied the belt to his bathrobe. He had spat on his moustache and swept it to the left and to the right with his fingertips. He felt abler to cope. But he suffered a setback almost immediately when he found the young man making himself quite at home in the kitchenette. He appeared from behind the door carrying in a glass a concoction which resembled some waste product from a surgical operation. 'Just swallow this,' he said, and Leonard's gorge leapt like a hart in protest. 'I know it looks terrible,' said the Samaritan (showing his first resemblance to a human being), 'but it will settle your stomach.'

'But I –' Leonard began feebly.

'Don't quibble, drink it right down.'

Leonard found himself clutching the glass and swallowing the slick fluid, which had a certain unity about it, leading Leonard to suppose that it was based on a raw egg. It descended to his stomach as dubiously as a paratrooper entering enemy territory, and then, to his surprise, settled there rather comfortably. 'Thank you,' he remarked tardily. 'Ah – very kind of you.'

'I know just how you feel,' said the young man, and producing a notebook and pencil, sat down in Leonard's chair again. 'Look, I'm sorry to bother you at such a time, but I've got to cook up some kind of tale about this poetry reading before I lose my job. This is a hell of a murder, you know.' He was a companionable bastard, thought Leonard bitterly, retiring to the guest chair again. 'First I get myself in a jam involving the honour of this virgin up at the Infirmary. My paper thinks the story's wonderful, but unfortunately I have by that time got myself amorously involved with a strange and luscious tomato who can't see things the practical way quite as plainly as she might. Now the paper is after me for more about Molly Morrison, but my newly acquired and highly valued love life says thumbs down, so now I've gotta get a new angle. Any ideas?'

The young man was beginning to appear more bearable to Leonard. His monologue seemed without ulterior motive, and genuinely troubled. As his health improved, Leonard's heart filled with sympathy, and some idea began to work in the back of his mind – when his head really cleared it would be plain just what its nature was. 'Perhaps,' said Leonard timidly, 'you could do a piece about the poetry.'

'That,' said the young man, 'was the general idea. Although how happy my boss is going to be to get a piece of literary criticism instead of a new suspect, I'll leave you to imagine.'

'Perhaps,' ventured Leonard, with unprecedented boldness, 'you may – ah – be able to – ah – supply your – ah – boss with both.'

The young man sat forward in his chair. 'So?' he said, cocking his cropped head.

Leonard drew himself up in his chair, frowned, and touched his moustache. 'Can I trust you not to quote me if I simply relate to you certain notions which have entered my mind as to the possible murderer of Kevin Boyle?'

'I guess you can sue me for libel if I do, since we haven't any witnesses,' said the reporter wearily.

'Personally,' said Leonard impressively, 'I found the entire notion of the poetry reading last night a very suspicious business.'

'How so?' said the young man, holding his pencil suspended over his pad.

'For one thing,' said Leonard, 'the entire English Department was given to understand that part of the purpose of the gathering was to have Philip Frisbee, one of the editors of Cornish House, hear Mr Boyle's poems read. Yet Mr Frisbee did not appear.'

'Oh, that could be explained very easily, I'm sure,' said the reporter, looking disappointed.

'It was explained,' pronounced Leonard impressively. 'To me. By Mrs Cramm. After the party. She knew from the beginning that Frisbee was not coming.'

'Well,' said the young man pensively.

'But that is not all,' said Leonard. 'She admitted this to me in conjunction with a number of other remarks which seemed to me very much out of the ordinary. About murder. She said to me flatly and in so many words that there were not enough murders, and that in this case the murderer would never be caught.' He paused impressively and folded his hands on one knee.

'She may be right on both counts,' said the young man, biting his thumbnail.

Leonard sniffed irritably. He was beginning to dislike

the young man again. 'While mulling over Mrs Cramm's very *odd* remarks this morning, I was trying to reconstruct my own impressions of the departing steps of the murderer. I heard him – or her – leaving Boyle's apartment, you know.'

'Yeah, I know. I interviewed you once before, but it was with a bunch of other reporters. Donelly's my name.'

'Oh,' said Leonard correctly, 'how do you do, Mr Donelly?'

'Not very well, thank you,' said the young man abstractedly. 'How's *your* health?'

'Better,' replied Leonard. 'That – that *thing* helped me.'

'What were you going to say about the murderer leaving Boyle's place?'

'*Well*,' continued Leonard with renewed eagerness, 'I got to thinking about the footsteps. I got to thinking about how there was no way I could remember whether the footsteps were those of a woman or a man. Now if they had been the footsteps of a – well, a *slender* woman, in high heels, it would have been quite simple to distinguish them from those of a man, wouldn't it?'

'Sure, I guess so,' said Donelly.

'*However*,' said Leonard, leaning forward, 'had the steps been those of a large woman wearing brogues, they would have been *very difficult* to distinguish, wouldn't they?' He leaned back triumphantly.

'So?' said Donelly, unimpressed.

It seemed to Leonard that he had gone quite far enough – the reporter's lack of enthusiasm dashed him a bit, but he pulled himself together and went on. 'Boyle used to talk to me a good deal,' he said. 'He used to talk to me about – ah – women. I was quite conversant with the type he preferred. He frequently and graphically described it.

Among other less relevant characteristics were those of good legs set off by high heels, and willowiness.'

'That's what *I* used to say to myself,' said the reporter in a puzzled voice.

'Breathes there a man with soul so dead, Mr Donelly?' quipped Leonard boldly.

For a moment the reporter's face looked almost irate; Leonard wondered what on earth he had said wrong this time. 'Look,' said Donelly at last, 'are you trying to say you think Mrs Cramm did Boyle in?'

'I think,' said Leonard coldly, 'that I have gone quite far enough. You may make what use you like of my deductions.'

The reporter rose exhaustedly and put on his coat and hat. 'It doesn't cook,' he said. 'I always knew there was no story in the poetry angle. There isn't any story, and that's the long and the short of it, because there aren't any clues – unless you take this Morrison girl, and I can't take the Morrison girl or I'll lose my girl, and I don't think I want to lose my girl,' he muttered on in an amazed undertone, 'because I *think* I might want to marry her.'

Deep pity rose in Leonard's breast for Donelly's troubled spirit. If he had been writing himself in a book, he would have had himself clap Donelly on the shoulder and say, Don't worry, old man, it will all come out in the wash; but in real life this seemed both unrealistic and impertinent. He followed Donelly to the door, commiserating silently. Just as he had his hand on the knob, the reporter turned suddenly on Leonard. 'By the way, Marks,' he said, 'what was that paper you tore up and put in your pocket on the sun porch at Freda Cramm's last night?'

The room reeled, the reporter seemed to leer at him like the wolf from Grandma's bed, the Kafka-esque quality of the encounter increased a thousandfold.

'Paper?' gasped Leonard feebly. 'Paper?' and making a hopeless upward gesture, turned and fled to the bathroom, where he threw up the Prairie Oyster in the toilet.


## Chapter 18

'DR Forstmann, Mr Bainbridge,' said Miss Seltzer, sticking her head around the door, and disappeared to admit the tall, dripping figure of the psychiatrist. Bainbridge came round from behind his desk.

'Hullo, Julian,' he said. 'I'm as glad to see you as any of your anxious patients.'

'A good deal gladder than most, I assure you,' said Forstmann, shaking out his trench coat, knocking the drops off the brim of his hat, and standing his wet umbrella in a corner.

'Julian, this business of the Morrison girl becomes more and more pressing. Sit down.' Bainbridge went behind his desk again and sat down, passing and repassing his hand over his bald spot. 'How am I going to keep that idiot Flaherty from arresting her?'

Forstmann sat down and lit a cigarette. 'I suppose that if it were absolutely necessary he could put a police guard outside her door at the Infirmary.'

Bainbridge shook his head. 'I'd hate that, and so would the trustees. Lord, what a scandal! I wish I could just ship the girl home.'

Forstmann grinned. 'Flaherty would love that.'

'Oh, I know, I know; but I'm at my wit's end. Now you must tell me what *you* think about her.'

'Think about her? That's a poser. I think it probable that she could and should undergo a successful analysis. But as to whether she's a murderess or not, I have no more idea than you. Her Rorschach shows her to have a high intelligence, but low productivity. She is very much introverted, and has great difficulty in making contacts with people, even to the point of showing paranoid tendencies.'

Bainbridge groaned. 'Pity my grey hairs and translate, Julian.'

'Delusions of persecution,' said Forstmann sharply. 'Lucien, do you know what a hepcat is?'

'Why – ah – yes, I believe I do,' said Bainbridge, amazed. 'It's approximately – ah – a jitterbug, isn't that correct? Good heavens, what has that to do with the Morrison child –'

'It has only to do with your affected ignorance of psychiatric terms which have long since become common parlance, Lucien. From your overprotestations I sometimes suspect that one morning I'll come to the office and find you on my couch.'

'Not if I see you first,' said Bainbridge colloquially. 'And you seem a little touchy yourself.'

'If you want to be convinced of my humanity,' said Forstmann, 'I had a flat tyre on the way over, and I'm catching cold.'

'Patient shows a tendency to wander away from the subject,' murmured Bainbridge.

'All right, all right,' said Forstmann. 'The picture of Molly Morrison that I've gotten from three visits with her is this: Her father is Miles Morrison, as you know, and a very distinguished painter who is not successful financially. Her mother makes no bones about having married him on the assumption that he would one day be rich and famous; when he failed to become so, she became very much embittered and took out the frustration of her social ambition on both the father and the child. Wait a minute.' He unzipped the brief-case that was on his knees and withdrew a manila folder. He scanned a sheet and then began to read from it.

'There were constant recriminations, and Morrison evidently felt a good deal of guilt about his own inability to make money, which Molly shared with him. Molly also seems to have gotten the idea that if she had never boon born, things would have been easier between her mother and father. She came to Hollymount actually dreading to leave home, but feeling that if she did leave, relations between her mother and father might become smoother. She is strongly attached to her father, and I should imagine that her feeling for Kevin Boyle was a pretty direct transference of her feelings for her father to a nearer object. Her relations with all women are fearful and inhibited, as a reflection of her dealings with her mother – she seems to have had literally no strong relationships outside her home in all her life. When she speaks of her housemother, of the nurses in the Infirmary, or of the students in her dormitory, her sense of persecution is intense – she imagines she is always being ridiculed, scorned, despised. It's interesting, for instance, that her feelings about Flaherty during the interview in which she made the confession are nowhere near so violent as those she has about Miss Sanders taking her to the Infirmary, which she felt was just another move in the conspiracy of women – mothers – to get rid of her.'

He broke off, shuffled the pages, began again, 'About the confession – she will tell me nothing about it – simply refuses to discuss it. I haven't thought it wise to press the point, because I am most interested, at the moment, in building up her confidence in me.'

'But, Julian, you'll have to,' said Bainbridge worriedly. 'You'll simply have to find out something about it. Because it's the confession that's Flaherty's entire weapon in the case. And, of course, to a literal mind, it has a striking weight. Even to my literal mind.'

Forstmann replaced the papers in the folder, frowned and shook his head. 'The confession may be gospel truth or pure confabulation, for all I know. The girl is not psychotic; I can say that fairly flatly. But does that make her incapable of murder? I don't know. Look at suicidal types. There is some truth to the old saying that depressives who talk a great deal about suicide seldom actually kill themselves. Yet the fact remains that once in a while one does destroy himself – perhaps simply by accident. The same is just as probable of murder. I'd say from what I've seen of Molly that it is very unlikely that she killed Boyle. The act seems quite untypical of her personality as I've had occasion to see it. But I've only *had* occasion to see it three times.'

Bainbridge picked up a pencil and beat the eraser against his front teeth. 'God,' he said, and sighed heavily. 'God. What kind of people do commit murders, Julian?'

'Murderers,' said Forstmann shortly.

'Isn't there a criminal type or something?'

'Balderdash,' said Forstmann.

'How about Lombroso, or whatever his name is?'

'Nineteenth-century nonsense.'

'Oh dear,' said Bainbridge, 'I really know a good deal about Milton, you know. Also about seventeenth-century poets. Why did I never turn my mind to some more practical field which would come to my aid now?'

Forstmann shook his head abstractedly, staring out at the level lines of rain.

Suddenly the president extended his pencil at arm's length. 'A double personality!' he cried.

'What?'

'Maybe she's a double personality – you know – Dr Jekyll and Mr Hyde? Or is that,' he finished weakly, 'just nonsense – I mean, do people have them?'

'Oh yes – not frequently, but they do.'

'Well, how about the Morrison child? Is she the type to have one?'

'Type?' said Forstmann, who was thinking of something else. 'Oh, I don't know. You don't see them nowadays. Not in my kind of practice, anyway. Hysterics, or schizophrenics.'

'Well, could this girl be – what about all those diaries? Aren't they always supposed to do automatic writing and so on?'

'The diaries!' said Forstmann, suddenly galvanized. 'That damned tyre put them out of my mind. Did you get them?'

Bainbridge shook his head sadly. 'Miss Sanders said she turned her room inside out and didn't find anything but school notes and papers. Not even letters from her family.'

'Hmm,' muttered Forstmann.

Bainbridge rose, came round his desk, and began to

pace the floor, his hands in his pockets. Suddenly he stopped in the middle of the carpet and extended his short arms. 'Look, Julian,' he said, 'I wish you'd do something for your fat fee besides sit around and look cryptic.'

'I'm wide open to suggestion,' said the psychiatrist sadly.

'Well, *do* try to get some kind of answer from her about the confession,' said Bainbridge.

'I'll try to-day,' said Forstmann; 'but if she says she *did* commit the murder, she'll only be repeating what she's already said to the police. I really can't see how that's going to help you – however, I'll try. Meantime, I think you should conduct a recheck on anyone who might possibly give her an alibi – have the housemother talk to all the girls in the house to see if anyone could definitely state that she had seen her at the time of the murder. Because she might very well admit to me that the confession was false, but what influence would that have on the police?'

Bainbridge sank into one of the armchairs and groaned again. 'None at all. I can't think straight. The *Messenger's* printed another story – *What's Become of the Morrison Girl?* or some such. After my childlike faith in that young man. Although I must say they didn't mention the confession. But you can imagine the frenzy this will stir Flaherty to.'

'Well, at least I'll see what I can do,' said Forstmann, rising with a loud sneeze. 'I'm on my way to the Infirmary now. You see what you can do in the way of getting an alibi. So far as I can see, that's her only real hope, other than having someone else confess to the murder.'

'If all else fails, I may as well do that myself,' said the president gloomily, helping Forstmann into his sodden coat.

## Chapter 19

THE bed had been turned so that the foot was toward the window, and Molly, lying propped on pillows, stared out aimlessly over the rolling, dun-coloured fields that stretched beyond the river to the misty mountains. Forstmann closed the door behind him, took off his hat and coat, and stood his umbrella in a corner. 'Hullo,' he said.

'Hello,' she answered listlessly, not turning her head.

The wicker chair stood ready for him, a little behind the head of the bed. But to-day he drew it to where he could see her face and sat down. For a moment neither of them spoke. Then, a little to his surprise, she broke the silence. 'The fields are like a cow,' she said in a monotone. 'Like an old brown cow, lying down waiting for you to lay your head against its flank and be comforted. With a big warm udder full of milk hidden between her legs and a warm stupid sort of look in her eyes.' She paused. 'You could just put your head against her and go to sleep.' He thought that what she said was almost beautiful, but her voice had the sound of exaggerated grief and self-pity to which he was so used that it voided any emotional content which might have reached him, leaving only the sickness for his mind to deal with. He followed her gaze out the window to the drenched fields. 'That would make a painting, too,' he said, half jocularly.

'Oh yes,' she said, and turned toward him with a spark of animation in her eyes. 'I was thinking that. Like those paintings that are two things at once – a landscape and a face – you know what I mean.'

He nodded.

All at once her face turned pink, and she looked down at her hands. 'I'm glad you're sitting there,' she said. 'Where I can see you.'

'I'm sitting here because I have something special to say to you,' he said, a little wearily.

She looked up, her face pale and drawn again. 'What?' she said anxiously.

He smiled at her. 'You won't like it.'

'All right,' she said tensely, 'all right. Say it. What is it?'

'About the confession you signed for Flaherty,' he brought out, not at all sure that he had been right to go at it quite this way. And as if to confirm his self-doubt, she hid her face in her hands and turned from him.

He looked out at the fields again, and put his hand over his eyes. 'Listen,' he said, 'listen to me for a moemnt, Molly. I'll try to explain. I shouldn't have to ask you this. You ought to be allowed to take your time, and to talk about this when you get ready to. Psychoanalysis doesn't go on the theory that suffering purifies – it makes it plain that when people have to suffer beyond their strength it warps and scars them, so that it takes them a long time to heal – if they're lucky enough ever to do so.' This was not what he had planned – he could not remember what he had planned, but he went on. 'It's against anything that I want to push you into a position of making you go back to something which hurts you so deeply as the thought of this confession plainly does. But unfortunately, your cure is not the only issue involved. You have got mixed up in a complicated situation over which I have almost no control. You're tangled in the law. And I can't help you unless you help me.'

She kept her hands over her face and rolled her head

from side to side. 'I don't care, I don't care!' she wept. I don't care what happens to me. It doesn't matter, it doesn't matter!'

He would have liked to put aside his therapeutic imperturbability and tell her not to be a little idiot, just for once in a way. The course he must steer was so delicate, running between the necessities of the police and of his patient – on the one hand a need for immediate action, on the other the need for infinite patience. He groped and fingered among his thoughts for the right word, the exact degree of gentle firmness. 'It matters,' he said. 'It does matter; but I'm going to have a hard time trying to explain to you how, unless you will listen to me very patiently and trustfully. Yet I am perfectly aware that you have no reason for trusting me – you've only seen me three times in your life. Ordinarily, Molly, you would have the time to try me out and find out whether or not you thought you could count on me before you exposed anything you found painful to expose. But because of the pressure of the police, I have to try to push you, although it's against my better judgment. Will you listen to me, Molly?'

She had turned her head while he was speaking, and drawn her hands down her face until her eyes stared at him over her fingertips. 'I'll listen,' she said tragically, through her hands. 'But it doesn't matter.'

Now he marshalled his forces and blew his nose. He recrossed his long legs, looked at her for a moment. She stared back, her eyes flickering, frightened, but steadfast on his own. 'You're saying,' he began finally, 'that your life doesn't matter – that it doesn't matter whether you live or die. But you're not sure. You have before you in the world too many examples of people who have preferred life to death to be able to say quite flatly that there's little to choose between them, or that death is preferable.'

'But –' she began, taking her hands away from her mouth.

He raised his hand to silence her. 'Will you just listen for a moment while I lecture?' he said, smiling a little, but firm. 'It would be much easier if I could tell you that your life mattered to me, or to your mother, or your father, or some other person. And of course it does, in many ways. But the person to whom your life is really important is yourself. Much more important than your death could possibly be.'

She made a little moue of scorn and began to speak, but he went on without letting her. 'Death has certain incontrovertible advantages which I shouldn't for a moment undertake to deny. Death is a sure thing, and life is a risk. Death might even represent for you a small but definite improvement on the *status quo*.' An amazed look came over her face, and he was childishly pleased. 'You're miserable now; if you were dead, you'd at least be at peace.' She nodded and nodded, agreeing vehemently. 'I've got everything your father ever learned, everything your mother ever learned, and most of the things you ever read to fight when I try to sell you life, Molly. I wish I had a nickel for every time somebody in the last generation and the generation before said that: You can't demand happiness of life. I think you can. Once you've found out that happiness is learning to work with the materials at hand and to grow and develop in proportion with your own abilities. Once you've found out you have a right to your own importance.'

Her hands lay on her lap, her white face gazed at him,

and a flat look of utter contempt was on it. As he watched her, he saw her raise her eyebrows and shake her head slowly and hopelessly. Outside the rain poured on the window pane, on the brick terrace, on the dingy fields. He felt tired and mistaken. What he had done was like giving a patient a six-weeks' dose of medicine in one day ... Six weeks ... six months ... sixteen ... 'All right,' he said wearily. 'I know. It sounds idiotic to you. It even sounds idiotic to me. I've tried to give you a *Readers' Digest* version of *War and Peace*, or something like it.' He sneezed ignominiously, blew his nose, and rising, took his overcoat.

'You have a cold,' her voice came to him suddenly, small, flat, and female.

'I have indeed,' he said stuffily.

'You shouldn't run around without rubbers,' she said softly. 'You're worse than my father.'

He stopped in the midst of thrusting his arm through a sleeve, then made himself go on calmly. When he had buttoned his coat and taken his hat and umbrella, he turned. 'All the same,' he said, 'I wish you could have told me about the confession, Molly.'

She looked down at her hands, rolling and unrolling the edge of the sheet. 'All right,' she said, almost inaudibly. 'I didn't kill him. Of course I didn't. But I might as well have. And it doesn't make any difference.'

He took a step towards the bed, striving to keep his voice even. 'Where were you at the time the murder was being committed, Molly? Do you remember at all?'

'I went back to the house and stayed there all evening,' she whispered, bending her head even lower over her moving fingers.

'All right, Molly,' he said gently. 'That's all. Good

girl.' Quietly he let himself out the door, without either of them saying good-bye.

Good old transference, he thought irreverently as he strode out of the Infirmary to his car.

## Chapter 20

As he pushed the big library door and stiffened himself to brave the rain, Hungerford met Leonard Marks, who, with sighs and puffings of relief, was folding his umbrella under the shelter of the vestibule. The younger man looked peaked and drawn, with an unattractive oyster-like pallor. Hungerford remembered having been beastly rude to him once when Marks had approached him in his repulsively eager fashion. And he remembered, too, that Marks had been kind to him the night after Kevin's murder. So he made a point of stopping and speaking to him, instead of passing on.

'Hullo,' he said, and twisted out a wry friendly smile. 'Glorious New England autumn, isn't it?'

'Oh, Christ,' said Marks miserably, 'it's awful.'

'How did the reading go at Freda's?'

'I read,' said Marks.

'Yes, I know. How did it go?'

'Oh,' said Marks bitterly, 'everybody wished it had been you.'

'Rats!' said Hungerford, embarrassed and annoyed. 'As a matter of fact, Miss Austen was just telling me how well you read. How did Frisbee take the poems?'

'He wasn't there,' said Marks, a peculiar expression passing across his face.

Hungerford raised his eyebrows. Because he felt sorry for Marks and wanted to make a demonstration of friendliness, he said frankly, 'Why the devil do you suppose she gave the thing?'

Marks drew his face into a mask of exaggerated suggestiveness. 'That is something I should like to know very much myself,' he enunciated.

The poor blundering idiot! Hungerford thought with annoyance. He made it so impossible to be decent to him. What in the world was he trying to imply? Hungerford's own mood of benevolence was not ample enough to impel him to coax out hidden meanings. Instead he sought to change the subject. 'Wonder who's to be your new neighbour in Kevin's place,' he threw out. 'I don't imagine there'll be any difficulty in finding a tenant for it in this enlightened community, in spite of its tragic associations.' He felt his face contract for the tic. I'm tired, he thought, I must get home and rest. The constant chill and dampness of the day were enervating. Still and all, he had felt well to-day – better than for a long time – better than he had since Kevin's death.

He saw Marks' depressing countenance fall into lines of self-abnegation and doglike devotion which would have been moving had they not been so abject. 'I wish,' said Leonard with humble hopelessness. 'that *you'd* move in there, sir. It's an awfully good apartment – sunny and all, and the fireplace.'

Hungerford smiled, and made ready to go, 'I'm pretty well off where I am,' he said. 'It's a gloomy old place, but it suits me, somehow. Give me a ring and drop in to see me one of these days.' And he was off down the granite steps, erecting his umbrella against the downpour. God, he thought, he'll probably come.

Sometimes, he found, rainy days pleased him. They carried the well-worn childhood recollections of staying indoors by the fire, of reading three or four novels in a day, of having his mother surprise him with a tray of cocoa and cookies as he sat curled in the old wing chair. She had liked the rainy days too, shutting the two of them off from the world ... Ah, he knew their relationship had been perverse and warping, but how beautiful, my God, how loving! True, he had grown up like some small white stunted plant beneath a stone, but he had loved the secrecy and privacy of his warm underground world – sometimes he thought the brilliance of that filial passion he had known was worth the torments it had caused him. Things he could not have told a psychiatrist, who would have made them obscene, he treasured as the loveliest moments of his life. Sitting on the stool of his mother's dressing table while she lovingly brushed his long blond curls over her ivory fingers. He could not have been more than four or five – his earliest memory. She had dressed him in kilts – even then a little out of date – and velvet suits. 'I wanted a little girl,' she had confided to him. 'That was before I knew how nice a little boy could be.' Their warm, plush-carpeted privacy ... his mother, her auburn hair tumbling down over her peignoir, coming in to light his gas log as he lay in the big mahogany bed ... A neurotic, sex-terrified widow, almost insane in her withdrawal from the world. Those things were true, he recognized them. He recognized the irreparable damage her strangeness had wrought on his spirit. Yet how was he ever to explain to anyone, ever, the vivid pure pleasure of their companionship, the mutual harbour of their love? She was the great passion which more than his work, even, had justified his existence; for her he had remained

virgin during the fifty years of his life, regretting nothing
.. nothing he had missed.

Wrapped in his thoughts of warmth and love he had
walked unnoticing through the dripping streets and found
himself at his own doorstep almost before he knew it. The
old house held its grim face up to the rain in a kind of bleak
resignation; it seemed to him like a person awaiting his
return, like some long-faced spinster housekeeper, unsmil-
ing always, yet devoted and welcoming in her own queer,
unyielding way. Silently, he returned the silent greeting.

In the hallway an old-fashioned lamp shaded·by a
crimson and gold painted glass globe throbbed dimly in
the gloom. To the left and right were the closed doors of
two apartments occupied by very old ladies. He climbed
the stairs to his own rooms. Opposite his own was the
apartment of an emaciated and ancient professor
emeritus of Greek who ate health foods and would, if you
allowed him, discourse for hours on the benefits of eurhy-
thmics and Dalcroze. On the third floor, in what had
formerly been the servants' rooms, lived Miss Penny, the
landlady, who was quite as elderly as the rest. Among
them, Hungerford was a youthful sprig, a mere boy of
fifty. He smiled as he turned his key in the lock. Downstairs he could hear Miss Belcher's radio tuned to
'Orphan Annie,' while across the hall Samson Ellerbee
engaged in audible slumber. He felt a kind of peace and
protection in the queer old place. He snapped on the
gooseneck student lamp on his desk. The blotter was neat
and vacant; at once his heart began to pound and he
could not catch his breath. He became aware that all his
protestations of peace, his memories of protection, had
been a barrier erected against fear – the fear that he
would find the notebook awaiting his return.

He sat down in his armchair, slumped over like an old man, panting. Fear. Why should he be so frightened? What was there to fear? Was not death the ultimate thing that people feared? And was he afraid of death? No. Then what? Guilt, he thought involuntarily. What kind of guilt? Of what was he guilty? His breath began to come in heaving, audible gasps. He hid his face in his hands. Of nothing – nothing but his mother's death.

And yet he was not. Surely he was not. That was pure madness to blame himself for what must have come with or without him one day ... Ah, but it had come without him! He had left her; she had died helpless and alone, surrounded by strangers, calling for him. If he had been there to comfort her, to stay her with his love, perhaps she would have lived again, and died in peace some later day, dropping off to sleep and never waking, as one might hope. There he had been, enjoying heartlessly the things she would so have loved to share with him, basking un-abashed in Sicilian sunshine, gone abroad to write on a fellowship, while she lay pierced and gasping with pneumonia in the bitter New England damp. His breath came rasping from his chest. God, had he not paid sufficiently? Since that day, when the cable reached him, he had not written another word. For three years now he had been nothing but a living corpse, waiting to be buried.

He could not stand these thoughts; as if to purge one pain by inflicting another, he rose, went abruptly to the desk, drew out the notebook, and began to turn the pages of mad scrawled writing. Slowly he dropped into the swivel chair at his desk and began to read the entry dated November 5.

George Hungerford (it said) went to Kevin Boyle's tonight. He sat down by his fire and put his feet on his fender. He talked to Kevin Boyle about his work. Oh, says he, in his whining meaching voice, all Christlike, all crucified. You must get away from here. For the sake of your work, he said. Hoh! He said for the sake of his work! If I told all I knew how his fine speeches would fly out the window. The martyr, suffering about so they will comfort him. Oh no, Mr Hungerford, don't got there! You're too weak, too feeble – let us take care of you, we understand. So he goes to Kevin Boyle, all love and fawning. I come too. I knock at the door, I beat on the window. Will I tell Kevin Boyle to go away? No, I will not! I will tell him to stay here, to lie on my breast, to know what warmth is – not sit by the fire with dry old men. Oh, Kevin Boyle! I cry, but George Hungerford will not let my voice be heard. He is all Go Away, and For the Sake of Your Work. Old hypocrite! I will finish you ...

The writing was so large that this entry covered five pages. When Hungerford turned the last of them, his hands were shaking. He laid the brown-covered notebook on the desk. Why should it disturb him so – beyond the mere fact of its presence, which was, to be sure, disturbing in a realistic enough way. It was hostile, unfriendly, hating. And who should hate him so? Who was his enemy? And how had his enemy such secret access to his house? And if to his house, perhaps to his thoughts ... Already this had occurred to him. This enemy seemed almost to read his thought ...

He rose and paced the floor. The room was gloomy with only the small puddle of light from the desk lamp to illuminate it. In the dark corners the furniture loomed threateningly, with semi-human faces. He wished, for once in a way, to think this through, scientifically. He tried to remember how each discovery of a new entry in the journal had come about.

The discoveries had these characteristics in common. They occurred on his return from supper, which he usually ate down-town, in the cafeteria of the Harlow Hotel. This, of course, was the logical time for an outsider to gain access to his room. It had occurred to him that it would also be possible for the girl – or woman – to enter the room while he took his regular afternoon nap, but this he had dismissed as too improbable a notion. Besides which, since he had thought of it, he had taken to propping a chair underneath the knob of the door, which, had it fallen, would have awakened him even from the drugged sleep he slept. She could even, he thought, as he walked up and down the floor with a rapid and erratic tread, write the entries while he slept, for all he would know of it. For always when he woke his head would be thick, his consciousness muddy; it was his custom to put his clothing and wraps in meticulous order before lying down so that when he woke there would be no need for concentration; he could simply stumble into his things blindly, wash his face, and stagger out into the night, where the fresh air would revive him. But that was improbable – highly improbable. No, the most likely thing was that she came while he was at dinner. No one would notice her. The old ladies downstairs were half-blind and deaf, besides which one of them always had a radio roaring. As for Mr Ellerbee, he was always either sleeping or practising Yoga. And Miss Penny, supposing that she heard footsteps or an opening door below, would have no reason to suppose that it was not one of her regular tenants. The question was not so much the how as the why. What curious and subtle mind had devised this form of torture? Who knew him well enough to know how utterly undone this odd means of persecution would render him? Who cared enough?

For a moment he halted at the rain-streaked window and stared into the thickening twilight. One hunched figure under an umbrella passed on the opposite side of the street; a red truck rumbled by. Yet the strangeness of the thing grew, for though he thought of the torture in terms of a subtle mind, nothing said in the entries indicated subtlety of mind except with regard to means of causing pain to himself. There was one detail of the business which haunted him with such implications as he dared not think about straight-on. The name of the writer – for she sometimes referred to herself in the third person – or the name she had assumed, was Eloise. Just why this should terrify him so he did not know, yet it made him tremble in his deepest being – Eloise was the name of his sister, who had died when she was six months old, before he was born.

How long was it to go on? How long must he bear it? Something must be done before – before ... He whirled about and faced the dark room, his hands against the window-sill, like a criminal at bay, facing his tormentors. The furniture seemed to take on the appearance of people he knew. The spindle-backed straight chair was Samson Ellerbee, all bones and no flesh; a well-picked skeleton existing in polite madness. The studio couch was Bainbridge, stolid, overstuffed, unperturbed, unheeding. The bookcase was the dog-faced librarian, herself half mad, who lashed out at him in invective when he brought in books that were overdue. The telephone was Leonard Marks, extending his lips in a great black over-eager kiss. But in the corner – ah, in the corner! There stood a square-shouldered, apelike figure, clenching its fists and lowering its head, grinning a broad brass-edged grin, seeming to move, to swing its weight from hip to hip – the golden-maple highboy, like Freda Cramm, waiting to pounce on him!

He fled across the room and opened the door to the hall. There too it was dark, but through the banisters he could see the hall lamp shining its fiery eye malignantly. Downstairs the radio had been turned off, and all was very still. It seemed to him the latch of the outside door clicked gently and a step sounded in the hall below. In panic he slammed the door and propped Samson Eller-bee – the straight chair – under the knob. He switched on the ceiling light, and the room suddenly glared. He was panting and trembling. He went to the telephone and thumbed clumsily through the college directory, then dialled a number. 'Hullo,' he said breathlessly, at last. 'Hello, Marks? This is Hungerford. Look, I wondered if you would do me a favour. Speak to Miss Stone for me about Boyle's apartment. Tell her to hold it until I see her. On thinking over your suggestion, it seemed it might not be a bad idea to make the change.'

## Chapter 21

THERE were ten tables of six girls each in the dining-room. The talk flowed on in a water babble of female voices – you could become fascinated by the collective effect if you ceased to listen to the individual sense. It was bright and warm there, snug with the knowledge that the rain was coming down outside. The dining-room was full – no one wanted to eat out when the weather was so horrible, in spite of the meal, which consisted of creamed chipped beef, baked potatoes, beet, and canned fruit cup. There was a short conference among the girls at the head table, then they banged on their glasses with their spoons to quiet the dining-room, while Miss Sanders, at the head of the table, rose.

'There will be a short house meeting after dinner in the living-room, which it is imperative that you all attend. Roll will be called. It will only last a very few minutes, and it is terribly important.'

She sat down again, blinking her pink-rimmed eyes nervously, while the stream of talk took up its course with added volume. The house president, seated at Miss Sanders' table, looked at her in some surprise, since she was usually asked to call any meeting of the girls in the house. 'What's the meeting, Miss Sanders?' she asked curiously.

'Why,' said Miss Sanders, blinking her eyes almost frenetically, 'I'd rather just wait and have you hear it with the rest, if you don't mind, Marjorie.'

Slightly wounded in her dignity, Marjorie addressed herself to her fruit cup.

With a short nervous titter, Miss Sanders asked one of the other girls how the try-outs for the Dramatic Association play were coming along, and the conversation resumed its irritatingly innocuous course.

When one of the maids gave her the signal that all the tables had finished their dessert, Miss Sanders rose and conducted the stream of girls out of the dining-room.

Chattering and jostling they idled after her, the procession held up by the bottleneck created while each girl waited to thrust her rolled-up napkin back in its cubby hole. During the dinner hour the last mail of the day arrived; a second halt occurred in midstream during the trip to the living-room when each one stopped to look despairingly or delve triumphantly at her mailbox. At last they were established in the living-room, on the couches, on the chairs, on the floor, with Miss Sanders behind the coffee urn and several self-appointed Hebes moving about with demi-tasse cups, sugar, and cream. A slight stir of curiosity and impatience was beginning when Miss Sanders pulled out a sheet of paper from under the tray, and perching a pair of reading spectacles on her beaklike nose, began to read out the names.

'Ackerman ... Allen ... Bastion ... Bellini ... Burton ...'

Several were missing, in the Infirmary or out to dinner. These names Miss Sanders carefully marked on her list. When she was done, she folded up her spectacles, looked at all of them apprehensively, and cleared her throat.

'Girls,' she began in her high nasal voice, 'I want to ask a question to which you must all give your most serious attention, as it is – ah – in the most *literal* sense a matter of life and death.' She paused and looked around at their faces, now frozen utterly dumb with surprise. 'I want you each and everyone to try to remember if she saw Molly Morrison on the day that Mr Boyle was – ah – killed.' The silence following her speech was absolute. Faces turned up to her, round and amazed, many of them open-mouthed. 'If any girl *does* recollect seeing Molly about the house on that day, will she please report to me in my apartment. I'm going to my room now.' She rose and left the living-room in the midst of a dead silence.

After her departure the talk started up again slowly, first a buzzing murmur around the room, then aloud and confused. 'God,' one little redheaded girl kept saying, 'I live right *next* to her and I didn't see her ... No, I'm sure I didn't see her!' 'Do you suppose she *did* it? Do you suppose ... ' Kate Innes, sitting on the sofa beside Honey Sacheveral, beat one fist on the other palm. 'Oh, Lord,' she kept saying over and over, 'I *couldn't* have. I was at a meeting of the *Holly*.'

'Gee,' said Marjorie, the house president, hopelessly, 'how can they expect anyone to remember at this point? It's nearly two weeks ago. Anyway, nobody ever noticed her, and that's the truth.'

They sat chattering anxiously for some time, then one or two got up and drifted out the door, then more. Each time someone left the room there was a general craning of necks to see if the departing one turned into Miss Sanders' doorway, but none of them did. The rest stayed on, conversing desultorily, draining off little by little. When the room was nearly empty, Honey, who had been staring broodingly into space, turned to Kate with sudden animation. 'Did you see the new article about Molly Morrison in the *Messenger*?'

'Yeah,' said Kate tonelessly, 'I saw it.'

'Know what I bet?' said Honey eagerly. 'I bet that little ole boy we met in the Harlow wrote those stories. *I* thought *he* was *cute*.'

'He's a stinker,' said Kate. 'An old fourteen-carat stinker from way back. You, Sacheveral, are more or less innocent because you don't know what you're doing. He knows.' She rested her elbows on her dungareed knees and put her head in her hands. 'They'd never have gotten that stuff about Morrison if it hadn't been for me.

*I* did it, I did it all, and then I so miserably misjudged that rat's character ... oh, I could shoot myself!'

'Don't feel bad, honey,' said Honey.

'Why the hell not?' said Kate ungratefully. She pulled viciously at a strand of her drooping hair, then sighed and pushed her glasses up her nose. 'If only somebody had seen her. She must have been around here. Somebody must have seen her. It wasn't the time of day when a person's ordinarily out wandering around.'

'When was that?' said Honey vaguely. 'Was that a Monday?'

'Of course it was a Monday, you cretin. A week ago last Monday.'

'Now let me see,' said Honey. 'On Mondays – yeah, I ride. That's it. When it's rainin', Miss Hoogle comes and picks us up on the corner by The Coffee Shoppe.'

'You mean,' said Kate, momentarily distracted, 'you actually know a character named Hoogle?'

'Oh, honey, she's *real* sweet – she comes from Atlanta.'

'Not Miss Scarlett O'Hoogle?'

'Uh-uh,' said Honey seriously. 'I think her first name is Mary Margaret. She teaches riding, you know.'

Kate groaned, but Honey went on undeterred. 'Now let me see,' she mused, cocking her beautiful head so that the golden feathers of her hair curled over one shoulder of her pale blue sweater. 'Did it rain that Monday?'

Kate shook her head abstractedly.

'That means we were in the outdoor ring. Miss Hoogle was teaching us about leads.'

'Do you have to call her that – that name?' snapped Kate, rousing momentarily from her reverie.

'Honey, I can't help that's what her name is. And you know what? I think she's queer.'

'How do you mean, queer?'

'Oh, *you* know. Regular sort of queer. I mean, she has such a deep voice, and she goes around in pants all the time.'

'So do I,' said Kate morosely.

'Oh, but honey, you're like my mama says – full busted.'

Kate threw her hands in the air and collapsed against the back of the sofa, closing her eyes. In a moment she might have been seen to open one of them a trifle to view her own contours as they were spread before her. Meanwhile, Honey went on placidly.

'O.K., so that Monday we were in the ring. That was until five o'clock, or ten of, or something. Then I walked home from the stables – that takes about twenty minutes, I reckon. Then I took my clothes off and put on my robe – only it seems to me the tubs were all full and I had to wait. Seems to me I went all the way down the hall and Dibby and Jane or somebody had the tubs. No, it couldn't have been Dibby, because it seems to me she has choir practice Mondays ... '

'Gee,' said Kate, 'you're awfully boring, but I wish I could be wondering like that what I was doing last Monday. The least I could do would be to produce an alibi for the girl. If only I hadn't been in that damn *Holly* meeting!'

Honey went on as if Kate had not spoken. 'And then it seems to me I went back down the hall to my room to wait for the tubs to be empty, and I plucked my eyebrows for a while, and then I came out again and ... '

Kate got up abruptly and stretched. Honey stopped and looked up at her. 'What's the matter with you, have you got a photographic memory or something? People aren't supposed to remember that well what they did two weeks ago.'

'Oh,' said Honey complacently, 'it's very easy. That was the day I fell in love.'

'In love?' said Kate, sitting down again and looking more curious than she would have liked.

'With little ole Petey Jones,' said Honey dreamily. 'Honey, he drove all the way over here from Amherst, and he had two flats on the way. And I was thinking about him, all day. About whether I would fall in love with him or not. And I did.'

'So that's the way it happened,' said Kate shortly.

'Yes, it did,' replied Honey. 'Darlin', isn't it *mysterious*?'

The room was empty now. Kate fished in the crevice between the sofa cushions for her cigarettes and pulled herself forward, preparatory to rising.

'Then,' said Honey, rolling on like the Mississippi, 'when I finished plucking my eyebrows I started back down the hall again, and –'

'Oh, shut up,' said Kate rudely, and rose. 'You don't take my mind off my troubles worth a nickel.'

'But Ka-ate!' cried Honey aggrievedly. '*That* was when I saw that little Morrison drip! Isn't that what I'm supposed to remember?'

'You *what*?' shrieked Kate, and plumped down again. 'What time? Where did you see her? What was she doing?'

Honey nodded her flaxen head complacently and smoothed her skirt. 'I surely did,' she said. 'I remember it just as plain, because she nearly took my head off. She was coming out of her room with a great, big, old pile of notebooks, and I said to her, What are you up to, fixin' to make a bonfire? and didn't she just lay into me – what was I doing snooping around her room, and why was everybody always spying, and – oh, I don't know what all. She just blessed me out for sure, and I never did a thing – just was coming down the hall to take a bath and met her with all those papers and stuff she was carrying.'

'Well!' gasped Kate. 'Well! Could you say – is there any way you could tell what time it was?'

'We-ell,' said Honey doubtfully, 'I didn't look at the clock or anything. What time *ought* it to be?'

'Between half-past five and six to do her any good.'

'Well, honey, it's *got* to be between half-past five and six, because I couldn't have gotten home earlier than ten after five, only more likely, it was twenty after, and then I got dressed, only Jane and Dibby were in the tubs – but it couldn't have been Dibby –'

'Oh, the hell with Dibby,' said Kate joyfully. 'Honey Sacheveral, could you swear all that on a stack of Bibles?'

For answer, Honey turned her blue eyes upward and raised her slender right hand in the air. 'I, Honoria Sacheveral, do solemnly swear to tell the truth, the whole truth, and nothing but the truth, so help me God,' she intoned dramatically, 'that on the night of – Monday night, whenever that was – I saw Molly Morrison in the hall of the second floor of Birnham House at the time the murder was being committed.'

'Amen,' finished Kate religiously, and taking Honey's arm, dragged her to Miss Sanders' apartment.


*Chapter 22*

WHEN Kate had finished directing Honey's evidence as it was given to the excited Miss Sanders, she slowly climbed the stairs to her floor and locked herself in her room. There she sat down at her desk and stared at the open copy of the *Messenger* that was lying there. WHAT HAS BECOME OF THE MORRISON CLUE the headline read – not a big headline, or on the front page, but still, there it was in plain view. It didn't have a West Lyman date-line. It was mostly a rehash of old stuff. There was no mention of the confession. But who else could have written it? It must have been what needled the police so that it was necessary to find an immediate alibi for Molly. Thank God for Sacheveral. She had really expiated her sins – which was more than some people could say. Deliberately she took off her glasses, laid them on a corner of her desk, put her head down on her arms, and began to cry. How could he be such a heel?

In the middle of a loud snivel, the electric buzzer in her room rang alarmingly. She jumped and put her glasses on, snatched a Kleenex, and blew her nose. The buzzer meant she had a caller, who was, she judged, the man from the printer's here with galley proofs of the December *Holly*. Yes, it must be that, and *whoever* it was, she disdain-ed making up her face for him. She unlocked her door and went thudding down the stairs to the front hall.

Jack stood there, looking somehow dejected, with his hat on the back of his head, reading *PM* as he leaned against the mail desk. Kate stopped halfway down the last flight of stairs. She said very distinctly, 'I don't want to talk to you.'

Jack looked up at her and folded up the paper. 'Yes, you do,' he said, without smiling. 'Go put your face on and we'll go somewhere.'

'I'm sorry,' said Kate, 'there isn't anything I have to say.'

'You don't need to say anything. I'll do the talking.'

'You've verbalized quite enough,' she said, with excessive dignity, and turned to go upstairs again.

Jack made a sprint and caught her by the wrist. 'Look,' he said, 'I'm in no mood for explanations here and now. Will you go up and make yourself presentable, or shall I take you up and wash your face for you?'

She stood quite still, looking into his eyes. 'I don't feel like joking,' she said, 'not about anything, and especially not about Molly Morrison. I just don't want to see you any more. Will you let me go, please?'

He released her wrist. 'I've never seen the dignified side before,' he said, sounding a little more natural. She was on the landing when he called after her, 'Would it make you feel better if I said I'd lost my job?'

She turned and looked back at him, her face still stern. 'When?' she asked.

He laughed shortly. 'You ought to be a lawyer,' he said; 'think of everything, I lost it after I turned in a piece of literary criticism on Kevin Boyle's poetry. The thing you're sore about was written by a colleague who was more willing to ride along with the boss.'

'Oh, Jack!' she said, transfixed on the landing.

'Now will you go fix your face for me?' he grinned.

'Yeah,' she said, flushing, 'yeah!' and turned to fly up the stairs when he caught her on the landing and kissed her resoundingly.

'Take those damn pants off,' he said, smacking the logical place, 'and drop them in the nearest incinerator!'

'Young man! Young man!' came a sudden, scandalized voice from the hall below. 'Men are *not allowed* on the upper floors of the dormitories!'

'Miss Sanders!' gasped Kate, scarlet.

'Kate Innes!' gasped Miss Sanders, the same colour.

'Now, Miss Sanders,' said Jack soothingly, ambling down the stairs as Kate fled up them, 'I assure you that my intentions were most honourable.'

'Well!' spluttered Miss Sanders. 'You must remember that appearances count as well as intentions, young man! Although,' she remarked over her shoulder, as she trailed off toward the dining-room, 'I must say I've always thought that a little more of that sort of thing was just what an intellectual sort of girl like Kate needed.'

In something more than a jiffy, Kate reappeared, looking respectable in a sweater, skirt, and cosmetics. She took her polo coat from the coat rack and they went out of the door in silence. When they were in the car, Jack said, 'I'll have to be going back to New York.'

'You could work for the West Lyman *Star*,' said Kate without conviction.

'Not and start saving for Junior,' he replied, looking at her so meaningfully that they almost cannoned into a traffic light. After this they drove soberly and silently to the Harlow bar.

It had stopped raining, but the raw New England wind ripped around the street corners, whipping at skirts and cutting the breath. As Kate and Jack were precipitated through the glass door of the Harlow by a gust, they ran into a man coming out, head bent to meet the blast.

' 'lo,' said Jack.

Amazingly, the figure swept off its hat and made a low bow. 'My dear sir,' it intoned, 'the clumsiness is entirely on my side. Think nothing of it, nothing of it!' and went off muttering into the night.

'Why,' gasped Kate, 'that was Mr Marks and he was pie-eyed!'

'Drunk as a skunk,' said Jack cheerfully, removing his gloves. 'Good evening, Stanislas.' The bartender nodded morosely.

'But he's the quiet type!' said Kate, unable to get over her surprise. 'I mean, you should see him. The most utterly inhibited white mouse you ever saw!'

'I know,' said Jack. 'We've met. I suspect that somebody suggested a touch of the hair of the dog, and he's been chewing dog hair ever since.'

'Since when?' demanded Kate.

'Since Freda Cramm's party.'

'Was he potted that night? He sounded perfectly sober when we were listening.'

'I regret to inform you, my respected fellow sleuth, that we walked out of that gathering just before things got hot. I deduce from later findings that our Leonard stayed on after the rest of the guests had departed.'

'Oh, Jack, that's incredible! You don't mean –'

'My dear young woman, I don't mean any such thing, having a strong sense of reality to balance my highly coloured imagination; but when I went to interview him the following morning he was most horribly hung and gave evidence of having had a private chat with Freda such as he had no opportunity to have during the rat race that was going on while we were there.'

'Well, well, well!' said Kate.

They sat down in a booth in the taproom, and Jack gave the order for two whiskies with soda. 'Beers,' said Kate firmly. 'This is not on the expense account.'

'That's my little woman,' said Jack, grinning idiotically.

'Don't be so possessive,' Kate pushed her glasses up her nose and leaned on her hand. 'Marks,' she said pensively. 'Leonard Marks.'

'Shall I let you in on my secret theory?' asked Jack rhetorically. 'I'm suspicious of that guy.'

'*Him?*' said Kate.

'Yes,' said Jack. 'Him. Or *he*, as we used to say back at City College. Here's the story. I went to see him last Saturday morning, after a cold night spent on a sun porch where I was so adequately heated that I failed to catch even the slightest sniffle.'

'Shut up,' said Kate. 'Go on.'

'I said I wanted to get some dope on the poetry, which, as a matter of fact, was the God's truth – I wanted anything I could put down on paper that didn't include Molly Morrison.'

Kate blushed. 'You're very sweet,' she said primly, 'but just by the way, what ever happened to our Freda Cramm story? I mean, that seems a little more substantial than the poetry reading.'

'Nothing at all, dear,' said Jack grimly. 'It went right into the waste basket. Mrs Cramm has a nice hunk of *Messenger* stock. Embarrassing, isn't it?'

'Not to me!' said Kate hotly. 'Why, that's –'

'The way of the world,' finished Jack. 'Be quiet and listen to my story. I went to Marks' place, as I was saying, and found him green as an uncooked lobster. Hung? says I. Yes, says he, and promptly rushes off to shoot his cookies. So I went into his kitchen and fixed him a little remedy. He swallowed it, it stayed down, and I rose in his estimation. Then he began making mysterious noises around the subject of la Cramm.'

'What sort of noises?'

'It was a little hard to make out. That she had made a lot of suspicious remarks to him about murder in general, and this murder in particular, and some sort of wild deduction that since the footsteps of the murderer couldn't be distinguished as either those of a man or a woman, therefore they must be those of a heavy woman. Beer!' Jack broke off irrelevantly.

'Beer?' said Kate. 'What's that got to do with it?'

'You can't have beer! It has too many calories!'

'Why you –!' exploded Kate, looking about pointedly for something to shy at him.

But he signalled the waitress and ordered coffee for her with utter disregard of all her splutterings, and then proceeded calmly. 'He was trying to pass the buck a little too hard. It sounded very phony. As a parting shot, I asked him what the paper was that he tore up on the porch. His reply was a rush to the bathroom.'

'Maybe he really knows something about Cramm. Maybe he really has something on her.'

'If he had something on her he would have either spilled it or have been more mysterious,' said Jack, shaking his head. 'He was trying very hard to make something out of nothing for some ulterior motive. I suspect him.'

'Oh!' Kate disagreed. 'Really, why do people always have to have the least likely person as a murder suspect? It's sort of a new development in logic, if you like.'

'It makes the customers feel they're getting their money's worth, I guess. But I want to know what that paper was he tore up so carefully on the porch there.'

'Probably an old cleaners' bill he found stuck on his coat. He's just the type that would be embarrassed about a thing like that. My money's on Freda Cramm. Look at her – she's a big battle-axe who could wield a poker – and please keep your associations to yourself – she's a woman of violent emotions, she hung around Boyle, she has no alibi – alibi! I forgot to tell you that Molly Morrison has an alibi!'

'No!' cried Jack. 'What is it!'

'Well, it's the irony of fate, or something. Honey Sacheveral saw her in the corridor at Birnham between five-thirty and six the day of the murder. She couldn't conceivably have walked over to Boyle's place in time to have conked him.'

'I should telephone old Knucklehead! I would, too, if I thought he'd reverse the charges for me,' said Jack dazedly.

Kate clasped her brow. 'Hoogle! Knucklehead! What a day! Who's Knucklehead, and is that really his name?'

'Naturally not, stupid! It's Smith, and he's my ex-boss.'

'Well, gee,' said Kate concernedly, 'oughtn't you really? I mean, isn't it sort of a scoop? You'd probably get your job back.'

'Yeah,' said Jack, 'and get stuck in it for the rest of my life. I believe in fate or something.'

'Don't tell me you're now free to write the great American novel,' said Kate suspiciously.

'Not at all,' snapped Jack. 'I'm just tired of being a sob sister, and also of administering digitalis to the entire staff every time the New Deal is mentioned.'

'All right, dear,' soothed Kate meekly.

Jack leaned across the table, grinning like a monkey. 'Baby, you're wonderful.'

'Fine,' said Kate composedly. 'Now I've been sweet for to-day and I'll have that beer if you don't mind.' She collared the mug and deftly substituted the coffee cup in Jack's hand. He sighed resignedly and signalled the waitress.

'Everybody was concealing mysterious papers,' mused Kate after a moment's silence. 'Molly with her notebooks and Leonard with his cleaners' bill, or whatever it was.'

'That was no cleaners' bill,' said Jack. 'Otherwise why did he scrape up the pieces after he'd already dropped them in the waste-basket?'

'Some unfashionable cleaner, perhaps,' suggested Kate.

'You've got foam on your lip, and if you get on the scales to-morrow morning, you'll find out what you're doing to yourself. The trouble with you as a detective, baby, is that you get a preconceived notion of a character which you stick with through thick and thin, at the risk of tossing aside objective clues. You see Leonard Marks as a Caspar Milquetoast, and you refuse to even try to imagine him as a killer. You'll never make the homicide squad that way. You have to let your imagination play.'

'Well,' said Kate stubbornly, 'I just can't see Marks as a killer. It's too unconventional. The notion of the unfavourable publicity would make him faint before he ever picked up the poker.'

'Ah, but can't you bring yourself to imagine that in his breast there rages an uncaged beast? Even the rabbit will turn and snarl when cornered!'

'If there's a beast in his breast, a rabbit is just about the size of it. And rabbits don't snarl, Frank Buck; in my recollection they can't even squeak.'

'I'd still like to know what that paper was.'

'Why don't you search his tuxedo pockets?'

'Maybe I will.'

'What I'd like to know – out of idle curiosity rather than detective spirit – is what those notebooks were that Molly had. I'll bet those were psychiatric documents.'

'Classroom notes, probably.'

'Honey said she carried them downstairs toward the door. It sounded as if she were taking them to the trash baskets by the kitchen door. And she could ill afford to burn class notes when she was flunking four out of five subjects.'

'Maybe she was taking them to the library or somewhere.'

'Honey said she had no coat on.'

'Well, she's got her alibi now, so it can't matter much.'

'Oh, I know. I was just taking a psychologist's interest, in my amateur way.'

Kate drained her glass and Jack looked at the clock. 'It's ten to ten,' he said. 'We'll have to start back if I'm going to have a chance to kiss you before lights-out.'

'O.K.,' said Kate, roseate.

They shouldered their way back to the car through the blustery night and drove through the quiet empty streets to the quadrangle. There the new trees shivered in the blast, in spite of the protection of the neo-Georgian buildings. Now and then a hunched figure pedalled by on a bicycle, or a group of girls rushed by chattering and giggling. Inside Jack's car the heater gushed forth hot air. At ten-fourteen they drew apart, and Kate pushed the handle of the door. But Jack caught her face in one hand and forcibly turned her jaw toward him. She tried unsuccessfully to wriggle away. 'Look at me,' he said, and she deliberately shut her eyes. 'Seems I'm in love with you.'

There was a silence in which a window rattled up in its frame and the electric bells in the dormitories could faintly be heard sounding curfew. Her jaw was beginning to hurt between his fingers. 'Seems it's mutual,' she said at last, and sliding out the door, ran into the house just as Miss Sanders was locking up.

## Chapter 23

THERE was a row of small, diamond-paned casement windows across the front of the room; the 'sun poured through them prodigally, illuminating towers of books piled on the floor, and suitcases set in a corner, empty and ready to be stored in the cellar – or the attic, perhaps, depending on Miss Stone's custom. There was a kind of infantile joyousness in this morning to Hungerford. He found himself particularly sensitive to weather on all occasions; one way or another his mood was always intensified by the day. What he hated most were days of sun and shade, indeterminate, when, in the midst of glorious brightness, clouds passed across the sun and the spirit was dashed to earth even as it rose. To-day the heavens were as clear as a blue glass bell; crystals of frost made ferns about the mullions of the windows. He whistled what was intended for a theme from a Mozart sonata as he worked at arranging his books in the bookshelves where formerly Kevin Boyle's had stood. He wondered idly what had been done with Boyle's things, since he had no family. For sentiment's sake, there were one or two of Kevin's volumes he should have liked to own – a first edition of Yeats he had noticed. An issue of *Transition* with a fragment of Joyce as it had first appeared. He would have liked to have one of these to finger, to say, Kevin Boyle chose these, owned these, thumbed these. ... In retrospect he was surprised at the violence of his feeling when he had first heard of Kevin's death. Now he felt sweetly mournful, for he had enjoyed the boy's company, but no more. Who was he to begrudge a man's death, after all? The Mozart theme rose androsein his head like a fine trickle of water in the bright steam-heated air, but his whistle cracked, only air came from between his pursed lips, as in his ear he followed the complication of sound and rhythm. He congratulated himself on owning the New York edition of James as he packed its faded rose and gold volumes evenly into the bottom shelf of one of the bookcases. His mother had given it to him on his fortieth birthday. She had always given the most beautiful, sensitive presents in the world. That was an art, if you like. To make a study of those you love so delicately that you anticipate their desires before they are themselves aware of them. He had dedicated his book on James to his mother because it was in the truest sense her book – somehow, without her gift, he thought he would never have written those pages, have come to love so passionately the high, pure perverse *noblesse* of Milly Theale, the inflamed voyeurism that inundated *The Sacred Fount*. He had been passionately happy in the writing – passionately! He had found himself singing over and over fragments of an old hymn –

> *Amazing grace – how sweet the sound*
> *To save a wretch like me.*
> *I once was lost, but now am found –*
> *Was blind, but now I see.*

He knew no better words to explain the passion of creation. It was like divine grace – whatever your virtues you could never be worthy of the joy of it. Each time it flowed was as miraculous as if it had never been before, would never be again ... His face drew together and twitched sideways in the tic. He straightened from his work and looked up into the blinding sun.

*He who has eaten ambition*
*Accepted it into his person*
*Cannot un-eat or reject it ...*

There was an intent clumsiness about Kevin's words that
expressed what had run as an undercurrent to his thinking. The proof of it all was the completeness of the dark
when the light of his creativeness had been withdrawn –
as if God had turned his head, and the light fell else-
where ... as if a shadow had crossed the sun, and the sun
remained dim.

He stood up, the back of his legs stiff from squatting, to
light a cigarette. He looked at his mother's ormolu clock,
now standing on Kevin Boyle's mantel where the coloured postcard of van Gogh's young man in a straw hat had
once stood. He remembered somebody saying once that
where you found that picture you would find a homosexual, and he could see why that remark had been made
– there was a kind of glow of narcissism on the sensitive
face – but it certainly bore no reference to Kevin Boyle.
He had had the kind of deep self-love that one might
mistake for the prelude to – the other, but on the whole –
no, it was not so. In spite of the overprotestations of
potency. In spite of the role of professional erotic so
ardently played. Sometimes he thought that perhaps
Kevin Boyle was as pure as himself, though it was hardly
probable that this could be. He thought that Kevin must
have been pure and timid like some wild animal, making
the camouflage of ordinariness, but underneath it
primitive, and frightened, and wild ...

His mind finally took in what the face of the clock was
saying to him, and with a muttered, 'God!' he went to
the bathroom to wash the dust from his hands before

going to class. He had fifteen minutes to spare, but he wanted to think over his lecture quietly for a space before plunging out to it. He sat down in the wing chair and riffled through the pile of folded papers that lay on the table beside it, held together by a rubber band. His reader had marked them and he should have looked them over. He skipped past the B's and C's, paused at an A-minus. He pulled it out of the pack, glanced at it. It was a paper on Hawthorne. It said very little that had not already been said better, but this seemed to be the aim of education as it was practised on the eastern seaboard – and on the western and in the Dust Bowl, for all he knew – to enable the mediocre mind to paraphrase the wise and pseudo-wise. Well, this was no time for bitterness, when he was about to have to go look into their shining young faces ... Damn it, he was in a good humour this morning! That he had moved – it seemed to prove that he was still capable of action, of decision ... that he might become able to move again.

A knock sounded at his door. 'Come in!' he called cheerfully.

The door, made of panes of frosted glass, opened, revealing Leonard Marks' putty face. 'May I come in?' he asked hesitantly.

'Yes, come in, come in!' welcomed Hungerford. 'I won't apologize for the mess. I didn't even try to begin putting things away yesterday.'

'Of course,' said Leonard nervously. 'Naturally. I stopped by to see if I could lend a hand.'

'That's awfully good of you, but I'm just about to leave for class,' said Hungerford. 'Are you going toward the campus soon?'

'Yes,' said Marks. 'I have an eleven o'clock too. But

your clock is fast, I think. We have quite a little time. The College Hall clock just struck ten-thirty.'

'In that case sit down,' said Hungerford. 'Have a cigarette.'

Marks cleared himself a space on the book-crowded sofa and twitched a cigarette out of the pack Hungerford extended to him. His nervousness began to make Hungerford nervous. 'Moving is hell,' he said, trying to make some sort of start to set the younger man at his ease. 'I'm taking it very slowly, like a convalescent. Yesterday, the actual removal of my belongings occurred. I saw them well strewn over the living-room floor, paid the movers, and promptly went to sleep.'

'You must have been pretty irritated by your caller,' said Marks, smiling a little for the first time.

'Did you knock?' said Hungerford. 'I'm terribly sorry, I didn't hear you. I sleep so foully at night that I always take a sedative in order to get a before-dinner nap. That seems to be my best sleeping time.'

'Oh no,' said Marks. 'I didn't knock. I thought you were probably fed up by then – I was going to, but then I heard your voices and went away.'

'As a matter of fact, I was completely done in,' said Hungerford, his mind wandering to the pile of papers. Oh well, they were marked – he would hand them back without reading them. He would like to be kind to this Marks, for some reason. He always made one think of the white rabbit in *Alice* – a furtive look of guilt behind his spectacles proclaimed his awareness that somewhere, always, some ever-avenging duchess was furious. 'Yesterday I felt depressed as a boulder – fatigue, I guess. To-day I am full of hope for the world – I go around congratulating myself on my courageous remove from one house to another over a prodigious space of four blocks.'

'It's too bad you had to be bothered yesterday,' said Marks shyly.

'If it were done when 'tis done, then 'twere well it were done quickly,' said Hungerford banally. Suddenly a sense of confusion entered his mind. He wondered if he had quite understood what Marks had said. 'I mean, you were talking about my moving, weren't you?'

'Why, no,' said Marks, with an embarrassed laugh. 'I meant your caller. You must have been ready to kill her.'

'But I had no caller,' said Hungerford, his face suddenly drained of expression.

Marks blushed very red, his eyes watered, and he rose. 'I'm sorry,' he mumbled. 'I didn't mean –' he made for the door.

'No! Don't go!' cried Hungerford sharply. 'I had no caller. What made you think I did?'

'Oh please!' said Marks. 'I didn't mean to be inquisitive.'

Hungerford rose too, and went toward him. 'Don't be a fool, man,' he said sharply.'Will you please sit down and tell me what gave you the impression that I had a caller?'

'Why, Mr Hungerford,' said Marks, clasping his hands nervously, 'I heard her voice.'

Suddenly his knees buckled, his face twitched violently, and Hungerford sat down again in the wing chair, his hands dangling between his knees.

'Oh, Mr Hungerford!' cried Leonard Marks contritely. 'It was probably just Miss Stone! What's the matter?'

'Sit down, Marks,' said Hungerford dully. 'Sit down, sit down! Listen, this is very important. Miss Stone was not here yesterday. This morning she came and apologized profusely for her negligence. It seems she had to go to a church meeting and couldn't oversee my moving, for which I was profoundly grateful. What makes you think this was a woman's voice you heard, and what time did you hear it?'

Leonard paused a moment, seeming to put his thoughts carefully in order so as to answer the questions exactly. 'I came back from my last class,' he said, 'it's a five o'clock class. That means it was over at ten to six, and it takes me just about ten minutes to walk here from Raleigh. I didn't speak to anyone on the way, so it must have been just about six when I got home. I came in the front door, and I thought I would look in on you and see if I could do anything for you. I – I thought' – he fumbled – 'you might be willing to have supper with me. But I heard a woman talking inside, so I went to my rooms instead, thinking you'd have enough confusion with your moving, without two callers.'

'Six,' said Hungerford dully. 'Six. Ordinarily I take my nap at six. Yesterday I was done in and lay down as soon as the movers had gone – at twenty minutes to, or so. I must have been completely out by six o'clock. It's a pretty heavy dose of sedative I take.'

'You mean,' gasped Leonard, fumbling his way back to the couch at last, 'that somebody was in your apartment while you were asleep? Oh, Mr Hungerford! Hadn't you – I mean, suppose – oughtn't you to tell the police?'

Hungerford did not answer, hearing only the meaningless outline of the words. He rubbed his hand across and across his forehead. At last he rose, warily, and went to a carton that stood in a corner beside the books. The string which had tied it hung loose about it. 'I left it tied,' Hungerford muttered. 'I know I left it tied. And who

would have known which —' But just as he had expected, the papers that filled it were disordered, as if
someone had gone through them looking for something,
and on top of them lay what he had carefully packed at
the bottom, the limp, brown, cardboard notebook. He
did not open it, but held it in his hand. Then he closed
his eyes and began to shudder violently. He held the
notebook at arm's length. 'Look in it!' he ordered
Leonard. 'Look at it and see if there's an entry dated
with yesterday's date!' He felt the notebook removed
from his fingers, and buried his face in his hands.

'Mr Hungerford,' came Marks' questioning voice, 'it's
a journal – do you want me to –'

'Yes, yes,' he said impatiently, 'do as I say!'

'Yes, sir,' Leonard's answer came to his ears, 'there is.'

'Oh, God!' said Hungerford.

'Oh, Mr Hungerford, sir,' Leonard Marks' pleading
voice came to him in the darkness. 'Please, sir, let me do
anything I can! I'd do anything for you, anything – I
can't tell you how much I've always admired you and
your work! If there's *anything* –'

Yes, thought Hungerford, still standing among the
towers of books with his hands over his eyes, there is
something. You can listen. I have to tell someone. I can't
go on alone with it – not if it's to follow me ... 'Listen,'
he said, 'ever since the school year began, that journal
has been turning up in my rooms. It's a form of persecution – read it if you like. It's horrible – maybe it
won't seem as horrible to you as to me, but somehow it
has grown into such a nightmare in my life – I don't
know how to describe it. It disgusts me utterly. At first I
thought it must be some student who held a grudge
against me – though I couldn't think who or why. Then –

then – I didn't know. I don't know. It seems to be some-one who hates me so utterly as to be indecent. A person who knows my most secret weaknesses. Each time I find it open again I wonder if she will not have discovered the most secret crime in my heart – the crime which would still be secret to me. It's a woman. She calls herself Eloise. She's insane. That's all I know.' He took his hands down from his eyes, and leaning heavily on the corner of the table, on the back of a chair, he made his way back to his seat.

'But Mr Hungerford!' cried Leonard Marks, the note-book clutched between his palms, his voice thrilling with horror, 'why don't you show it to the police?'

'Look at it,' said Hungerford wearily. 'Glance through it. You'll see why I might not care to.'

Hesitantly Leonard let the notebook fall open, and began to read. His face blanched and his lips parted. 'Oh,' he said. 'Oh.' Then he slapped the book shut and rose from the sofa, came and leaned urgently over Hungerford's chair. 'Look, sir. This can't go on. But now there'll be two of us to catch her. You must tell me every-thing – when she comes, how you think she breaks in, everything! Then we can set watches, the two of us, and catch her at it!'

Hungerford's muscles relaxed and he felt a sense of gratitude. even affection for the unattractive young man. 'What can we do when we've caught her?' he asked.

'We can have the police on her for housebreaking. We – oh, we wouldn't have to show the notebook, sir! You could have me for a witness that it had existed, and just burn it!'

Hungerford lay back in the chair, exhausted, and looked up into Marks' eager face. He smiled faintly at the younger man's excitement.

'Oh, Mr Hungerford,' said Leonard, leaning down close to Hungerford, 'I would do anything for you!'

## Chapter 24

SINCE the reading, he did not know how he had lived with himself. It was not the things that he thought, somehow, but the things that he did not think, the things which lurked on the periphery of his consciousness, half exposing themselves to his awareness, then fleeing back to the shadows of the unknown. And a good thing. For if they had come whole into the light, he would not have been able to bear them – this much he knew. They would have led him to such wholesale self-condemnation as no man can stand. He grouped them under the mass heading of having behaved like a fool, and strove to forget.

He could not forget. It was not how he had behaved. He had not behaved so very badly. Not so badly as many men behaved without harming themselves in the least. It was what he had *thought*. It was what he had dared – albeit tacitly – to *demand*. And she had known. She had looked right through his skull into his brain – he had no illusions about that. She had looked into his most secret hopes and ambitions, his most indecent considerations, with her wicked, X-ray eyes, and had allowed him to go on in his idiocy until she had no more use for him. Then, in a grand gesture of contempt, she had let him know what she had observed, stripped him bare, revealed his silliest delusions of grandeur, and left him derelict on the shore of his own self-knowledge. Pipsqueak! she had cried.

And why? For what reason? For if he had behaved like

a fool, her own behaviour was open to some question She led him on. There was no reasonable, rational doubt but that at the first, at least, whatever it was that now shamed him so – his hopes of elevation, his dreams of affection – she had approved and fostered. Had she not asked him to read Kevin Boyle's poems? There were at least five other men in the department who could have read them as well as he. Had she not encouraged him to stay alone with her in her house when the others had left? What meaning had he been expected to read from that, but the obvious one, which she had subsequently so brutally denied? And when had it all changed – how had she become so different?

*Are you lying?* she had rapped out, rising on her elbows. ... Lying about what? About whether Kevin Boyle had spoken of her. Oh, was it not all becoming plainer and plainer? And now this latest. This horrible persecution of George Hungerford.

Leonard Marks' office was in the round tower of one of the older campus buildings: high, hideous, and pseudo-Gothic, it stood at the intersection of one of the campus drives with the little street of shops that ran downhill toward Miss Stone's. From his office window, Leonard could almost see his own roof, could watch the passers-by on the sidewalk of Witherspoon Street – girls jostling and pushing each other at the between-class interval, piling their bicycles like a heap of scrap metal in front of The Coffee Shoppe, or, during class hours, idling past the shop windows where feminine frivolities were displayed. It was four o'clock in the afternoon; dimly, at the edges of the day, twilight was creeping up the sky. Leonard was not sitting at his desk, but was pulling his straight chair to the window, where he sat surveying Witherspoon Street with a vigilant eye. Parked half-way down the narrow way was Freda Cramm's elaborate automobile. Freda herself he had seen disappear into The Coffee Shoppe a half-hour ago. He was waiting for her to come out, although he was not sure what he would then do.

No doubt existed in his mind as to whose voice he had heard last night as he stood hesitantly outside Hungerford's door. It had come from far back in the room, so that the words it spoke were indistinguishable. But the tones could have belonged to no one he had ever known but Freda Cramm – low-pitched, harsh, almost like a man's for deepness and decisiveness, yet poisonously feminine in their purring persuasion. Oh – the violence of his feeling made him rise from his chair – she was a bad woman! Yet he meant to be calculating and cool, not carried away by emotion. He sat down again.

Coolly and calculatingly he had considered it: it seemed to him ultimately probable that Freda Cramm had murdered Kevin Boyle. She had, he thought, been carrying on illicit relations with the young man. She had been afraid of indiscretions on his part, and had murdered him to shut his mouth.

Here a snag arose in the flow of his reasoning. Why should she fear indiscretion, loud-mouthed advocate of liberty and modernity that she was? Would one not have expected her to override, even to flaunt that sort of revelation? Leonard frowned, his eyes fixed unseeingly on the shining black car. He thought he had the answer. He thought he had hold of the explanation which, if one accepted it, made the premise of Freda as murderess quite tenable. This was that he had not been wrong in his drunken assumption on the night of the reading that under her free talk Freda was a puritanical woman. He thought he could offer some evidence on behalf of this hypothesis. Otherwise, why had she repelled his own advances? Leonard straightened his glasses and smoothed his moustache to one side and the other. 'I am quite,' he said to the empty room in a tight voice,' 'an unrepulsive young man.'

At the moment, in the street below the door of The Coffee Shoppe opened and a large flame-headed figure in a russet coat came out. Leonard started and rose, for it was Freda. He did not know what to do – had not made up his mind. If she got in her car, there was no use following her. Impossible. Well, if she got in her car, he would go straight back to his own apartment and keep watch on Hungerford's door. But she was not crossing the street. She was walking straight down Witherspoon Street, lingering at shop windows. In a frenzy of decision, Leonard snatched up his hat and coat and sped down the stairs. There were three long flights; when he reached the street corner, the figure of Freda Cramm was out of sight. He stood panting at the corner, wondering which way to turn. Here Witherspoon Street formed one of the branches of a Y, with Main Street the base and Jeffery Street the other arm. If she had turned down the hill to Main Street, she was simply walking down-town – there was no use following. However, if she had turned up Jeffery, there was a lane she could take, leading straight through the backyards to Miss Stone's. At once he paced determinedly down Jeffery. If he could not see her, he could take the lane himself, give up the chase, and simply get washed for dinner. He would have covered all the possibilities of her reaching Hungerford's apartment unseen. It was, Hungerford had warned him, unlikely that another entry would appear in the journal for weeks. But

Leonard did not mean to count on that. He meant to watch her every moment, to prevent its ever happening again, and somehow to expose the whole of her criminality by means of that vicious little manuscript. And he, wished he had not said what he did about burning the journal. He thought that it should be preserved as evidence. He thought a handwriting analyst could undoubtedly prove the script to be Freda's, and that then it could be shown to have some bearing on Boyle's murder. He had not read more than the last passage in it, but Hungerford had told him that there was mention of Kevin Boyle earlier – incriminating mention. In any case, he could not entirely understand Hungerford's sensitivity about its being seen. It was vulgar, crass, even obscene, but the references to Hungerford did not appear so serious or shameful to Leonard as they seemed to have struck their subject. They reflected on the writer, after all, not on her innocent prey.

Jeffery Street curved down a hill. To the right was a row of dingy frame houses built at the turn of the century, styleless, graceless. To the left the hillside flowed away to the river bottoms, which were swampy and rush-grown, now brightly sanguine with reflection of the evening sun. The sky was pink in the east, flamingo in the west, and overhead, a pale dusty blue. The day's wind had died, but chill was rising in the air. The sidewalk Leonard hurried down was empty except for himself, clear to the curve of the road. He came to the lane to Miss Stone's, where the houses began to be set far apart. Here for the first time he could see round the bend. At quite a distance he made out Freda Cramm, striding easily up the rise that came at the margin of the open farmland around the town. Leonard caught his breath and walked faster.

The houses were all left behind now; he followed the macadam road into the open country. The fields full of out-croppings of rock, the distant mountains, the occasional low-lying farms were all bathed in red evening light. It was a cold redness, cold and bleak, promising snow, although the sky was clear. It was an ominous, unfriendly sort of light, not like the mid-western sunsets Leonard could recollect. Near his home the farm land had been rolling and rich; here it was rocky and poor, stretching miserably to the foot of the Berkshires. The road wound away from the town, out over the flat fields; the macadam ended; a dirt surface began. The river disappeared in a thicket of willows off to the left. The road ran along flat and then began to climb. Far along it, growing dimmer as the evening deepened, Leonard made out Freda, still stroking along with a hiker's stride. He was a little winded himself, but followed bravely.

The woods, which had resembled sparse stiff hair on a recumbent animal's side while the hills were in the distance, now appeared as a heavy copse of saplings and second growth. The road curved around the foot of the mountain, and Freda disappeared from Leonard's sight. He paused and panted. He had lost sight of his objective – not only Freda, but why he was following her. Now he was only consumed by a strange sense of urgency that seemed to press on him from all sources, from the bloody sunset, from the darkening woods on the mountain slope, from the strange luminescence of the pebbly road as it caught the slanting light. He began to walk faster and faster until he almost ran around the bend at the foot of the mountain, but still Freda was nowhere to be seen. He felt a sort of panic. How could he have lost her? Where had she gone? He could imagine that he would run on and on in this foolish way, pursuing nothing, but obsessed with the notion of his pursuit. Then suddenly there appeared a break in the woods, and a branch of the road ran up the mountainside. Gasping with relief, he turned up it and began to climb.

In the woods darkness had already begun. Darkness collected like a mist around the boles of the trees, rose in a vapour from the dead leaves that carpeted the forest floor. Suddenly there was a rustling, a small dark shape ran across the road. Leonard started, and stood frozen for a moment before he could reassure himself that it had only been a chipmunk, disturbed by his passing. As he paused he listened for footsteps, wondering if he were within earshot of Freda. But he heard nothing – nothing but a vast resounding silence, punctuated by the small mysterious cracklings of the woods and their secret life. He pushed on, less and less knowing why.

Then suddenly, the air was lighter, the trees thinned, and Leonard paused, for he could see that ahead of him the road stopped at the edge of a clearing. Now that the woods had come to an end, he felt disinclined to leave their protection; prodded by he knew not what impulse, he struck away from the road and through the trees, across the floor of leaves to the edge of the clearing. There, standing a little behind one of the few old trees in the wood, he looked out at the open field, at the house that stood there, and at Freda Cramm, suddenly close enough so that he could make out her features, sitting on its doorstep.

The house was an ancient saltbox with a fanlight and the date 1700 carved over its door. Half of the panes of the windows were gone; the rest, facing blindly westward, blazed crimson into the sunset. Clapboards were warping away, paint lay only in leprous patches over the walls, and a great black wound gaped in the shingles of the roof. Freda sat on the only remaining step of what had once been a flight of three leading to the front door. She seemed to be staring out at the panorama of river and valley that lay below her. As she watched a shape detached itself from the woods at the other side of the field, came streaking across the grass and leaped into Freda's lap – an enormous tortoiseshell cat, whose head she touched absently, and murmured.

It seemed to Leonard he had stood for years watching her stroke the head of the cat and wondering what he was to do – it seemed a mystery to him that night had not fallen in the long, long moment of his watching. The strangeness was too much for him; he could not bear it; he found himself shaking and clutching the trunk of the tree. Then, without his intention, the words formed themselves in his mind: I must get away from here. He saw a star, shining tentatively in the twilight. The sun was fading from the chequered glass panes of the windows of the house. He took a step backward and trod on a dry stick. Suddenly Freda Cramm rose, dropping the big cat unceremoniously from her lap.

'I hear you!' she cawed out, standing like some big, broody bird in the midst of that lonely place. 'Come out of the woods there! I hear you!'

He could turn, he could flee, but behind him the woods were dark and darker. Stumbling, he came out of the trees and stood at the edge of the clearing, a distance from her.

'Come over here!' she commanded. 'Come where I can see you!'

Like a hypnotized animal, he crossed the desolate yard, picking his way among the rusted tin cans, and stood before her. She glared at him as he approached with eyes which seemed to him as bright as hawk's or owl's. The cat wound itself purring in and out around her ankles. 'Well,' she sneered, in her deep harsh voice, 'it's little Mr Marks – our Leonard!'

He was unable to speak, but only stared at her dazed, like a schoolboy caught in a misdemeanour. She set her fists on her hips and looked at him, tilting her head so that she seemed to look down at him, although actually they were of a height.

'Well,' she said finally, 'what are you doing here?'

He caught his breath. 'What are you?' he piped.

She looked at him and cocked her head to one side. 'I can't see how that concerns you.'

The darkness was deepening. Freda's hair shone brazen, catching what little light was left. A chill came over Leonard – he felt himself facing a bare reality – he felt it was now or never; he must speak. 'I followed you,' he said, his throat dry. 'I came after you. I don't know what you're up to, but I won't let you do it. You've done enough. You're a bad woman.' His breath was coming fast.

'So?' she said expressionlessly. 'How so?'

'Boyle,' he said, scarcely able to speak. 'Kevin Boyle. And now Hungerford. You leave Hungerford alone or you'll be sorry – I'll make you sorry!'

He thought he saw the shadow of a malicious smile hover on her face. 'So you think it was Boyle and then Hungerford,' she said. 'Oh, my little Leonard Marks!' She seemed to swell and tower over him in the darkness. 'Do you know what happens to little peeping-Toms like you? Do you know what happens to bad little boys?' she put her face close to his, her lips drawn back from her teeth. He could distinguish each golden blot in the saddle

174

of pale freckles across her nose. The gentle prettiness of her small features was horrifying to him in combination with the malevolence of her expression. She leaned over him as if she had grown taller as she stood there; it seemed to him her hands were moving upward, gauging the roundness of his throat. His knees began to tremble – he imagined her brandishing the poker, striking upward to the base of Kevin's skull. All at once something pressed against his leg, as if hands were reaching up from the ground to pinion him, hold him fast. He gave a wild, shameless yell, spun around and ran, kicking the cat in this flight. After him rang the shrill laughter of Freda Cramm, pursuing him through the trees, resounding in the darkness as if to warn him of the hopelessness of escape.

He ran and ran, blindly stumbling in the ruts of the uneven road. He could see nothing, he only trusted the feel of the ground under him. The road through the wood stretched endlessly – it seemed the trees would never end. Just as he thought he must fall down for want of breath, his hip struck something with a metallic sound, he doubled over with pain, and a hand took his elbow. 'Here, here,' a voice said softly. 'What goes on?' It was Donelly, the reporter, beside his car. In a frenzy of relief, Leonard threw his arms about him, like a French diplomat honouring a hero.

## Chapter 25

DR. Forstmann had made arrangements to have one of the doctor's offices in the Infirmary in which he could see Molly Morrison. The nurse had gone for her. He sat looking over her charts. Her temperature had been normal for two days; nausea had ceased; crying fits during the day had given way to lethargic depression. Sedative still administered at night. He wondered what was to be done with the girl. It seemed unlikely she could continue her college work. He doubted that the family could pay for a sanatorium, and sending her home appeared to him the least advisable course of all. It seemed very strange that the mother had not answered Miss Sanders' letter with some show of concern, but there had been no word from her. He heard footsteps in the corridor and rose. Molly knocked and came in. Her hair hung lankily in oily strands. Her face was white, her lips pale. There was a stain on her sweater, as if she had spilled food. 'Hello, Molly,' he said, and smiled.

'Hello,' she answered dully, her face unmoving. She went to the couch and lay down, like an animal moving mechanically to its stall. Then she pulled something out of the pocket of her skirt, raised herself on one elbow and held it out to him. It was a letter. 'Here,' she said. 'I got this this morning. Read it.'

He took the letter and she sank down on the couch.

Dear Molly (he read): A week or so ago I had a communication from your housemother from which I made out that you were down with something which she vaguely describes as 'mental disturbance.' I trust you will have become undisturbed again by the time this letter reaches you. It seems to me that you are hardly in a position to allow yourself the luxury of a nervous breakdown, if that is what you have in mind, since your staying in college depends on your scholarship, and the continuation of your scholarship depends on your academic standing.

He stopped reading for a moment and glanced at Molly. She was twisting her hands together, her eyes were closed. He glanced at the envelope, at the postmark, almost to reassure himself that she had not written the letter herself – it fitted almost too perfectly with her expectations of persecution. He had to remind himself that this was the mould in which those expectations had been cast.

... As you are aware, after twenty years of marriage to your father, I am not so inclined to be sympathetic with this sort of 'disturbance' as I might once have been. There are always people in the world who can make their moods the excuse for failure and irresponsibility. There are others who are unable – or unwilling – to indulge quite the same moods, because they refuse to make themselves a burden to those around them. You are no longer a child who can lie on the floor and have temper tantrums. If you try to do so, you will find yourself in the embarrassing position of simply being allowed to kick and scream and make as much of a fool of yourself as you like.

I have kept your housemother's letter from your father. I do not wish to trouble him with it, as there seems to be some chance of his getting one of the post office murals after all, and I do not know what this kind of upset might provoke him to do.

As I reread this letter, I am aware that you may find it cold and harsh. I must confess frankly that I feel no sympathy for you, only deep irritation. I have lived in poverty and sordidness because of your father's highfalutin notions of his art, being the one who scraped and met the creditors while he indulged his soul. I would feel that I had failed in my duty as a mother if I encouraged you in a path which, for the twenty years I have watched your father follow it, has brought nothing but misery to both of us. The scholarship at Hollymount is your chance for some better kind of life than your parents have known. I will not have you pass over an opportunity of that life.

I am concerned for your welfare only, Molly.

Mother.

He folded the letter and returned it to its envelope. 'Well?' he said.

'Well,' she repeated dully.

'Tell me how the letter made you feel,' he said.

'How would it have made you feel?'

'Why,' he considered, 'if I were you, it might have made me feel in one of a number of ways. I might have been very angry at it. I might have been hurt. I might have thought she was right.'

'Oh,' she said desolately. 'You think she's right!'

'No,' he said immediately, 'I think she's wrong. Because I don't accept the premises and standards from which she argues. But try to tell me how you felt about it, Molly. Tell me how it was when you got the letter – how you felt when you opened it – from the beginning.'

'From the beginning?' she said. 'Oh ... well. Miss Justin said I could get up this morning. She said did I want my breakfast in bed. I said I'd get up and dress first. So I did. Then she brought my breakfast on a tray. I was sitting on the chair with the tray on my lap when she brought the letter. She said, You have a letter from your mother. Then I spilled the egg on my sweater.' She put her hands over her eyes and began to cry, sobbing without sound, but violently, so that the convulsions shook her body.

'Why does that make you cry?' he asked softly.

'She hates me!' she cried, her voice suddenly loud. 'She always hated me! She never would admit it – she was always saying how she loved me! But nothing I ever did ever pleased her – ever! I used to pretend I'd been invited to somebody's house for meals and then go without because she nagged me so. She always said I was sloppy, and I knew she would be watching me to see me spill something, and then I would. I know you think that's silly, I know it's silly, but I can't help it, I can't help it!' She was gagging and gasping hysterically. He said nothing; at last her sobbing subsided. 'Once she found my diaries,' she said finally. 'That was the worst, I think. I always wrote in them when I was angry with her. I tried to say all the things she would hate most. I tried to describe her the way she was – so cold and accusing and inhuman. I tried to write her so that she would be ashamed to read it if ever she did. She did, all right. But she wasn't ashamed. She just got that terrible cold look on her face. She held the book out to me, and she said, Is this yours? as if it were some stranger's hat she'd picked up in the street. But she wouldn't give it to me. She showed it to my father. She never said anything about it. She never said a word. She just looked at me – just looked at me – as if I were beneath contempt.' She had begun to cry again. 'And then she took it out on him. She knew that would hurt me most. I heard them in the night. Oh, I hate her so!' She was caught in another convulsion of weeping and could not speak. When she was quieter, she said tensely: 'She'd kill me if she dared. Do you know that? I've seen her looking at me as if she were – were taking the measure of my throat – to choke me!'

'Do you really think that's true, Molly?' he said quietly.

'Oh,' she cried, 'you don't believe me, I knew you wouldn't, but it's true all the same! She wished I'd never been born, and then she could have left my father and married someone who would have made lots of money! But she couldn't bring herself to leave me, too – she couldn't forget her Presbyterian upbringing to that extent! She couldn't leave me, so she stayed and tortured me the rest of her life! I tell you, she would have liked to kill me!' She paused, drew a grubby handkerchief from her pocket, blew her nose and wiped her eyes. 'She was always saying my father was a failure. She never could see he was a great painter – a really great painter! He is! She was always talking about how we lived, how it was so sordid, how he didn't care enough about his family to support us – I don't care! I don't care! He's a great man. It didn't matter if we did live sordidly if he could paint! I'm not ashamed!'

He looked at his watch. 'Your way of life may have seemed sordid to your mother because the kind of rewards it offered weren't within her understanding. I imagine from what you say that she doesn't care a great deal about painting.'

'Oh, she doesn't, she doesn't!' cried Molly eagerly. 'She pretends she does! She used to teach art appreciation in high school before she met my father. Art appreciation! *How* she can talk about brushwork and impasto and chiaroscuro! But just ask her what a painter is saying or what his work means! Just ask her! She looks as if you'd asked some question that was between obscenity and stupidity ... '

'Molly,' he said, 'I want to talk to you a little about plans. Have you thought at all about what might be best to do?'

'Best to do?' she said in a frightened voice. 'What do I have to do? Will I have to leave? Do I have to go back to Birnham? Do I have to go home?'

'You don't want to do either of those things, do you?'

'No, no, I don't, I don't!'

'Your mother's right about one thing, Molly,' he said. 'It would be a shame to lose your scholarship. I thought of this. I think that in a while you may feel ready to go back to Birnham — but I don't want you to go back before you do feel absolutely ready. I shouldn't like to think of you staying at the Infirmary and doing nothing at all, seeing no one. Dr Abby tells me that there's a clerical job open that you could do for an hour or two a day if you liked. The rest of the time you could try to get caught up in your school work a bit, and maybe do some painting. And I want you to get out and take a walk once in a while. Talk a little to the other girls in the Infirmary I won't put you in a ward, but wander around and chat, if you can.'

'They don't want to talk to me,' she said sullenly.

He leaned forward in his chair. 'They have nothing either for or against talking to you,' he said. 'They will like to chat with you as much as with any other chance acquaintance they make, because they happened to have caught flu at the same time. You have a great deal to offer, Molly — an unusual background and an unusual knowledge.'

'Very unusual,' she said bitterly.

He ignored her. 'And get some air. Would you like to do some outdoor sketching?'

'No,' she said. 'I don't want to go out. I don't want to walk.'

'Why not?'

This time there was no sobbing, but the tears began to leak slowly from her eyes. 'I want to be very still. I don't want to move myself. When I move, it's like dragging a great stone. I don't want to look at a lot of things. I don't want to look down streets. I want to look at small areas, like my hands, or a page of paper. You know where I like it best? I like it in corridors, when there's nobody there. A corridor is nowhere. It's just a between place. Nothing can happen to you there.'

'What are you afraid of having happen to you, Molly?' he asked.

'I don't know,' she said. 'I don't know.'

## Chapter 26

SHE had made the decision. She had been very brave. She had been brave almost beyond her own power. She had taken her coat and scarf and put them on. She had walked to the front door. She had opened it. 'Where are you going, Molly?' Miss Justin had cried from the desk, with hygienic cheer. 'For a walk,' she had answered. For a walk. She had stepped out on the stoop. She did not look down the street, she only looked down at her brown moccasins, he tan socks, her cold bare legs. She watched her own feet walking down the brick walk. She was very tired. She walked slowly and dragged her feet. She was cold too. Her teeth chattered and her muscles contracted against the wind. She heard a group of girls pass on the other side of the street. She did not look up from her feet. She heard them begin to laugh. They were laughing at her, at what a fool she was, walking there all hunched over with cold, looking at her feet. A lunatic. In the Infirmary because she was crazy. But she wasn't really. If she had been really crazy there would have been some excuse. She was just indulging herself saying: I can't stand it, when what was really true was that she wouldn't try hard enough. But something had to be worth trying for. You couldn't try in a vacuum, try for nothing. Now she had something to try for – something to take a walk for. She knew where she was going. It took a great deal of courage, but courage was what she must force herself to have. Oh, how she despised the coward that she was!

It was getting to be evening. The winter sun was nearing the horizon, salmon-coloured among violet clouds, promising snow. For a moment Molly looked up from the ground; it seemed to her the world was turned to a vast, ominous, but beautiful dream landscape. The white frame houses took on a luminousness in the evening light, standing in their drab dead lawns among the skeletons of trees. She had reached the corner and turned out of the side street. Now there were a few more passers-by, bundled against the cold, intent upon their secret errands. And she knew that, as in a dream, though their faces seemed strange to you, you knew that somehow they were your enemies; secretly they peeped at you from under their eyelids, from over their furs, and mentally noting your appearance, your patent guilt, they hurried on with news of your treason to the great mysterious one who held your fate in the hollow of a palm, who totted black marks against you, and would at last pounce, strike ... She walked faster, hearing footsteps behind. If she walked quickly, got to where she meant to go, warmed herself with a fire, perhaps, and talked – the kind of talk she longed for so, then everything would not seem so threatening and evil.

She recognized the house, set back on its lawns with a dark antique elegance. For a moment when she first saw the iron Saint Bernard, she was stricken with a new fear, thinking that it was real, and she would have to pass it. But as it continued to stand so still, with one paw raised, she saw it was only a statue, and let her breath puff out, milky on the cold air. Now she was close enough to see the lamp gleaming amethyst and ruby through the coloured glass panes of the front door. The house towered above her, high and stern, with its flat roof, its beetling eaves, its cupola. It seemed to hold her at a distance, to ask her business. Her heart pounded, she could not catch her breath. 'Courage!' she whispered to herself, and turned up the walk. The bell at the high double door was the sort you have to pull. At last she found the trick of it, and heard it pealing, far back in the hollow reaches of the house. Oh please ... she prayed. She waited a long, long time before footsteps sounded within, far away and slow, then closer and shuffling. Finally the door opened and an old, old woman peered out. She said nothing, but stared at Molly, as if she too were participating in the dream.

'Please,' said Molly faintly, after a long silence, 'is Mr Hungerford ... ?'

Still the old woman did not answer, but stood there staring at her in the twilight. At last it seemed true – this was a nightmare, the horror was about to come. Then the old woman spoke. 'Well, miss, speak up!' she said sharply.

Don't be a fool, said Molly to her pounding heart.

she's only deaf! 'Is Mr Hungerford in?' she said loudly.

'Doesn't live here any more,' said the old woman flatly, and began to close the door.

'Oh, please,' cried Molly, 'can you tell me where he lives?'

The old woman drew the door a little farther open again. 'He moved over to West Street,' she said grudgingly. 'He moved in where that young man lived who got murdered. I don't recollect the number.' And closed the door.

She had to stop and press her mittened hands against her breast, standing there on the high step, panting in the cold. He lived at Kevin Boyle's house … he had moved there. … It was beautiful – like a gift! Now she could go, could ring his bell, could go in the room where he had stood, had lain … lain dead. She ran down the steps lightly before her weariness caught up with her again. She crossed the street and took the short cut down the hill toward where she knew so well.

As she walked toward Kevin Boyle's house she had no choice but to think of the thing that had brought her out – out of her hole. It was a strange thing, something new, something she could not understand, something terrible, a new kind of death. In the last days she had forgotten Kevin Boyle.

She had forgotten the way he looked. Or how it felt to walk to The Coffee Shoppe with your heart exploding like electric shocks because you did not know if he would be there. Or how it was in class, watching him talk, seeing the way his hands moved. She could remember *that* it had been, but *how* it had been was gone.

The thing that had come over her had begun with grief, but it had been worse than grief, worse than any live pain. It had been like a stone on her heart, a negation of life, of love. She began to wish fiercely that she could feel grief as she had felt it in those first days after his death, but even the memory of the sharpness of it was gone from her. Grief had been a thing like love – clear, and with a certain purity. What had come over her was allied only to death. Depression, Dr Forstmann would say, who always had the word for everything. Almost she could hate him too, though he was her only friend. Sometimes she felt that if she had not talked to him she might have preserved the beauty of her grief and kept the life from running from it. Now she had two things to mourn – the death of Kevin Boyle and the death of her grief. And since the first was irreparable, it seemed the second was the harder to bear. She would not, *could* not bear it. So she had tried to think of what would be a restorative for her dead grief. She thought if she had a picture of him ... but she could not think where she would get one. Or a letter he had written – just some impersonal thing ... but that was just as hard. And then the perfect thing had come to her. A poem. Just a copy of one of his poems. And she knew where she could find that, too. Only – how many ages ago? – two weeks ago she had heard him tell, sitting in the booth at The Coffee Shoppe, Mr Hungerford was reading his book of poems, was kind enough to offer to submit it to his publisher. Mr Hungerford. He had a kind sad face. And a poem. A poem was like a painting. In it you said a thing so dear and tender and secret you could not venture it straight out in plain words ... If anything could revive her dead grief, it would be Kevin Boyle's poem. She had begun to long and long for it. Longing had made her brave. Longing had drawn her out ...

It seemed strange to her to see the college girls pushing their bicycles up the hill past her or walking in long, striding steps. A long time ago she had been one of them – in name at least – sharing their common routine, their meaningless activities. What meaning could they have? To go in a library, to look in a book, to write words on a paper ... Was that life? Was that any sort of preparation for life? Once in her father's studio there was a young man with a beard, one of the wild-talking ones who made her want to hide for not knowing what to say. 'What do *you* do for a livelihood?' he had asked, looking down his crooked nose patronizingly, stroking his too thin beard. 'I – I'm going to college in the fall,' she had stammered. Suddenly he began to pace round the studio as if he had gone mad. 'College!' he had cried. 'Education! All they care for is knowledge – all knowledge and no wisdom!' At that moment she had scorned him, had heard her mother's voice speaking in her own thoughts, saying. Why do artists think they have to behave like maniacs? Yet he had been right. That was all that was here. Knowledge, and no wisdom. Now that Kevin Boyle was dead ...

She was at the corner of West Street. There was a hedge full of red berries, running along by the walk. Then the house. What was she to say? Yet she must speak. She had come so far ... She would blind herself to everything ... She could scarcely gasp air into her lungs as she plunged round the corner, ran up the steps on to the porch. His name was still on the mail-box on the card tacked over the bell. She pushed it desperately, and closed her eyes. She heard the door open and looked quickly. There was Mr Hungerford, his thick grey hair rumpled, his tie loosened, his face haggard. 'Yes?' he said, in a strange, far-away voice. Now she was here. Now she must begin.

'Mr Hungerford?' she said. But of course she knew him. 'I'm Molly Morrison. I'm the girl who ... ' but she trailed off, not knowing how to say, I'm the girl whose name was in the paper; I'm the girl who confessed to murdering Kevin Boyle, only it wasn't true; I'm the girl ...

'Oh,' he said, 'yes, of course. Come right in.'

Now she knew it was a dream. This was the strangest thing of all. He acted as if he had been waiting for her, as if he had known she was coming. *Of course what?* she wanted to demand of him. But she followed him into the dim hall. This was not a nightmare part of a dream. This was a warm, good part. This was the way she would have wished to be welcomed to Kevin Boyle's rooms, as if she belonged there, as if it were natural that she should come.

French doors with glass panes opened off the hall. One of them stood ajar. Preceding her, Mr Hungerford stood in the entrance and said, 'Won't you come in?' She followed him. He turned to her. His face seemed very tired and very kind and very sad. 'Excuse the mess,' he said. 'I'm not properly moved in yet. I was just lying down for a moment.' He passed his hand across his eyes. 'Then you rang, and I was glad. I couldn't sleep. I can't seem to sleep here – not any more.'

She stood clutching her hands together in front of the dying fire. For the first time in days, feeling assailed her heart, as if a half-healed wound had broken, and warm beautiful blood were pouring out once more. She saw everything with terrible intensity, as if each object were surrounded by a ring of light. It was Kevin Boyle's room she was standing in – where he had stood; perhaps where he had died. And Mr Hungerford there, his face hanging in such weary and despairing folds ... How she knew that look! How she had lived with it! It was her father's look, standing at the easel, his brush dropped to the floor, staring out of the dirty panes of the slanting skylight ... 'Can't you work?' she asked softly.

'Oh,' said Mr Hungerford, a sudden little smile of surprise lighting one corner of his mouth, 'that. No. Not for years. My God, child, how did you know?'

She tossed her head in embarrassment. 'I just knew.'

'Here,' he said, 'take your coat off. Pull up to the fire. Get warm. Are you one of my students? To tell you the truth, I don't yet know one face from another.'

Then she grew cold again inside. No, it was not a dream. It was only a mistake. He thought she was one of his students. She must tell him at once, even if then he would not like her any more. Her face contracted with anxiety. 'No,' she said, 'I'm not one of your students. I'm – I mean – I –' and against all her most fervent intentions, she began to cry. She put her mittens up to cover her face.

'Oh, my goodness, child!' she heard his worried voice saying. 'Don't cry. Just tell me what it's all about. You're very welcome, you know. You don't have to be one of my students to call on me!' he gave a little laugh. 'I'm delighted to have a strange young woman in ... my ... ' His words trailed off strangely. She took her hands down from her tear-smeared face. He was looking off into space as if something were behind her shoulder, as if he were haunted. Again her heart grew hot with pity for him.

'Mr Hungerford,' she said reassuringly, sniffling at the remains of her tears. 'Is it embarrassing for you to have me here? I'll go away. I didn't know students weren't supposed –'

'My goodness, no!' he said, with heartiness to counter-act her sadness. 'Take your coat off like a good girl and tell me what it is you want. ' He put his hand to the knot of his tie and pulled it closer. 'Tell you what,' he pushed on, 'this is really against rules – to offer a student alcohol – but let's have a glass of sherry; by now we both need it.' He did not wait for her answer, but took a decanter from the top of a bookcase and filled two of the glasses that stood by it. She took off her coat and laid it on the couch, then sat down on a stool by the fire, pushing close to the warmth. She stared at the hearth. On these bricks Kevin Boyle had lain. His blood had flowed here. And the truth was ... the truth was she had forgotten him. Her heart had gone dead. In all the confusion, the drugs, the confession, the weepings to Dr Forstmann, she had lost the wood in the trees. Nothing was about her but the confusion of the trees of her thought – her mother, her father, the shame of living among the girls at Birnham, Miss Justin, Miss Sanders, the newspaper reporter, the policeman – she wanted to make a sweep of them! She wished she could take a wet cloth and wipe her mind clean as a blackboard. She wanted to go back – go back to the sense of her love. She had lost her love – first she had lost Kevin Boyle, and then her love for him. The second loss was more desolate than the first. The first was human and bearable, in a terrible way. The second she could not stand. She could not bring back Kevin Boyle, but she must bring back her love for him ... 'Here's your sherry,' said Mr Hungerford's voice.

She looked up at him, almost startled, and took the glass. 'Thank you,' she said.

He pulled forward the chair opposite her and sat down. 'Now,' he said, raising the glass in silent toast before sipping from it. She sipped too, staring at him. His face was so drawn, so weary. And there was a strange indecency about seeing him with his streaked grey hair, usually so smooth, disarranged. He moved his lips together in little mumbling motions, like an old man. 'What's your name?' he asked kindly. 'I'm afraid I didn't listen when you told me before.'

'Molly Morrison.'

He looked at her, waiting for her to go on, she knew, but she was unable ... 'What class are you – shall I call you Miss Morrison or Molly?'

'Oh, Molly, of course,' she said, her tongue suddenly loosened. How kind he was! He seemed – he seemed so much more human, more understanding – something ... 'I'm a Freshman, I was in – I was –' she wanted to say she had been in a class of Kevin Boyle's, but her voice faltered and broke.

'And you aren't in any of my classes, but you came to see me – is it a guessing game?' There was an edge of asperity in his voice at last. His patience was going to end in a moment. She gathered herself together frightenedly. She did not know what to say, though – how to begin. She couldn't just ask him baldly.

'I've been in the Infirmary,' she said abruptly. 'They seem to think – I've been acting – they think I'm rather unbalanced.' But she did not want to give him a false impression. 'I may be, you know,' she said earnestly.

Suddenly he laughed, startling her. For a moment she thought her heart had stopped at the thought that he was laughing at her. Then he looked at her very, very kindly. 'That makes a pair of us, Molly,' he said. 'We should be friends, alone together in this neurasthenic garden spot.'

She did not know what he meant, except that they had

something in common, and he looked so very kind, so very sad. 'I didn't mean to be,' she said, saying at last to him what she had wished to say to all of them. 'I wanted everything to go right when I came to Hollymount – I wanted to be different, to make people like me, not be shy. But then it wasn't, and I couldn't seem to make it change – they hated me, and laughed at me, and then when – when Mr Boyle died –' She had done it again. She had begun to cry. She put her face down in her hands and let the tears trickle through her fingers. She cried a moment in silence. Then suddenly she heard a glass crash on the bricks of the hearth, and looked up, all tear-stained as she was.

She had heard the girls talk about the way his face twitched sometimes – how he would have to stop dead in the middle of a lecture to wait for it to be over – but she had not known it was as bad as this. The whole side of his face was drawn together in the most grotesque way – it was so strange and horrifying it almost shocked you to laughter. She saw his hands were shaking, and the sherry glass lay in fragments on the hearth. She felt terribly terribly sorry – she almost had risen to touch him, to comfort him – when suddenly the dream was back. Inwardly she shook herself, she implored herself not to let it come again, but inexorably – as inexorably as if she were asleep – she felt its atmosphere closing in. The warmth of the fire, the warmth of the sherry, the warmth of Mr Hungerford's kindness – all evaporated until her very bones were shuddering with cold at the knowledge that she was alone in a threatening world, a room in which each object of furniture conspired against her. Outside unknown pursuers were closing in, wicked enemies were ambushed behind the berry-red hedge; and here inside, even Mr Hungerford, even with his kind sad face, his tragic tic, his trembling hands, his hopelessness ... She should never have come out. She should have stayed in the safe white room at the Infirmary, where she lay like a corpse, with Miss Justin and Dr Forstmann praying at her wake. She got to her feet nervously. 'I came,' she said, because she must get it out at once, 'because I heard him – I heard Mr Boyle say once you had some poems of his. I came to ask – I came –' She was shaking all over, uncontrollably.

On the other side of the fire, Mr Hungerford got to his feet. Was it true that he was shaking too, or did she only imagine it was so because she shook herself? In any case, his face had not relaxed from its contorting grip, it stared at her gargoyle-like. Impossible to separate true from false – was he glaring at her, or did her fear read anger into kindness? Then suddenly it seemed to her something strange had happened to him. The tic left his face, but left it different, slacker, in strange new lines. His posture changed; everything was different, because of what she imagined she saw. She thought, quite carefully, I am going mad. She thought she must pick up her coat and scarf and leave here before she lost her mind in front of Mr Hungerford – as if she had to get to the bathroom before throwing up. She knew it was madness now, because suddenly, instead of the sad worn intelligence so like her father's that had first clothed his face, she now saw on his features the fierce, peering cruelty of her mother – the slack jowls, the drawn brow ... She slung her coat over her shoulders, mumbling foolishly, keeping her eyes on him, trying not to let him notice. 'I'll just –' she said. 'I'd better go now, I don't – I'm not feeling very – you'll excuse ... '

It was useless. Whatever it was that had been holding her together snapped loudly, like a log on the fire and he – she – Mr Hungerford – her mother – who? – took a step forward, hands raised, the way she had always feared. 'Why,' said a strange voice, a voice she had never heard before, coming from she knew not where, 'you little – it was you –' She closed her eyes to shut herself in darkness. Hands were at her throat as she had always known they would be. Her own hands were wrestling at them – or was it her own hands at her throat? A finger-nail drew a thin line of pain over her wrist. Back and forth she was battered, like a boat in a storm, battered by waves, caught in undertow – what? 'Oh, Mr Hungerford!' she gasped. She wanted to say she begged his pardon, but she had no breath.

Then at last she was loose. Something had fallen to the floor – someone – an inert lump. She could not stop to see what it was. It might even be herself lying on the floor there. She flung open the door and fled. The cold night air tore in her lungs. And all the time she ran she was thinking foolishly, He'll never believe me. Meaning Dr Forstmann. Meaning she was mad.

## Chapter 27

THE first snow of the season was floating down through the blue air, catching pinkness from neon signs, yellow from shop windows. It lay in unmelted crystals in Kate's hair, gently removing the curl. She blew an upward blast at her forelock to send it out of her eyes, and passed through the glass door of the Harlow bar. Stanislas was, as usual, morosely mopping, but Jack was nowhere to be seen. She pushed on to the gloom of the taproom, where Jack promptly popped out of a booth as soon as she crossed the threshold. 'Hello, gorgeous,' he said, winking elaborately, 'we've got company.'

When she came around the back of the booth, she perceived Mr Marks, drooping low over the table, hiccupping gently. 'Good God!' she said *sotto voce*, clutching Jack's arm, and then loud, politely, 'Good evening, Mr Marks.'

'Mum mum mum,' said Leonard Marks indistinguishably, then suddenly straightened and threw his arms wide. 'Good evening,' he enunciated, clearly and 'oudly. Then he relapsed to his former posture. 'Mum.'

Jack gave Kate a rather hideous wink, and summoned the waitress. 'Mr Marks seems to have a bit of dope on the murder,' he said.

'Oh, now listen,' said Kate, 'fun's fun, but do you have to go digging up old dead murders *every* night? I'm sick to death of it.'

'Climbing and climbing,' muttered Leonard, looking cross-eyed. 'Following and following. Up, up, up. Black as the pit. Like wrestling with Lucifer!' he slumped a little lower.

'Wrestling with Lucifer!' whispered Kate, not quite sure how near to the surface of consciousness Leonard was. 'What in hell is he talking about?'

'Beers,' said Jack to the waitress, 'and a highball for the gentleman. Lucifer, in this instance, is La Cramm. Just keep listening, pet, and a very interesting saga will be unravelled – has been about three times already, and each time it starts over, it has a little something added.

He's still holding something back, I don't make out just what.'

'If that's the case,' said Kate, 'for heaven's sake get him coffee, not whisky, before he's out like a light. Look at him!'

Leonard's face leaned closer and closer to the initial-carved table top, a look of utter despair spread over it. 'Venusberg!' he said suddenly and distinctly. 'The temptress! The whore that sitteth upon the waters!' His eyelids drooped.

'By golly!' cried Jack, suddenly recognizing the danger, and slid out of the booth to run after the waitress.

Suddenly Leonard hoisted himself a notch and looked straight though blearily at Kate. ' "Thy ruddy breasts, thy rosy thighs, thy snowy flesh incarnadine!" ' he remarked.

Kate turned perfectly scarlet and edged toward the end of the booth. 'I beg your pardon?' she inquired desperately.

'The whore that sitteth on the waters!' pronounced Leonard again, and slumped lower.

Jack reappeared, carrying the cup of coffee himself. 'Here you are!' he cried briskly. 'Swallow this down fast and you'll feel like a new man!'

'The guilty flee where no man pursueth!' mumbled Leonard, but toyed with the handle of the cup.

'Quick!' cried Jack. 'Drink it up!'

Obediently Leonard drank the whole cup down, steaming as it was. Then he passed his hand across his eyes, reeled slightly. A sweat erupted visibly on his brow.

'Let me get this straight again,' said Jack, businesslike. 'You were following Mrs Cramm and she *attacked* you, you said?'

'Oh, Mr – uh – Mr – uh – well, I really forgot your name, but not in the ordinary sense of the word, I assure you!' cried Leonard earnestly, leaning across the table and swaying gently. Kate recoiled a bit.

'Well, just how *do* you mean?' pressed Jack.

'Oh,' groaned Leonard, 'it all began that dreadful night, that dreadful, evil night!'

'Which night?' chorused Jack and Kate.

Suddenly Leonard's eyelids went down to half-mast again. 'Watch it!' cried Kate, but amazingly, Leonard shot to his feet and pressed his right hand to his left breast.

'Thy ruddy breasts, thy rosy thighs, thy snowy flesh
   incarnadine –
O nymph, thou art a pearl, I'm swine!'

he declaimed vociferously, and collapsed again, staring vacantly into his empty coffee cup, the sweat forming in little rivulets on his temples.

'Oh, Jack!' cried Kate. 'That's the second time!'

'Baby,' said Jack, 'it's the first for me. Would you mind repeating that, Marks?'

Suddenly, dismally, Leonard's countenance was contorted as by a drawstring, and in addition to the perspiration, two tears brimmed over his eyelids. 'Oh,' he snivelled, 'I'm so ashamed! Please forgive me, Miss – ah – Miss – ah – please forgive me! I'm just drunk, that's all, disgracefully, disgustingly drunk!' And he sobbed bitterly.

'Not at all,' said Kate, reassured. 'I'm very interested. Can you give me the source of that quotation, or can I find it in Bartlett's? Thy –'

'Oh, don't!' wailed Leonard. 'Please forget I ever said it! Please! It's that dreadful night! It's that dreadful woman! Please!'

'Now you've *really* got my curiosity roused,' said Jack. 'What *is* all this – what terrible night?'

Leonard sank his face in his hands. 'The reading,' he muttered. 'The night of the reading. Kevin Boyle. Kevin Boyle's poetry.'

'You mean *that* was Kevin Boyle's poetry?' demanded Kate.

Leonard kept his hands over his face. 'No,' he whispered, 'no.'

'Then whose *is* it? What's it all about? What's it got to do with – Freda Cramm?' asked Jack irritably.

At last Leonard raised his face and peered through steamy glasses at Jack and Kate. 'It was the beginning of everything,' he pronounced. 'That poem. You know who wrote that poem? It was in with Kevin Boyle's. *She* read it. *He* read it. They laughed at it. I found it there that terrible night. The night – the night of the reading. I didn't find it until I was right in the middle of the reading. There it was, between two of *his*. I nearly lost my voice when I saw it. I shifted it to the bottom.' He paused and panted a moment, then looked at Jack with bloodhound eyes. 'Mr – uh – Mr – uh – '

'Donelly,' said Jack impatiently. 'Call me Jack.'

'Mr – uh – Jack, you remember when you came to my place? You remember what you asked me just at the end – before – before you left?'

Jack shook his head No.

'You asked me what was the paper I tore up on Freda Cramm's sunporch. You asked me – *that* was what I tore up.'

'*What* was what you tore up?' demanded Jack.

'That poem. I wrote it. Oh,' Leonard sobbed brokenly, 'I'm so ashamed. One should never be – never be *carnal*!'

'The cleaners' bill!' breathed Kate.

'Anyhow, that cleans that up,' replied Jack. 'How did it get there, anyway, Marks, and what's so awful about it? A little carnality makes the whole world kin. Did somebody swipe it from you?'

'Oh, no,' said Leonard miserably. He took out his handkerchief and blew his nose. His tears seemed to have sobered him up a little. 'I gave it to him – to Boyle – to read. I guess he got it mixed in with his own stuff. I can't tell you how it makes me feel. It's so – so *private*.'

'Not at all,' soothed Kate in womanly tones, 'it's in-dividual, but it's *also* universal, Mr Marks. You mustn't feel you're the only sinner in a pure world – you know better.'

'Oh, I know,' sighed Leonard. 'Boyle could do it. Boyle could get away with it. But I'm different. It's life – I guess it's the way Mr Hungerford feels about the journal.'

'What journal?' said Jack, beckoning to the waitress with his empty beer mug.

'The one Freda Cramm writes and puts in his room.'

'*What?*' cried Jack and Kate simultaneously.

'Yes,' said Leonard. 'Didn't I tell you? That's why I was following her. To catch her at it. I'm *sure* she mur-dered Boyle now. And she's trying to drive Hungerford insane. She poisons his life with this – I don't know how to tell you. She breaks into his room and writes a journal. Just an ordinary notebook – full of – evil!'

## Chapter 28

DR. FORSTMANN subdued Miss Justin's flutterings and left her outside the door of the room. The lamp was lighted by the bed. Under the white covering there was a large quivering lump. 'Molly!' he said. 'What happened?' In response, the quivering stopped and the lump was responsively still. 'Please come out, Molly,' he said. 'I want to hear about it.' The lump was still and solid as a boulder. 'Miss Justin told me you came in terribly upset from a walk. That's all I know. I have to know more to help you.'

'You can't help me,' was what he made out of the muffled voice coming from under the covers. 'Leave me alone,' or 'I'm all alone.' Something like that.

'That's what I'm here for, so you won't be alone,' he said, pulling up the wicker chair and sitting down. 'I came over from Springfield just as soon as I heard you needed me. How about it? How about telling me?'

He wasn't sure whether or not she could hear him. He sat silent for several minutes. He was gathering himself to utter some new bromide when the knot under the covers began to loosen; he saw the outline of Molly's legs extend under the blanket, and at last the frowsy top of her head and her two red-rimmed eyes appeared over the sheet. 'I'm so frightened,' she said urgently. Her mouth was still covered and he couldn't understand her very well. He was surprised at how quickly she had emerged. It put a new complexion on the matter. In a way it troubled him. He had expected a long, stubborn struggle before she gave in. 'Dr Forstmann,' she was saying. She even took a hand out of hiding and pushed the covers away from her mouth. 'Dr Forstmann, I'm so glad you came really. You can't help me, though. I'm really crazy.'

'I doubt it,' he said. Inadvertently, the thought of the dinner he had left steaming on his home table crossed his mind and he put more asperity into his answer than he had meant. Her lip quivered. 'You went for a walk,' he said quickly, with all the gentleness he could summon. 'Something upset you. Let's hear about it now.'

'Yes,' she whispered. 'Listen. I have delusions or hallucinations or something. Hallucinations, it must be. That's when you really imagine direct sensation instead of just sort of distant things like persecution, isn't it?'

He nodded, puzzled.

'I imagined,' she whispered, and seemed to choke, 'I imagined someone was strangling me. That's' – she caught her breath again – 'that's pretty far gone, isn't it?'

He was trying to think quickly, to go over the notes he had made about her without having them there to go over. What was this fear of having 'gone crazy'? Was it in response to the letter from her mother? Perhaps to convince the mother of the seriousness of her plight, she had produced more violent symptoms ... Possibly. Yet for some reason he had a feeling that something was unpredictably odd about her behaviour. She was somehow too straightforwardly glad to see him, too straightforwardly fearful of the experience she had had, whatever it was ... too little conflict ... Well. He had let a long silence lapse after her last words. Quickly he said, 'You've had an upsetting day to-day, Molly, what with your mother's letter and your first venture out of the Infirmary. Maybe if you could describe your – hallucination, we could piece together a good reason for its appearance.'

'Yes,' she whispered. 'Yes. Listen. I went to see Mr Hungerford. I walked to his house. But the woman said he didn't live there any more. She said that he had moved to where Kevin Boyle used to live. Oh!' she cried suddenly. 'Maybe he hadn't moved at all! Maybe I only dreamed that too! But it seemed so real!'

'Just tell me what happened first,' he said. 'Why did you want to see Mr Hungerford?'

She pushed her face farther out of the covers and lay back on the pillow. Her forehead contracted anxiously. 'I want to tell you everything,' she said. 'It's so complicated. He had Kevin Boyle's poems. I thought if I could see them I –' She stopped and looked at him, but for once she did not begin to cry.

'Go on,' he said, 'you thought if you could see them – what?'

'I thought – if I could have one – I might feel something again,' she said in a whisper. 'I thought I'd stop being dead.'

It was complicated. The roast veal he had been about to carve when the telephone rang kept coming back to haunt him as if he were an habitual glutton. His stomach uttered a loud and probably psychosomatic protest. 'Just tell it right along, Molly,' he said gently. I know there's too much to say all at once. We'll go back and pick up the pieces later.'

'All right,' she said faintly. 'So I went to – to the house where Mr Hungerford lives now. I rang the bell. Mr – Mr Boyle's name was still on the card. Mr Hungerford let me in. He was awfully nice. He even said I'd waked him up from his nap, but he didn't care. He wasn't trying to make me feel uncomfortable by telling me that. He seemed really glad to see me. We talked, and then I told him why I was there. He gave me a glass of sherry, but I wasn't drunk at all. I was almost –' the tears came up on her eyes, but hovered at the brink of the lids. 'I was almost happy. He was so nice. He was so human. He wasn't like a professor at all. He was like somebody you know, and you feel fond of – like a father, or an uncle, or something. And then the feeling came back.'

She stopped, but he did not prompt her, only waited.

'I guess I should have told you about the feeling I had. I guess it sort of fits in. I didn't want to go out, in a way. It was only thinking of the poems that made me able to go. All the time I walked in the streets I felt as if I were in a dream – when you're not sure what time of day it is, and you aren't certain whether you've seen the people you pass before, but it seems they look at you as if they knew some secret about you, and you know something dreadful is going to happen – they've found out something you've done, and you're going to be punished for it – you know the feeling?'

He nodded. 'Who was going to punish you, Molly? For what?'

'Oh, you don't know who, and you don't know for what! It's like when you were little, and your parents found out you had done something wrong, only you didn't know it was wrong, so you didn't know what it was they were angry about, or why they were going to punish you – only it's something worse than your parents that's going to punish you now!' Her voice was rising.

'So when you were talking to Mr Hungerford about the poems the feeling came back?' he cut in.

'Yes. I told him that that was what I had come for – I wanted him to let me read them. Then his face went funny – he has some sort of tic, you know. I guess that was what frightened me. It drew all to one side for a long time, and he dropped his sherry glass. And then, when his face went back again – that was when it happened.' She stopped.

'What happened?'

She closed her eyes and shook her head on the pillow. 'I guess I went crazy. I guess there isn't any other way to explain it. He looked all different. Before I had been thinking' – she blushed – 'I had been thinking he remind-ed me of my father. And then all of a sudden he looked like my mother. That just doesn't make sense, you know.'

'I think it makes a good deal of sense,' said Forstmann slowly, 'when you think about the letter you had from your mother to-day. I don't know why you should have thought of her in connection with Mr Hungerford, but I'll bet you we can find a reason. Was that all?'

'Oh no!' she cried, suddenly rising on her elbows. 'That's only the beginning! I shut my eyes because I was so frightened when – when I thought he looked that way, and all of a sudden somebody was strangling me!'

'Describe how that felt,' he said, sitting forward.

'Why,' she said, 'it felt just like somebody strangling me!'

'Do you mean you had a choking sensation – couldn't swallow or so?'

'Oh, no, no!' she cried. 'Somebody's hands were around my throat, and I could feel all the blood swelling in my head, and I was fighting with this – this person, only the terrible thing was' – she paused – 'I wasn't sure I wasn't doing it myself, or that nothing had happened at all, or that I'd just dreamed it. And then finally the hands dropped away, and it seemed' – she puzzled a moment – 'it seemed that something or somebody fell on the floor. And before that somebody said something.

About So you're the one. But it was a strange voice. I'd never heard it before.'

'Whose voice does it make you think of? Does it remind you of anyone?'

'Oh,' she said, 'oh, let me see! I can't think. It was sort of deep. But not a man's voice. Like some woman with a very deep voice. You know who it kind of sounded like? Mrs Cramm in the English Department. Do you know her?'

'No, I don't. Have you a class with her?'

'No. I used to see her in The Coffee Shoppe sometimes. She was a friend of – of Mr Boyle's.'

Her eyes were wide and her breath was coming fast, but there was a certain calmness, a kind of sureness about her which he didn't understand. Was she relieved at being able to produce so definite a symptom? Did she feel that now she would be justified in the eyes of her mother? Something must be done now about the parents. If he could get her father to come East, to talk to him. He couldn't see keeping her at the Infirmary at this rate. Nor could he think of sending her to the state hospital. It was possible some arrangement could be made to send her home and put her in the care of someone there – cheaper than a sanatorium. Certain doctors might be willing to take her on a sort of professional discount for the sake of Miles Morrison's work. He'd have to talk to Bainbridge – that was the next thing.

Unexpectedly she broke into his thoughts. 'I'm not worried, you know,' she said oddly. 'I'm the calmest I've been since I've been here. It's sort of the courage of desperation. Now I know the worst. I could even go to sleep now. I even feel sleepy.'

'Listen, Molly, the worst isn't so bad as you've made

out, that I know – I don't mean you haven't told the truth,' he amended hastily, 'but I doubt if its significance is so final as you imagine. You've been turning up a lot of violent emotions in the last few days which you've always kept far under the surface of your mind before. It's not altogether surprising if you get some violent reactions. If you can sleep now, I think that's the best thing you could do. I'll get Miss Justin to give you a sleeping tablet to take in case you can't. To-morrow we'll talk more about this. Sleep's the thing to-night.' He rose. 'Good-night,' he said.

She even smiled at him. It was almost the first time. 'Good-night,' she said. 'I'm sorry I made you miss your dinner.'

He grinned. 'Good-night,' he said again, and left.

## Chapter 29

WHEN Molly woke the white room was filled with dazzling white sun. White as a magnesium flare. She shut her eyes to recapitulate her dream. It was an old dream, almost an old friend of a dream, a nightmare, but this time (as always) with a new twist. She was walking through a wood. It was dark and tangled and dangerous. In the thickets behind the trees lurked danger, but what the danger was she never knew. But the sense of it was terrible; sometimes in the dream she dropped on the path and lay quivering in a ball, waiting for the danger to take her to digest her in its inexorable maw. Sometimes she fainted for fear, yet remained conscious all the time, not escaping the danger by her withdrawal from life.

But this time she walked on through the forest, in terror. Then all at once, an enormous beast came bounding from out of the bushes, roaring terribly. Suddenly she had turned calm, had drawn her sword and shot him three times, and had wakened, not with a sense of nightmare, but of curious peace.

Lying in the infirmary bed with her eyes closed, she began to laugh. Shot him with her sword! How ridiculous! The laughter took her by surprise, caught her unawares, carried her away. She was so delighted at the surprise of her laughter that the tears rose in her throat, of a kind of gratitude for being able to laugh. She opened her eyes and sighed. Then she realized the significance of the whiteness of the light. It had snowed. The sun was reflecting from snow.

Snow in the night is like a gift, she thought, and wished she had something on which to write this sentence. It came in the night like a gift, like an ineffable largesse of purity. It came like a reaffirmation of hope after despair. Like the premonition of a miracle. Like love. She began to cry with happiness because of the snow. 'I'm not dead! I'm not dead!' she said aloud, the tears running down her cheeks. She raised her hand to her cheeks, to cover her face as if she were blushing with love at the approach of her lover. Then she saw it.

Running across the back of her left hand was a long, deep scratch.

It all came back, like part of the dream. The threatening walk through the twilight. The Saint Bernard. The deaf old woman. The haven of Mr Hungerford's room. The fire. The sherry. And then, like a clap of thunder, everything changed, everything different: Mr Hungerford transformed to a wicked witch in an enchanted wood, standing on the hearth amid the bits of broken glass. She had closed her eyes at the sight of him – she could not bear that he had changed. And then the hands had been at her throat; she was rocking and struggling, straining to breathe. And all the time thinking: I am mad, I am doing this to myself, this is the final ultimate proof! Out of some skewed notion of self-destruction I am compelled to behave this way, wrestle with my own spirit! A fingernail had drawn a line of pain across the back of her left hand. And here was the scratch.

But her own fingernails were bitten to the quick!

The sun and snow blazed blue light through the windows, dazzling as revelation. 'Oh, oh, it was true!' she whispered. It changed everything! It changed the complexion of the whole world! Like the sun, like the snow, like the beast in the dream, like a gift presented to her unexpectedly! It was true, she had been right, and it made her feel nearly mad with excitement. She was not crazy – except almost crazy with happiness – someone – some real person – had actually tried to strangle her!

She leapt out of bed and shut the window. She stripped off her pyjamas and put on her clothes very quickly. When she was all dressed except for her sweater, she stopped and began to laugh, shivering in her slip and skirt. It seemed so insanely silly to be happy that someone had tried to strangle you! Maybe she was still crazy, only in another way. But it didn't matter, it didn't matter. ... This time she had been right. It was as if she were vindicated in all the thousand times she had made a stand, had said: You have mistreated me! and they had scoffed, What nonsense, what childishness, what selfishness! ... This is the birthday of my life, she thought, shivering with excitement.

When Miss Justin knocked on her door with the breakfast tray, her face was burning with anticipation. She ate in hasty gulps. When she was through, she took her coat and muffler from the closet, her mittens from the drawer, and dressed to go out. At once, at once, she must get to Mr Hungerford! She stopped, one sleeve of her coat still dangling. What a fool she had been! What a selfish idiot! Had he too not been in danger? What had she been thinking of, running off and leaving him, all cowardly with her own peril! God knows what could have happened to him by now, in the room like herself with those gripping hands, that grating voice! Perhaps he was even now ... like Kevin Boyle ... like Kevin Boyle, from her cowardice! She thrust her arm into the sleeve and ran out of the door down the corridor. Halfway to the front hall she nearly collided with Miss Justin, who was carrying a tray of thermometers and tongue depressors.

'Why, Molly!' she exclaimed, looking frightened in a curious way. 'Where are you going?'

'Oh,' she answered breathlessly, 'I'm going for a walk – I'm – I'm just going for a walk.'

Slowly, oddly, Miss Justin was edging in front of her, blocking the corridor. 'But, my dear,' she said, 'there's four or five inches of snow underfoot and you have no goloshes! None of the walks will be cleared at this hour.'

'It doesn't matter,' said Molly, starting to push past. 'I'll stop off at the house for my goloshes and another pair of shoes.'

'But, my dear,' said Miss Justin monotonously, 'why don't you let me phone one of the girls to bring over your goloshes? I mustn't let you go out in this way. We're not trying to drum up trade, you know!' There was a queer little rabbity look under her falsely facetious smile. No!

Molly told herself. I will not think it! I'm always thinking people are against me. I have to stop. I have to be reasonable.

'It's all right, I couldn't possibly catch cold in that little space, Miss Justin. After all, Dr Forstmann told me I was to go for walks –and it's a beautiful sunny day.' She smiled politely. There! That ought to convince her! It was probably the first time she had smiled at her for any reason.

'Oh, I'm sure Dr Forstmann didn't mean to have you go out with no overshoes into the wet snow,' said Miss Justin. 'We must remember you've been sick for a while, Molly – your temperature has only been normal a few days.'

She was beginning to tremble. She wanted to keep hold of herself, not slide away from the happiness, the plateau of reason which she had achieved in that waking moment. But already her face was flushing, her eyes preparing to fill with tears, her hands shaking. She managed to keep her voice even, though. 'I don't think he would mind, Miss Justin, really I don't. It's important that I go out this morning, you see. I'll tell Dr Forstmann all about it when I see him later. He – in fact, he already knows about it. I assure you it will be all right.'

But the rabbity look came even stronger on Miss Justin's face. A look of suspicion and secrecy and, strangely, of fear. Oh no, no! she thought. I won't see things like that! They're imaginary! And so subtle – who can *really* say what another person's face expresses? Nevertheless, the look was there. Fear, and wiliness. Danger. 'Molly,' said Miss Justin, 'you look a little feverish to me. Just pop this in your mouth, will you?' And drawing a thermometer from its antiseptic bath, she advanced it toward Molly's mouth.

Suddenly a great rage began to break the boundaries

in her; she felt like some small cornered beast who finally dares to bare its tiny teeth. 'That's fantastic!' she said angrily, backing away from the outstretched thermometer. 'Naturally I look feverish when you keep me standing with my coat on in a steam-heated hall. Will you please let me pass?'

'I don't think you'd really better —' Miss Justin began.

The tears conquered her. She was too weak. She slid back from the plateau. She covered her eyes with her mittened hand. 'He said I could go out!' she sobbed childishly. 'You call Dr Forstmann! He *said* I could go out! You're — you're exceeding your authority! Call him up! You — you horse-faced old bitch!'

'Well!' she heard Miss Justin's outraged voice. 'Well, I must say! I never expected to be working in an insane asylum when I came here! I see now ... Very well, miss, if you want to know, Dr Forstmann left instructions that you were not to leave the building. Do you want to go back to your room by yourself, or shall I call another nurse to help me?'

She turned and ran. There was a bolt on her door — they had not thought to remove it. She pushed it into place. Then she threw herself on the bed, coat and all, and sobbed and sobbed. Betrayed. He had betrayed her. Her last, her last ... This was the end. He believed it too. She was crazy. Dr Forstmann had said she could not leave. She wept wildly until she was worn out, and then she lay, staring at the patch of bright snow sunlight on the floor. A cool, contemptuous voice began to speak in the back of her head. Well, it said, what do you expect? How do you think you've been acting? Didn't you tell him yourself that you were mad?

But I'm *not*! she returned querulously. I'm not, and now I can prove it! He should have known, he should have known!

But how could he know? said the voice reasonably. You didn't know yourself.

Her eyes were blinded with sun. She raised her hand and looked at the scratch through a green haze of sun blindness. You didn't know yourself. Of course I didn't. He doesn't know about this. This makes it real. He couldn't know that. When he knows ...

Suppose he does not believe you? Suppose he thinks you have scratched your hand on something else, doesn't believe ... But I didn't, I didn't! It hurt too much – it was then, I remember! It was then, then!

Suppose it was just part of the dream – as when the alarm clock rings and you weave the ringing into your dream – invent a telephone or a doorbell to explain its voice.

She moaned. 'Oh, I must go, I must go!' she said aloud. Only one person could set her mind at rest – Mr Hungerford. If she could get to him, either he would support her, or tell her it had been illusion. And if it was *not* illusion, then he was in danger. Perhaps he was already dead. Yet if he had ... It was all too tangled. She must speak to him. She could not sit in solitude through the morning, waiting for Forstmann to set her right. Perhaps he wouldn't believe her, anyway. She rose from the bed, her head spinning and swollen with tears. It would be simple to get out. The room was on the ground floor. She had only to open the window and climb over the sill. Outside there was a brick terrace. Then where? Not the street. She would be seen. Across the field to the cover of the little wood that was behind the row of houses across the street. To the path along the river, then up the hill and across the athletic field to the back of Mr Hungerford's house.

She pushed up the sash, straddled the sill, and set her foot gingerly on the undefiled purity of the new-fallen snow.

## Chapter 30

'YOU see, it's just as sunny as advertised,' Leonard Marks said, and laughed nervously. Please, he seemed to plead silently, please, tell me what it is, let me help you!

Hungerford smiled at Leonard weakly, and tried to form a word, but he could not. He could not speak. He sat by the fire in an old dressing-gown, unwashed, unshaven. Every now and then he was taken with fits of shivering. The flu, Leonard said, and tried to persuade him to go to bed. But it was not the flu, and he would not go to bed. The curious thing, the thing which he could not tell Leonard, was that he himself did not know what the trouble was. He shivered and shook, he was nauseated with dread, he could not bear to be alone, but what it was, how it had come about, that he could not – or would not – conjecture. Since yesterday. Whatever it was had come up yesterday. And he simply could not remember. A girl had come to see him – a student. He had liked her at once. But he could not remember why she had come. And whenever he tried to recall it, he began to shake and shiver – he made Leonard bring him a tumbler half full of whisky.

The sun was streaming through the small, diamond-paned windows, blue-white. The fire he had lit seemed pallid in the brilliant morning light. He sat before the blaze, one side of his body heated, the other stiff with chill, and he thought irrelevantly of a passage in *Madame Bovary* where Charles comes to see Emma before they are married, and there is a description of the blue light coming down the chimney on to the dead ashes. But that was on a hot day, as he recollected – there followed a description of the beads of sweat on Emma's half-uncovered breasts. Hot. So hot you could sweat. So hot your bones were warm – you would not remember that bones could ever be cold. That intestines could run ice water. That feet could ache with cold inside woollen socks. Poor Leonard was looking at him like an anxious bloodhound. No. Dachshund. Well.

'I wish you'd let me call a doctor,' he pleaded, breaking the silence. Hungerford said nothing, only smiled weakly again. 'Oh, Mr Hungerford,' he finally burst, '*won't* you tell me what it is? Is it – it is something about the journal again?'

Hungerford shook his head, still unable to speak. He opened his mouth. His dry tongue clung to the roof of it. 'I seem,' he essayed thickly, 'I seem to have had – have had some sort of – sort of spell of amnesia. It has – it has rather undone me.' He felt the muscles of his face pulling anxiously, wishing to distort his cheek with the tic. But the fact was that he was too cold. It would have been like – like trying to pour molasses in January for his muscles to move his flesh that way.

'*Amnesia!*' Leonard was saying, his eyes starting behind his glasses. 'Is that – I mean, has that ever happened before?'

Hungerford shook his head in the negative.

'Then oughtn't you – I mean, really, Mr Hungerford,

really, sir, you've been working too hard! You aren't well enough! *Do* see a doctor!'

Poor Leonard Marks, Poor dear Leonard Marks! He meant so very well. Leonard, my dear, if I could only make you understand. You see ... But one must participate. One must have experienced to understand. ... One must have realized one's own participation. A mock professional voice spoke in his head. Mental illness, it said. Leonard Marks, he was sure, had had a thousand comparable experiences. He, Hungerford, was no more than a humble stockholder in the neuroses of the times. It was not that it was anything private, personal though it was. But to make it understood to one who was not *aware* ... His brain was cold. Thought flowed sluggishly and stiffly through whatever passages thought must flow through.

Marks had risen. 'Now really, sir,' he was expostulating, 'I'm just – I'm just going to *make* you go to bed! You're having a terrible chill! You're shaking like a leaf! Why don't you get covered up and have a hot-water bottle and some of that sedative you –'

A force – how else to describe it? – like a hand at the scruff of his neck, lifted Hungerford to his feet. 'No!' he was amazed to hear himself shout. Good heavens, he thought to himself, with a rather comic abstraction, what has got into me? Almost, he began to enjoy this illogical scene.

Leonard Marks shrank back – like a Victorian wife whose husband has asserted his authority. Almost visibly quaking, then, he pulled himself together, clasping his hands over the middle button of his vest. 'I know I'm being a pest,' he said bravely, 'but honestly, Mr Hungerford, I do so *deeply* mean it for your own good!'

Oh dear, oh dear. Better than a doctor, to be sure. But so ... Suddenly he thought of the girl who had been here yesterday, and an entire scene reappeared in his memory like an enormous bubble bursting on the surface of water. He saw her standing before him, twisting her brown mittens in her hands in an agony of embarrassment. They seem to think, she was saying, they seem to think I am unbalanced. How something frozen in his heart had melted at the sound of those words! How he had loved that child who knew too ... knew too ... He would like to talk to *her* now. Though for what purpose he could hardly say. He felt at the same time better and more perturbed for thinking about her. He felt that she was a key to his disturbance of to-day, if only he could fit her to the proper lock. He would even have sent for her, have made her tell him what had gone between them, if he could have remembered her name. Why had she come to see him? That he could not recollect at all. Perhaps one of his students. Perhaps if he went through the roll-calls of his various classes he would recognize a name.

Leonard Marks was looking anxiously between himself and the clock. He wanted to comfort Leonard, somehow, yet he was irritated that he was called upon to do so. 'Go along, go along, Marks!' he cried, his tongue finally loosened. 'You have a class, I know, and I assure you I'm *quite* all right. If I need anything, I've only to call for Miss Stone. I tell you, I wish you'd put a note on the blackboard that I won't be meeting English 24 this morning. It's in Room 33 of Framingham.'

'Oh, of course!' vibrated Leonard, delighted with his little task, yet still undecided as to whether he should leave. 'Are you quite sure ... '

'Go – get out – run!' he cried, trying to make his voice

teasing, yet annoyed within. And Leonard left at last, looking a little frightened, a little worried, a little relieved.

Now he was alone with the quiet, brilliant sunshine, the blue-white sunshine – blue. That meant it must have snowed. The windows were too high in the wall for him to see the ground from here; the shade to the one facing out on the porch was pulled down for privacy. But of course, if he had been in a mood for observation, he would have seen before that the bare branches that showed through the high panes had each a load of white, lying soft and precarious. As a child he had often been too delicate to go out in the snow, to play the rough games of sliding, wallowing, bombarding. Yet he remembered the sense of miracle that always came to him when he waked to find it had snowed in the night. Often he would lie abed until his mother came in to light the gas log. 'It snowed last night,' she would say, in a soft wondering voice. And he would answer, 'Yes, I know,' though he had not been out of bed to look through the window. There would be that whiteness in the air, that radiance. ·... He put another log on the fire and sat down beside it. He ran his hand over his rough cheek. In a moment he would shave. He felt better. Less cold. Because it had snowed, he felt less cold! What a nonsensical mood he was in to-day!

And then the doorbell rang. It gave a long sputtering buzz and stopped. He thought he would not go. He sat staring into the fire. It buzzed again. Still he sat. Then it occurred to him that he could peep through the crack of the shade and see who was on the porch. He rose and went to the window. A girl was standing at the door with her back to him. She wore a nondescript tweed coat, the usual socks and moccasins. Her hair hung lank over her coat collar – for the life of him he could not recollect ever having seen her. Just as he was about to let the blind fall back against the window, he saw her turn a little, beating the back of one brown mitten into the palm of the other. Brown mittens – brown mittens – probably a hundred pairs on the campus! But he had heard the voice saying again: They think I'm unbalanced. Oh, he must see her, must speak to her! Quickly, forgetting his déshabille, he rushed from the window, out of the French doors to the hall and the outer entry. He threw the door open, and sighed with relief and gratification. It was she – same face, same heavy bang, same frightened eyes. 'Come in!' he shouted joyously. 'Come in!'

She stepped back, looked a little startled by his exuberance, and by – he finally realized – his appearance. But she came forward again, crossed the threshold, silently walked through the hall to his room. He followed her, feeling so warm, so grateful. He remembered something new. When she had come yesterday, he had not known her name. 'Do you know something that's to my shame?' he said, shutting the door to his rooms behind him. 'I've forgotten your name again.'

But she had paid no attention to his remark. She stood in front of the fire as she had yesterday. 'Mr Hungerford, I *had* to see you,' she said, her grey eyes clouded with anxiety. 'I've run away. They don't know I'm here. I escaped. They really – now they really think I'm crazy. You have to tell me what happened yesterday!'

The strength went from his legs and he had to sit down. He looked up at her, opening and closing his mouth like a fish, unable to make words. She stared back at him, her face making ready for tears. At last he brought out, 'You mean you don't remember?'

Dumbly she shook her head, and he thought the floor was rocking under him. For if *she* did not remember, how was he ever ... 'Oh,' she said, 'I *think* I do. But it's all a hallucination. At least, I thought it was a hallucination. Dr Forstmann thought so too. He thought I was crazy. He told the nurse not to let me out. But then I found *this*' – she thrust her hand out toward him – 'and I couldn't tell any more if it was true or not.'

He looked down at the thin back of her hand, and saw an angry-looking scratch running across the back. He passed his hand across his eyes. He could make nothing of it. 'I don't understand,' he muttered.

'Then,' she said dully, 'there was nothing. I *am* crazy. I'd better go back.'

She started to move towards the door, her shoulders sunken. He jumped up and caught hold of the mantel to steady himself. 'No!' he cried. 'Don't go! You mustn't go! Tell me what it is you thought you remembered!'

She turned in the doorway and looked at him pitifully. 'Must I?' she said.

He went toward her unsteadily and laid his hands on her shoulders. 'Yes,' he said urgently, and almost tenderly, 'you must! Really you must!'

Obediently she came back into the room. She stood before the fire like a child making ready to recite a piece. Her eyes filled with tears, but she blinked them back. 'When I came here yesterday it took a lot of nerve,' she said. 'I don't know. I don't know if I can tell you.'

'Yes, you must, you must!' he urged.

'I'll try,' she whispered. 'You see, I don't know if you understand – it took such a lot of nerve just to go out of doors. I don't know if you'd understand that. It sounds so crazy. I guess it is crazy.'

He laughed a little, almost jubilantly. 'My God, of course I know, child! You get to the doorstep, and all you want to do is go back to your room and hide in the bed. You lay your hand on the knob and think you simply cannot ... '

'Yes,' she said in a surprised voice. 'That's just it – that's just it! And you're scared to walk in the streets – you think everybody – you think they're looking at you – you think they hate you. Oh, that's silly, I know. I just can't seem to help it.'

Hurry, hurry! he want to beg her, but instead he said comfortingly, 'I know, too well. Will you tell me what happened?'

'I'm sorry, I didn't mean to be so slow,' she apologized. 'First I went to where you used to live. You weren't there, but the woman told me you were here. So I came here. We were talking, and you were very kind to me, but then all of a sudden everything got ... I don't know how to – someone choked me! Or that was what I thought! Please, could you tell me what really happened?'

Now the tears were pouring down her face in earnest. He had taken his seat by the fire again. He let his hands drop between his knees. 'I don't know what happened,' he said. 'I can't tell you. I had some sort of fit of amnesia. I can't remember a damned thing that happened. I couldn't remember a thing except that you had been here. I recognized you when I saw you.'

'Oh,' she said, and stood in an attitude of utter gloom.

'Look,' he said. 'We must work on this, and maybe more of it will come back. Somebody *choked* you, you say?' All at once he began to be excited again. How had he

passed over her words so calmly? 'Tell me everything that
happened after you came here! What makes you say
you're crazy? What did Forstmann say to you? Oh, here,'
he cried, 'take off your coat and sit down!'

She peeled off her coat and threw it on the couch, then
sat down in the chair opposite his and thrust her feet
toward the fire. She clasped her hands in her lap and
began, 'I came here and you were very nice to me. You
gave me a glass of sherry. I thought you looked like my
father, and I liked you very much. But then all of a
sudden you looked different to me, and I closed my eyes
and someone was choking me – or I imagined it – and
then I ran away. I thought it was all a dream and that I
was really mad, and I told Dr Forstmann; only this
morning, I found the scratch on my hand. You see' – she
was getting excited, and so was he – 'the sensation of
choking was so plain, that I thought I must have done it
myself – taken hold of my neck with my own hands, I
mean. But I remember very plainly feeling my hand
scratched at that time – I remember that it hurt, but I
had to keep on struggling, and I couldn't get my breath.
Now, I couldn't have scratched myself, because' – she
blushed – 'I bite my fingernails so. So I thought that – I
imagined that might be a kind of evidence that something
had really – oh, and I forgot. I heard a voice. It wasn't
you. It was like a woman's voice, only deep.'

Suddenly he put his hands to his temples as if to keep
his head from falling apart. My God, my God! 'She was
here!' he said aloud, without meaning to.

'I beg your pardon?' she said.

'What's your name?' he asked, taking his hands down.

'Molly Morrison.' Her lower lip began to quiver.

'Molly,' he said,' you're not mad. I think it was quite

real. I think I see how it was. But I have to think. I have to figure it out. I —' He rose and began to pace the room. 'Go back home,' he said. 'I think — I think I'm going to find other evidence which will convince Dr Forstmann. Go back to the Infirmary. I'll telephone him to-day.'

She rose, looking bewildered, on the brink of tears. 'But —' she began — 'I have to know —'

Suddenly he was in a frenzy to have her out, to have her gone, to know for himself. 'You will!' he cried. 'You will! You must take my word for it! Now run along like a good child! I'll call Dr Forstmann within an hour.'

She took her coat and put it on slowly, biting her lip. She went to the door, turned and looked at him pitifully, her hand on the knob. 'You — you will?' she begged.

On an impulse, he rose and went to kiss her cheek. 'I will, Molly, I promise,' he said. Then she was gone.

A sweet child, a dear — but he had no time; feverishly he had jerked a whole row of books off the shelf and was scrabbling for — ah, he had it! He turned the brown cardboard cover and riffled wildly through the pages, the big scrawl staring up at him like a malignant face. Why had he not thrown it away? Why had he ... There it was. Yesterday's date. It began:

*And she came here, the little bitch, and how brazenly she faces up to me and says, Give me his poems. Ah, I cried, so it was you! And I took her by the throat, and I shook her like a dog in a fight, yes, in another minute I would have snapped her skinny little neck, but she broke away. Oh, the next time will I not succeed, the next time ...*

The unconsciousness overtook him, and he read no more.

When he came to, someone was dabbing at his face with a wet cloth. Slowly he became aware of Leonard Marks, looming into his consciousness like a ship over the edge of the horizon. 'Leonard,' he said faintly but urgently, 'now you can call a doctor. Call Dr Julian Forstmann in Springfield. Call him at once.' And as he closed his eyes it seemed strange to him that his first thought should have been of vindicating the little girl instead of calling the police, protecting himself.

## Chapter 31

FREDA Cramm was cleaning her desk. It was one of those small necessities which occasionally seem so pleasant as to appear self-indulgent. Across the top of the writing space was a row of eight cubbyholes assigned to paid and unpaid bills, answered and unanswered letters, receipts, and a great deal of miscellany – Christmas cards from years back, a wrist-watch which needed a new strap, a bunch of luggage keys, and envelopes full of snapshots and negatives. Freda sat precariously on a plump, plush slipper chair, humming and throwing papers on the floor. Sometimes the pile began to sprawl, so she gathered it up and threw it on to the fire that blazed pallidly on the sunny hearth. Then she would go back to the desk, to slit unopened envelopes, examine the contents of those already opened, filing some in the cubbyholes and throwing the rest on the floor beside her chair. Suddenly she made a little exclamation, and paused, smoothing a scrap of lined paper under her plump ringed hands.

Freda (said the small ragged writing), You're a big brute of a woman, damn you, and you can put a scare into a man. There it is, humiliating though it be: there is something about you that makes the words wither in my throat and my manhood on the vine. And I'm attracted to you, curse you. Forgive me, and come to tea to-morrow.

K.

She grinned at the paper, mirthlessly, musingly. She picked it up and dropped it on the wastepaper pile, then leaned and took it back again. *Memento mori*. She put it in her pigeon-hole with the envelopes of snapshots. She raised her chin in the air and ran her hand along the flabby flesh under it. 'I'm getting old,' she said aloud to the room. Outside the windows the evergreens nodded, loaded with snow. The sun blazed through the icicles that hung outside the panes. The room was too warm, with the sun, the central heating, and the fire on the hearth. Freda drifted into a half trance, bemused by heat and light. I am getting old, she thought, echoing her spoken words. She was forty-two. She had been a woman of vanity, in her prime, yet she had known so many of the satisfactions of the flesh that she did not grudge the years the weight and the wrinkles they had put on her. She was well aware that a woman's attraction lay in something beyond a slim waist and firm breasts, and if she chose this very day – well, it was no use pretending it was quite so easy as it once had been. But on the other hand, her appetite for experiment had long since been satisfied; she could now take her sex like a gourmet, sampling only the tastiest titbits. She laughed out loud, drily. She had never gotten a taste of Kevin, and that was the long and the short of it. Nor was it for want of trying, either. As he put it, there it was, humiliating though it be. Yet, when she considered the incident, she doubted very much if she had been as humiliated as Kevin Boyle. She had long since outgrown the capacity for that sort of humiliation, because she had long since learned to estimate her own strength, or attraction or whatever, and she was perfectly sure that it was great. Considering herself as a historical phenomenon, she thought she could stand as a successful example of a woman of the Freudian era – she had entered maturity in the storied twenties, and had been subject-matter for a good many stories herself. She had been married, she had been divorced, but the force of the blow of Michael's rejection had been so cushioned by the size of the sum he had settled on her that she could now meet him and his second wife with their growing family as amicably as though intimacy had never been. And if she had felt the need for reassurance, why, there had been lovers in Rome, Paris, London, Capri, Hendaye, and other places. Now she was basking in the warmth of her middle years like a fat cat resting after a long night's prowl; she enjoyed playing at being an intellectual, she enjoyed *épater les bourgeois* in this sleepy little town, and if a charming piece like Kevin Boyle slipped out of her grasp – well, no use mourning spilt milk. It made a good story, too. If only she could have told it to someone who would appreciate it.

She had first seen Kevin in the faculty tea room, cornered by Miss Austen, a colourless young woman from Rhode Island who was also in the English Department. They were discussing their respective sections of Freshman English, from all she had been able to overhear. Miss Austen was making sheep's eyes in a clumsy – even pathetic, if you could sympathize with that sort of thing – way. Freda had borne down on them like an expert polo player galloping in to take the ball, and in no time at all Kevin Boyle was driving home with her to borrow her copy of *The Tropic of Cancer*. In a week they had had three warm discussions of modern literature over her very excellent Amontillado. And then, just when she half expected him to attack, he withdrew. He began disagreeing cantankerously with her. He found fault with her way of life. She decided their relationship was ready to enter a new phase. She begged him to show her his poems.

In the guise of literary critic, she donned a new coloration. From dominating female, she shifted slightly to mother image. She was all warmth and appreciation. She invented new phrases of praise. She worked hard at the task of constructive criticism. As she looked back at it, she thought she had said some damned valuable things to him. His armour dropped. He was frankly adoring – in an impersonal sort of way. He was getting so he could not write without periodic injections of her approval. Then she began to be bored – bored with the amount of energy she was putting into him in proportion to the small returns she was getting. She had had the fullest intentions of sleeping with him from the start. She decided to stop the cat-and-mouse game and bring the thing to a climax.

It had become their daily habit to meet for sherry at her house in the afternoon, or tea at his, or coffee at The Coffee Shoppe. On this particular afternoon it was to be her place; she dressed carefully in a loose tea gown, and spent the afternoon in an astringent cosmetic mask. At four-thirty, when he was to come, the autumn dusk was descending, the fire was lit, the softer lamps were lighted.

He arrived. The maid took his coat and hat. She had not risen when he entered the room. She had not even raised her head, but only her telling eyes. She had taken in every inch of him, slowly, consideringly. She remembered his long sinewy hand rising nervously to the knot of his tie.

'Sit down, Kevin, sit down,' she had said. And she let him know with every syllable of it what she was up to.

They had sat and talked desultorily, he nervous, she slow and deliberate. At the end of their first glass of sherry, the maid had appeared in the doorway in her hat and coat, and Freda had risen to give her a cheque. 'I'm sending Margaret off for the week-end,' she let him know, as the door closed, and he had shivered, as if a goose had walked over his grave.

They had talked, as usual, about his poetry, but she had put very little of herself into the discussion this evening, only murmuring abstracted answers, agreeing, assenting. She meant business, and she thought he might as well know it sooner as later. She considered that men matured more slowly than women, and it annoyed her to have to wait for Kevin to bridge the ten or fifteen years that separated them; nevertheless, looking at his lean, odd sort of beauty, she thought he was worth the wait. But the talk wore on and on without any sort of move being made. His gestures grew more and more jerky, hers more and more unhurried. If he did not say something within the next five minutes, she thought, she would make the first move herself. She watched the hands move slowly across the face of the clock.

'I find you very disturbing, Kevin,' she interrupted then.

She had turned down the lamps, the room was in complete darkness except for the fire. They sat in the armchairs, facing each other, on opposite sides of the hearth. He was slumped low in his, his knees rising angularly, the shadows emphasizing the sockets of his eyes, the flickering light catching on his nervous fingers as they rolled and unrolled the end of his necktie. At her words, he sat forward with a jerk, his eyebrows flying up his forehead. 'Disturbing?' he echoed, in a high, tense voice. 'Why, how is that?'

She rose from her chair and looked down at him in silence a moment. 'I find you very sexually attractive,' she said at last.

His jaw dropped a little, then drew close again. 'Oh,' he said, 'thank you.' And sat there, looking up at her. She turned and left the room.

She stayed in the dark inner reaches of the house, laughing, and giving him a chance to gather himself together. Every now and then she would say, 'Thank you,' out loud to herself, and giggle uncontrollably. She supposed she *was* a bit of a shock. She wanted him to have time to get over the instinctive movement of withdrawal, and become a ravening male. When she judged he should be in that state, she came back to the living-room.

But he was standing on the hearth, wearing his overcoat, with his hat in his hand. She waited on the threshold a moment, taking in the situation. Then she entered the room and went about from lamp to lamp, lighting them all. When the room was bright and decided with electricity, she turned to him and said matter-of-factly, 'Must you go?'

'Yes – yes, I must,' he stammered. 'There's a – that is – I'm asked to a faculty dinner at – ah – at – ah – Barclay House to-night.'

'That's too bad,' she said. 'I had hoped you'd stay for supper.'

'Oh,' he said, making an almost epileptic gesture with his hat, 'that's terribly kind of you, but –'

'Of course,' she cut him short. 'Well, Kevin, I'll be seeing you at The Coffee Shoppe to-morrow, no doubt.' She led him into the hall and opened the door. 'Good-night.'

'Good – good-night, Freda,' he said, and stumbled off down the brick walk.

The next day the note she had under her hand had come, and she had gone to his house to tea. But it was not her game to be responsive at this particular move; she had arrived all indignant over her own affairs – had burst into his bravely loving mood (she had seen him steeled to approach her) with the letter over which they had quarrelled. She supposed, now that it was so long past, that he had reproached her out of irritation that she had not given him an opening to make up for his cowardice. And she supposed that she had got so angry herself out of a kind of misplaced and almost maidenly disappointment. She had meant to make it all up – make it appear to be a sort of lover's quarrel, by becoming his lover. But the next week he was dead.

It was strange how his murder had dropped out of sight in the life of the community, like a stone dropped into water. Only the outermost circles of the ripples it had created now remained to quiver on the surface. Perhaps the police were at work still, unearthing new clues. Perhaps the president had knowledge of new discoveries which were kept secret. But in the town, in the faculty, even the game of conjecturing about who could have killed Kevin and why had palled. It was a nine-days' wonder and the nine days were long gone. Curious that in so quiet a society violence should be accepted as a matter of course. She supposed it was because the group in the college was predominantly intellectual and accustomed to living the life of the mind,

so called. After all, the drama of Kevin Boyle was a
rather shoddy little business if you chose to compare it
with similar inventions of Dostoievsky, Euripides, or even
Poe. And murder, in order to be kept alive, had to be fed,
she imagined – with clues, or new murders, or something
of the sort. Here, Kevin Boyle had got hit on the head
with a poker, and that was the end of it. She felt somewhat foolish at her own anxiety over the letter she had
left in his rooms. But it had been natural to be hysterical
at first.

With a sigh, she rose, gathered up the new pile of
papers that had collected beside her chair, and carried
them to the black marble fireplace, trailing scraps behind
her. Just as she tossed them into the blaze, the doorbell
rang, and she went to answer it, hearing the hum of
Margaret's vacuum cleaner upstairs. There on her doorstep stood two youthful callers, a very intense looking
young man – somehow familiar, wearing regulation
college gear, and a roly-poly girl who was obviously a
student – who was, in fact, she realized in a moment,
Miss Innes, the editor of *The Holly*. 'Hullo,' said Freda
agreeably. 'What can I do for you?'

They had the violently defensive look about them that
she had seen on the faces of groups of students who feel
that their rights have been violated, and who have been
indulging their virtuous indignation until they reach such
a pitch as to call on sympathetic authorities for aid.
Among certain student groups, she herself was regarded
as an upholder of free living, and was not infrequently
called upon to right real or supposed wrongs of one kind
or other. She could not quite figure what the young man
had to do with the case – where had she seen his face? –
though on second thoughts, of course she could. Instead

of answering her, the two of them stood on the stoop, panting a little in the cold, and obviously trying to bring themselves to say something they had not as yet phrased to their own satisfaction. 'Well, come in, if the cat has your tongues,' she said finally, 'before we all freeze.'

'Yes, we'd just like to have a word with you, Mrs Cramm,' said the young man, suddenly glib and bustling as they crossed the threshold.

They refused to lay down their coats as she indicated, refused to sit down when they came into the living-room. They had a strange look about them as they stared at her; they began to irritate her a little. 'What in the world is the matter with you?' she snapped at last. 'You're staring at me as if I showed definite symptoms of small-pox or something. Is my slip showing?'

'Mrs Cramm,' said the young man after a dramatic pause, 'I'm Jack Donelly of the *Messenger*.' Of course, of course! That impertinent young idiot! 'I have a couple of questions I'd like answered about what you were doing in Kevin Boyle's rooms the night we saw you.'

Now she felt really annoyed. The whole scene came back to her – how she had come out the door of Kevin's house and had been half scared out of her wits by these two staring in the window of his apartment. She *had* been a fool about the letter – who would have cared if they had found it? It would have been slightly embarrassing at worst. 'What night?' she said sharply, not knowing yet whether she intended to lie or tell the truth.

The young man took a notebook out of his pocket and flipped the leaves. Why the Innes girl was here was more than Freda could make out. She thought she would report her to Bainbridge, since he had made such a point of having the students keep away from reporters. 'The night of

November seventeenth,' said the young man accusingly.

It was too ridiculous. She refused to lower her dignity by lying. 'I was looking for a letter I had left there,' she threw at the reporter. 'I had left it there one day when I left Mr Boyle's place in a rage because I'd had a fight with him. It was a letter from a poor relative of my late husband's, dunning me for money. Now you know as much as I do, and you may go, because I consider you fantastically impertinent and you are imposing on my hospitality. Miss Innes, I intend to speak to President Bainbridge about your collaboration with the press in a matter which he plainly does not want discussed in print.' As she talked, she grew angrier. What a pair of brats! — bursting in on her this way, and what a fool she was, deluded in thinking she was about to aid and abet a pair of errant lovers. And of course, the young man actually was attached to a paper, albeit one on which she was able to exert a certain amount of influence. Still, she could not be quite sure how much.

The young man was looking at her in a peculiar way — a very peculiar way indeed, as if he fancied himself a judge leaning down to lecture the prisoner at the bar. Which reminded her that she would very much like a glass of sherry before lunch, but she had no intention of offering any to *these*. 'And that was not your *last* visit to his apartment,' he enunciated, in the manner of a district attorney in a Grade B movie.

'*What* was not my last visit there?' Freda snapped back at him. 'The day I had the fight? No, it was not. I was at his rooms again on the night of November 17, as you just pointed out, looking for the letter I had left there. I hardly see how this can be of interest to your paper, Mr Donelly.'

'But,' the young man pressed in his overdone ominous tone, 'you have been back there more recently – *much* more recently!'

'No,' said Freda, with rising asperity, 'I have not. I think you'd better go now.' She raised one eyebrow and stared at them in her most quelling manner. Miss Innes shrank slightly and pulled at the young man's elbow, but he stood his ground.

Suddenly, looking at both of them, at their pale tense faces, Donelly's long and irregular, the girl's perfectly round, both of them with identical horn-rimmed glasses sliding down their very different noses, she wanted to laugh at them, but refused to do so. She saw it all now. They had constituted themselves a pair of detectives on the Kevin Boyle Murder Case, and she was their most likely suspect. She supposed the whole notion had grown that night they had caught her slipping out of Kevin's place. She supposed she had looked pretty suspicious. Suddenly her dignity did not seem worth maintaining. She rose abruptly and went to the secretary where the decanter and glasses stood. She poured three glasses and turned. 'You're behaving like utter babies,' she said amiably, 'but I'm so agreeable as to offer you a glass of sherry. Come on, sit down and tell me what this nonsense is all about.'

The Innes child had the grace to blush very red, but the reporter squared his jaw. 'What have you got against George Hungerford?' he shot at her. 'Does he know too much?'

'George Hungerford?' she repeated blankly, and stood still with a glass of sherry in each hand.

At that moment the girl gave a gasp and pointed to the desk. 'Look,' she half whispered, 'look, Jack, it's just like –'

Freda followed his finger, but saw only the mess of envelopes, returned cheques, and miscellany that she had just been sorting. But Donelly seemed to know what she meant at once. He dived at the desk and brought forth a brown cardboard notebook containing her monthly accounts. Suddenly she lost her temper completely and screamed. 'Here!' she yelled. 'What the hell do you think you're doing, rooting through my private papers? You get out of here before I call the police! Miss Innes, don't think you won't be disciplined for this abominable impertinence!'

The young man had actually opened her account book and was thumbing through it. A look of puzzlement came over his face. 'Oh,' he said weakly. Then he looked up at her. 'Is this your writing?'

'Of course it's my writing!' she said irritably, but unable to maintain her fury because of her growing curiosity. 'What in God's name did you think it was?'

But the young man's face renewed its fierceness. 'It doesn't prove a thing!' he cried. 'Anybody can change his writing. I'll just hang on to this. An expert –'

'Look,' said Freda. 'I won't call the police. I won't tell Bainbridge on Miss Innes. But will you for God's sake sit down and tell me what this is all about?'

'Where were you between five and six the afternoon of November 21st?' rapped the reporter, and glared at her, breathing heavily.

Deliberately, Freda set down the sherry glasses and went to her desk, extracted an engagement pad. 'I was,' she enunciated slowly, 'at a meeting of the Library Committee in Room 31 of College Hall. There are five other members of the committee, all of whom were present and will undoubtedly vouch for my presence. If you will call

234

Miss Austen, Mr Sancton, Mrs McGill and – um – Mr Horner and Miss Michaelson you'll find I have an iron-clad alibi for that period. and now, my good Holmes and Watson –'

The two looked at each other for a moment and sidled toward the sofa, sitting uncomfortably on the edge, as if to punish themselves. She handed them each a glass of sherry and sat down herself while they mumbled thanks.

'Well,' said Miss Innes resignedly, 'I guess it'll just have to be chalked up to reading too many detective stories. But honestly, Mrs Cramm, you looked like such a good suspect. Even Mr Marks – oh dear!' She blushed again, shutting her mouth quickly.

Freda lay back in her chair and roared. 'Oh, my lord!' she said at last, limply. 'Did Leonard Marks tell you I tried to murder *him*?'

Miss Innes was silent, but the young man, who on closer observation was neither as young as he looked nor as he acted, put in quickly, 'It wasn't only that, Mrs Cramm. Although what you were up to the day you scared the spit out of him up on the mountain is a mystery to me.'

Freda looked down at her sherry coyly. 'I frequently walk out to that wonderful old ruin. I'm thinking of buying it. That evening Mr Marks had come bounding out of the woods like such a beast from the jungle that I half felt I was protecting my virtue.'

'Bounding like a big fierce cottontail,' murmured Miss Innes, who was recovering her *savoir faire* as she absorbed sherry.

'It wasn't only Marks – or rather it was some other things he said that set us off,' said Donelly seriously. 'Someone has been systematically persecuting Mr

Hungerford. Someone who was – ah – rather intimate with Boyle. Hungerford won't go to the police about the thing, because the persecution takes the form of a journal which is planted in his room, full of – well, scurrilous statements about him.'

'Why in the world should *I* want to make scurrilous statements about George Hungerford, of all people?' said Freda in puzzlement. 'And if I did, why should I take the trouble to put them in a journal in his room? It seems to me that if a person wanted to make scurrilous – who started that word, anyway? – statements about another person, she would make them where they'd be heard.'

'Oh, I don't know,' said Kate Innes eagerly. 'It's the same principle as poison-pen letters; after all, nobody knows about *them* but the writer and the recipient.'

'Yes, but –' began Freda, and then threw up her hands. 'Well, it's just alien to my nature, that's all I can say. What in the world made you pick on me?'

The Innes girl blushed and played with her skirt, and Donelly cleared his throat. 'Well, it was a lot of little things,' he said belligerently.

'The story about the fight you and Mr Hungerford had before he went to the sanatorium was campus gossip,' the girl interrupted. 'Nobody knew just what it was about, or whether it was a real grudge or just that he was going off his rocker. And then this person who wrote the journal was a woman. She called herself Eloise, Mr Marks said. And she – she seemed – that is, she must have known Mr Boyle pretty well – wrote about it in the journal. And then Mr Marks heard her. He said – ' she stopped and blushed – 'well, he *said* she sounded just like you.'

But suddenly Freda rose and began to pace the floor. 'He actually *heard* the person?'

'That is why he followed you out into the country that day,' said the reporter. 'The day before, he had heard your voice – or what he thought was your voice – in Hungerford's apartment. On the same day a new entry appeared in the journal. That was when Hungerford told him all about the persecution – he'd been asleep at the time Marks heard the voice.'

'How in the world did Leonard hear a voice in Hungerford's apartment?' said Freda suddenly, stopping by the windows. 'Does he hang about the halls of that fantastic mansion waiting for Hungerford to appear?'

'Fantastic mansion?' said Kate. 'But didn't you know – Mr Hungerford moved! He moved to Kevin Boyle's apartment – just to escape the journal, he told Mr Marks. And then it followed him – even there! Maybe *especially* there! The woman actually gets into his rooms to write the thing!'

At last Freda was galvanized into action. She flew out to the coat closet and put on her coat. Then she whisked back to the living room and beckoned to the amazed couple there. 'Come along,' she said. 'You were quite right to feel some action should be taken. All this should have been in the hands of the police long ago. I'm going to George Hungerford's and get that journal!'

## Chapter 32

LEONARD had got him to bed, but by dint of a ruse he persuaded him to leave. He promised to go to sleep. He said he would not be able to sleep if he knew Leonard was in the other room. He pleaded that, after all,

Leonard would be just across the hall where he could easily hear him, and in any case the doctor would be here in half an hour or so. But after Leonard finally left, protesting and casting regretful backward looks, he crept from his bed like a naughty child and locked his outer door. For now he could no more lie still than he could cage a tempest. He was on fire, in flight, as dire as night, and everything about him was a little askew, as if the centre of gravity had shifted, as if he were climbing to the crest of one wave and down to the trough of the next as he walked across his once perfectly level floor; the imitation oriental carpet which Miss Stone had laid on his floor had suddenly become a jungle rioting with tropical plants and he was walking over the shifting treetops of the solid jungle, while the rhymes winged through his head like a flock of parrots, or a flight of pigeons in the draft between city buildings. He roamed and paced the rooms. He had a handkerchief in his hands which he was tearing to bits, dropping the shreds on the floor because he had to feel some kind of resistance, otherwise he would explode and fly into a thousand pieces before the doctor even came. At last he dressed. He felt he must dress. He shaved. 'Must lay the corpse out properly,' he mumbled. But he cut himself with the razor and bled. Corpses do not bleed. His hands shook. He was the corpse and the undertaker all at once. This is the church and this is the steeple. The sunlight coming through the diamond-paned windows was blinding blue, like the pointed rays of acetylene torches, burning through the bits of glass. And the snow, the delicate fragile snow, lying crystal on crystal like a thousand thousand lovers in a common bed, and the blue blue sky, blue as a steam whistle or a loud blast on a brass trumpet.

He was strung and humming, stripped like catgut, over bridge and around key. He shook and vibrated in response to the breath of the universe like the highest tautest violin string. He put a cigarette in his mouth and tried to light a match. Three times he could not strike the box, and when the little stick caught flame at last, he singed his eyebrow and did not touch the cigarette. He gave it up. He paced and paced the living-room with an uneven gait. Not the gait of a drunken man, for drunken men are loose and falling into stupor – but with the wild, twitching limp of an epileptic about to fall into a fit. In some far-off inner cavern of his brain where self-observation still resided, he knew he was beside himself. But outwardly he felt a queer joy in his own wildness, illness, madness. Never before had he felt so able to express the power in him that had gone muffled all these years except in his writing. It was as if at last the passion of creation could be taken off paper and put into life. In a rush of ecstasy he took the persecuting notebook and tore out half its pages, scattering them about the room. This was to symbolize that there was no more use for that kind of secondhand action, it could no longer touch him. Now let the murderess come herself, let Eloise attack him directly, for her mere paper words no longer had any meaning.

But the doctor was coming too. This he knew, and he knew he had something to say to the doctor, something which was absolutely imperative for him to say. Or pray this day one way ... He went back through the bedroom, pitching against the bed, steadying himself against the footrail. He clasped the edge of the basin and guided his hand to the knob of the medicine chest. By what feat of control he knew not, he extracted one of the sleeping capsules, separated its transparent halves, spilled out a little of the powder, and swallowed the rest. Then he went back to the living-room and sat down by the fire. He rocked back and forth in the wing chair, his head in his hands, simply because he could not be still. Suddenly he was roused by a pain in his foot. He looked down and saw his slipper smoking with heat, his foot almost in the fire. He began to laugh, but his laughter turned to tears, ran childishly down his cheeks. On the hearth beside his foot lay a black, curly head, pillowed boyishly on a folded arm. The intimacy of that hair, with the firelight defining each separate thread of it! To touch it, to feel it, to say: Kevin, come back ...

As the drug took hold, he became calmer. It did not make him drowsy at all, but only relaxed him a bit – thank God, otherwise he never could have said what he had to say to the doctor. Finally he would speak of the notebook, he would clear the girl of the change of madness; at last he would lay his burden in the hands of authority. He liked Forstmann. If it had not been too late, he would have gone to Forstmann long ago, to be cured. Once he had visited him professionally, indeed, and had approved that calm, sympathetic, recording face. But too late. He was too entrenched in illness by that time to be blasted out. Only in this hour of danger could he call on him. He must tell him of the danger in which they all stood. It menaced everyone, growing larger and larger, like ink spreading across a blotter. First Kevin, then the little girl – Molly – now himself – who next? Anyone, everyone.

On his mother's ormolu clock the minutes curled away. For a moment his mother came and stood beside him, her hand on his hair, in a way she had. But she did not speak. She only came the way she used to come to his study when he was at work, not speaking, not interrupting, but warning him that an interruption was at hand, that he must prepare for a meal or company. Then the doorbell buzzed. He twitched to his feet, jerked down his jacket, smoothed a hand over his hair. In the room a smell of burnt leather lingered from his scorched slipper.

He tried not to look too queer in greeting Forstmann, but gazing into the man's wide-set eyes, blue and magical as a Siamese cat's in his dark face, he had the feeling that already the doctor knew everything, there was scarcely need to say a word.

'Sit down,' he said, when he had ushered Forstmann in, his voice cracked, his hand making a tense upward gesture.

Slowly, gravely the psychiatrist took his place to one side of the fire, and Hungerford sat opposite. He imagined that in the black brief case on the floor might repose the mysterious implements to be used in administering last rites. Extreme unction. He cleared his throat, and restrained a titter, or a sob, he was not sure which. Like a fœtus miscarried before the sex can be determined. No. No sense in this.

'I wanted to talk to you,' he said, very slowly and carefully. He opened his mouth, but the wrong words came out. 'What's in your bag?'

'Notes,' said Forstmann, very calmly. 'Papers.'

'Oh,' he laughed foolishly. 'All at once I couldn't imagine what it would be a psychiatrist would carry. What sorts of implements, I mean.'

'What did you imagine might be there?' asked Forstmann conversationally.

'The things – whatever it is a priest carries for dying

people,' said Hungerford promptly. 'Of course, you know that's not what I meant to talk about at all.'

'No?' said Forstmann. 'What then?'

'It's about that little patient of yours – that little girl – Molly Morrison – is that her name? Strange, I couldn't remember it earlier. Now it's come back.'

'Yes, Molly Morrison,' said the doctor, twitching at his trouser leg. 'She told me about coming to you. I couldn't make much of it. I'd be very much obliged if you could throw some light on the matter.' But the cat's eyes were looking at him in frank scrutiny, saying, of course I know that this is not what you wish to talk about at all. However, they held infinite patience and ability to allow him to go his own gait.

Hungerford paused, picking his way among all the galaxies and myriads of dangerous words that swarmed like bees for him to choose from. 'First,' he said slowly, 'I must tell you that I am unable to give a clear account of what happened the day she – the day she first came here, because I seem to have – I seem to have suffered an attack of amnesia for the period of her visit.' He drew a breath, but Forstmann only nodded judiciously. 'Nevertheless,' he pushed on, 'I have reason to believe there actually was an attempt made on the girl's life.' He stopped. 'Just as she described it.'

Forstmann moved in his chair and cleared his throat. Would he never show emotion? 'You mean,' he said, 'there actually was an attempt made to strangle her?'

Something took hold of his own throat, as if he too were being strangled. In silence, he nodded. They both sat quietly until he could go on. Strange shiftings and undersea earthquakes were taking place on the floor of his brain, but he tried to maintain a surface calm. 'I found evidence,' he said at last.

'What sort of evidence?' asked Forstmann.

How was he to explain? It was so bald. 'First I must go back a bit,' he began, and stopped.

'Yes?' said Forstmann, after allowing him a pause.

He chose his words very carefully. 'All during this year,' he said, 'someone has been persecuting me. A woman. A woman named Eloise.' Again he had to stop. Why was it so hard?

'An acquaintance?' asked Forstmann. 'Someone who you believe has reason to dislike you?' He tactfully behaved as if he believed the whole thing.

'She's my sister,' blurted Hungerford, and then began to titter, for it had come off his blundering tongue without his having the least intention of saying it. 'How silly! I mean to say, she has the same name as a sister who died before my birth. Which leads me to believe this person must know a *great* deal about me – a great deal more than I can explain. I have no idea of who it is. No idea at all.'

'What did you say her name was?'

'Eloise,' said Hungerford. .As he said the name, he suddenly knew what she must look like. Like an idiot girl who had lived in the town where he grew up. Huge and hulking, built like a fat adolescent boy, with big flat feet and a strange walk, little pig's eyes ...

'What form does this persecution take?' said Forstmann matter-of-factly, quite as if he thought Hungerford were sane. He wanted to go and shake the doctor's hand for his fine performance. But instead he rose from his chair. The notebook was under a table where he had thrown it, with the leaves he had ripped scattered about. He gathered them up and put them between the covers, handed the book to Forstmann. 'A journal,' he said. 'A journal which has been appearing in my rooms ever since the beginning of the college year. I have come to believe this woman must have had something to do with Kevin Boyle's murder. And now that she has made this attempt on the little girl ... ' Suddenly his face contorted in the tic, and he was unable to speak until the tyrannical muscles released their grip.

Forstmann was thumbing through the notebook. 'If you believed this had to do with the murder,' he said thoughtfully, 'why didn't you show it to the police?'

The tic was doing a new thing. Instead of contracting only his face, it seemed to have taken hold of one whole side of his head, even of his brain, and was squeezing tighter and tighter. But he felt he must answer. 'Read – it – ' he forced out. 'I – couldn't.' He could see Forstmann's eyes staring at him, large and limpid. He heard his own words only faintly. He thought he could count on Forstmann to understand, to carry on, to ... Because he was at the absolute end. He might even be dying. This time he was not sure. He was being sucked down a corridor by an irresistible draught, to a broad, flat, grassless, treeless plain. And from the plain he looked up to a mountain which stood ominous and purple against the horizon. That mountain was his brain. And as he watched, he saw a crevice begin to open down its side, a terrible wound from which the bowels of the earth in all their foulness came spilling out, engulfing him in their sliminess, stifling him in their stench, like the patient under the ether cone, but his lungs were breathless, he was slipping sideways into space, his face contorting sidewise, his whole being changing, altering, crying out, Mother! like a dying man. Faintly, through the roar surrounding him, he heard Dr Forstmann's matter-of-fact voice saying, 'And you have no idea who the writer might possibly be?' And then he went altogether away.

## Chapter 33

'Of course I have,' said the voice irritably. 'I wrote it myself.'

Forstmann's whole being said to him: Don't show surprise! He grasped the notebook more tightly, and sat forward a bit. 'I thought you said you didn't know who wrote it,' he said very quietly.

'Not at all,' said the voice. 'I said no such thing. *He* did.'

The sun was pouring through the windows behind the chair where George Hungerford sat so that his face was dim in the shadow of the wing chair. But Forstmann could see that the tic had abated, leaving the face curiously lax. Had he known the man better, he would have said that there was something totally uncharacteristic about the expression on his face, but having seen him so seldom, he could not risk such a notion. Still, the face seemed to him to have a curiously secret smug look which drained it of all the tragedy and intelligence that made it so admirable ordinarily. 'Who is *he*?' he asked, as quietly as he knew how.

'Hoh,' said the voice scornfully, 'he, him, Jesus on the Cross, Prince Mishkin, our George, George Hungerford, who else?'

'And who are you?' asked Forstmann, very cautiously, very quietly, scarcely above a whisper.

'Why, I'm little sister Eloise,' simpered the voice,

nearly falsetto now, utterly horrifying in its grotesquerie, issuing from George Hungerford's mouth.

## Chapter 34

BAINBRIDGE sat at his desk, his head in his hands. Outside the windows the snow whirled dizzyingly. 'Please God,' he remarked devoutly, 'don't let the newspapers get hold of this.'

'I see no reason why they should,' said Forstmann. 'I see no reason why the police should, either. Let the whole thing simply dribble off, as it would have in any case. Hungerford is in a place where he can't do anyone any harm, anyway – there's no reason why he should be taken out of the State Hospital for the Insane, tried, and put back in again. And since he is in a condition which could legally be attested to as insane, there's actually no further evidence that he murdered Kevin Boyle than there was before.'

'Yet you're convinced that he did?' said Bainbridge curiously, lifting his head.

'Or that she did,' said Forstmann. He shook his head incredulously. 'Honestly, Bainbridge, this case has Miss Beauchamp, Doris Fischer, Dr Jekyll and Mr Hyde looking like a bunch of malingerers.'

'But George Hungerford,' wailed Bainbridge, 'was always the quietest, calmest, least troublesome – that is, with the exception of the nervous breakdown. Forstmann, if this were a joke, I assure you it would be a very bad joke, even in the rowdy medical circles which you frequent.'

'It's not a joke,' said Forstmann, looking serious. 'I've had Hungerford under observation for two weeks. I have placed him under narcotics about once a day. Each time I do so, the second personality – Eloise, as she calls herself–'

'Eloise!' exclaimed Bainbridge disgustedly.

Forstmann sat forward. 'That's one of the most fascinating sidelights on the whole thing. In his waking state – or in the role of George Hungerford – he is unable to remember any of the history that obviously gives rise to the second personality – Eloise. But in the guise of Eloise, he tells a perfectly connected story about how as a small child his mother called him by the name of the sister who died in infancy, dressed him in girl's clothes, and encouraged him to assume female characteristics altogether.'

'It just doesn't sound reasonable,' said Bainbridge, shaking his head bullishly. 'Hungerford has none of the ordinary homosexual mannerisms. God knows we've had enough around for me to recognize the signs when I see them.'

'He rejected the female elements in his nature so violently that they actually regrouped themselves into a second personality – that's the only way I can think of to describe it,' said Forstmann.

'Why?' said Bainbridge. 'Most men have some womanly characteristics, just as most women have some manly ones. What's the harm?'

'The harm is when a man has such a large admixture of the female in his nature that his whole sexual status becomes endangered. As near as I've been able to make out, Hungerford was encouraged to develop his female potentialities, so called, far beyond his male ones with his mother. Yet outside the home, the atmosphere which he lived in was so rigidly conventional that he knew he stood in terrible danger from not only his schoolmates but other adults, and, in a strange way, even his mother. She couldn't have given him a better background for psychosis if she'd known what she was about. For the first four or five years of his life he was actually called Eloise by her. (As Hungerford, he remembers none of this, by the way.) Then, when it came time to cut off his curls and take him out of Lord Fauntleroy suits, even his mother recognized that he must become a boy. So that then she began to rebuke him for behaving in the way that she had encouraged.'

'You *couldn't* be making this up,' groaned Bainbridge.

'Well, in a way I am,' said Forstmann. 'I'm trying to make something clear to you that isn't clear to me at all – I'm making very tenuous connections seem strong, and I'm reading in interpretations which may be quite incorrect. I'm taking bits of other cases of multiple personality and grafting them on to this one, simply because if I couldn't make some sort of sense of the business there'd be nothing for it but to say the man was possessed of a devil.'

'That's much the better explanation,' said Bainbridge emphatically.

'It's certainly easier,' admitted Forstmann, 'and I'll admit freely for a moment I might have been tempted to accept it myself. I always had a great admiration for Hungerford and his work. When I went to see him that day the first thing I thought was what a noble sort of head he has – like a Roman medallion. He was obviously extremely confused and on the border of some sort of maniac state. But when I heard that eerie falsetto voice coming out of his mouth, saying, I'm Eloise, I must confess that my hair rose on my head.'

Bainbridge sighed and shook his head. 'Well,' he began again, 'why hasn't Eloise appeared before? You mean she's been – I mean, he's had a double personality all this time and it never came out before? How is that?'

'I would take a guess that there may previously have been some sort of minor somnambulistic state in which she appeared, but never with the same distinctness as after his return from the sanatorium when he began to use nembutal to put him to sleep in the afternoons. It's possible that the reason for his insomnia at night at this time was the fact that Hungerford felt that Eloise was more out of his control than ever before, and he feared what she would do when she made her appearance.'

'Why should she have got worse all of a sudden? What happened to him?'

'I don't think it was all of a sudden. First came the death of his mother, about which he had terrible and quite conscious guilt feelings. His lifetime devotion to her stands as nothing in his mind beside the fact that he was not at her deathbed. This cut off his creative ability – evidently as a form of self-punishment he found himself unable to write after her death. Then his life was terribly empty of affection without her, until Kevin Boyle came to the college. In the role of George Hungerford he became very fond of him. In the role of Eloise, he fell madly in love with him.'

'But as Eloise, how did she know about Kevin Boyle? Eloise never saw him, did she?'

'He had what is not uncommon in cases of dissociated personality – partial amnesia. As Hungerford he had no recollection of the existence of Eloise, but as Eloise, he had total recall of his life as George Hungerford. In fact, Eloise seems to regard herself as existing at the same time as George Hungerford, but under a sort of spell, so that she cannot act.'

Bainbridge, who had been frantically rearranging his desk, twisting bits of paper, and sharpening pencils with his penknife, now could sit still no longer, but rose from his swivel chair and paced round the desk to lean over Forstmann, who sat deep in his chair, his knees jutting. 'Julian,' he said desperately, 'may I smell your breath?'

'Certainly,' said Forstmann, grinning, and blew at him.

Bainbridge sighed and went back behind his desk. 'The world would have seemed so much more *stable*,' he said wistfully, 'if you had been drinking.'

Forstmann stopped smiling and spoke soberly. 'Hungerford used a phrase that impressed me very much: the poetry of unreason. He said he had been unable to come to a psychiatrist, even though he knew he was mentally ill, because he never found one who could grasp the poetry of unreason. Well, I could make a different diagnosis of why he didn't come, but what he said would remain true. Because psychiatrists aren't intended to be poets, they're scientists, they're obliged professionally to take the dew off the rose and analyse it as $H_2O$. That's their function. But when, on my busman's holidays, I've thought of madness, it seems most easily explained to me as poetry in action. A life of symbol rather than reality. On paper one can understand Gulliver, or Kafka, or Dante. But let a man go about *behaving* as if he were a giant or a midget, or caught in a cosmic plot directed at himself, or in heaven or hell, and we feel horror – we want to disavow him, to proclaim him as far removed as possible from ourselves.' He stopped suddenly and looked at Bainbridge. 'For God's sake, Lucien, stop staring at me with your mouth hanging open as if you took my every word for gospel!'

Bainbridge shut his mouth and made a noise which sounded like 'humph.' 'Well,' he said more audibly, 'and when did he – she – tell you about killing Boyle?'

'Almost immediately,' said Forstmann. 'We were talking about the notebook. First Hungerford was speaking as Hungerford. Suddenly that very distorting tic he has came over his face and he reappeared in the personality of Eloise.'

'Wait a minute,' cried Bainbridge. 'I thought Eloise only appeared when he was asleep or under the influence of a drug.'

'It later appeared, when we examined him, that he had taken some nembutal before my arrival. Not enough to put him to sleep, but enough to release the personality of Eloise, who must have been awfully close to the surface even before he took the drug, to judge from Leonard Marks' description of the state he was in earlier in the morning.'

'What sort of person is Eloise?' asked Bainbridge curiously. 'I mean, can you tell?'

'She's a pretty unattractive female,' said Forstmann, 'if you'll pardon the loose use of the term. She is, I should say, brutal, ruthless, cunning, passionate – a real Mr Hyde type.'

'But that's so opposite to anything Hungerford could ever possibly be!' cried Bainbridge.

'Maybe if he'd found it easier to be some of those things he wouldn't have found it necessary to develop Eloise,' said Forstmann. 'Do you want me to give a lecture on the protestant ethic in education and its role in the formation of neuroses of our culture, or shall I just make out a reading list?'

'Spare me,' said Bainbridge quickly. 'I'm too old. But I still want to know about this murder.'

'Well,' said Forstmann, leaning forward and opening the zipper of his brief-case, 'read this.' He pulled out a few lined sheets of paper, covered with great toppling calligraphy, and handed them to Bainbridge. 'Begin here.'

Bainbridge frowned, looked at the sheets, pulled a pair of reading glasses out of a leather case and set them on his nose. He formed the words with his lips, trying to make out the strange writing, and then he began to read aloud:

Dear Dr Forstmann, old kid old coffin-face old mortality, this is the letter of how I killed Kevin Boyle – my sweet my lovely, but he would not have me no, he turned his face away. Listen, I said to him, I said Listen Kevin, I am your love your lovely, but he could not see me, he could not see me for the Other One that was without, that enemy, that tomb of ice in which I lay betrayed, our Hungerford. Listen, Kevin, I said, I am free, now no one can stop me (for this was the first time of my coming into the light) but he could see none of me, he turned from me, from my woman's heart, he turned and I could see that he hated me, that there was disgust and horror in his face and this I could not stand. You do not know how terrible this is because your heart is ice, you do not know how it is to be a woman, you are nothing but a nothing a nothing a no. So I took the poker up from the hearth and crushed his head in as he was going to the door. How

did I do it? Simply like this. I took the poker and I hit
him. And there he lay with his dear sweet head
mashed in like a tender little eggshell, like an egg with
the chick all unborn and oozing out the crevices ...

Bainbridge laid the papers down on the desk and whistled
long and low.

'The poetry of unreason,' said Forstmann softly.

'The poetry of unreason,' echoed Bainbridge.

## Chapter 35

HONEY Sacheveral sat in the Harlow Taproom looking
like an angel and drinking an Alexander. Petey Jones of
Amhurst, sitting opposite her, heaved a sigh which
caused the button of his dizzyingly plaid jacket to fly
open. 'Gee, Honey,' he said, 'If I sat on that side, I could
hold your hand. If I sit on this side I can look at you.
Gee, Honey, I don't know *what* to do.' In desperation, he
drank off half his glass of beer.

Honey giggled, threw back her plumes of hair, and
finished her Alexander. 'Silly,' she said, 'you could hold my
hand *across* the table. Can I have another Alexayunduh?'

Petey Jones sighed again and took the white hand
(magenta tipped) which she extended in one of his own
rather grubby paws. With the other he surreptitiously
counted ready cash under the table.

'Know what?' said Honey complacently, after Petey
had summoned the waitress and ordered her drink, 'Mr
Hungerford's gone crazy. They took him to the State
Hospital.'

'Gee,' said Petey, 'George Hungerford?'

'Uh-huh,' said Honey.

'Gosh,' said Petey reverently, 'we used a book of his in a Sophomore English course. Crazy, huh?'

'Uh-huh,' said Honey. 'But then, intellectual people are more likely to go crazy than other people.'

'Yeah,' said Petey, dazzled, 'I guess they are, at that.'

'It's because they *think* too much,' Honey elaborated. 'I don't think it's a good idea for a person to think too much. Even for a man.'

'Kinda wears your brain out, I guess,' said Petey, and swallowed some beer.

'That's right,' said Honey. 'My mama says a girl never should think too much. Just have a good time and leave the thinking to the men. My mama says a woman's place is in the home, and who in the world wants to just sit around home and *think*?'

Petey Jones leaned over the table ardently. When he felt ardent, and also when he drank beer, his left eye became slightly crossed. 'I like my women *feminine*!' he said, as if he were supporting a harem.

'My mama always brought me up to be a feminine sort of girl,' said Honey complacently. 'Can I have another Alexayunduh?'

'Sure,' said Petey nervously, feeling in his pocket to where there was a dollar and seven cents in change.

'But,' said Honey contemplatively, 'you can't honestly say an intellectual girl *never* gets a man. Now you take Kate Innes.'

Petey signalled the waitress for another Alexander and took a very small sip of his beer. 'Innes?' he said. 'Do I know her?'

'I don't guess so,' said Honey. 'She's the editor of *The*

*Holly*. Now she's a right messy lookin' sort of a girl, and *real* smart, so's you'd never expect her to do anything – well, you know, *foolish*. But I'm blessed if she didn't up and elope with this cute little ole reporter we met right here in this very booth!'

'You mean right *here*?' asked Petey meaningfully. 'Maybe it's an omen!'

'Omen?' questioned Honey.

'*You* know,' explained Petey, 'like there they were in this very booth and *they* eloped, and now here we are, too.'

'Why, Petey!' said Honey appreciatively. 'That's right romantic of you! Can I have another Alexayunduh?'

'Gee, Honey,' said Petey nervously, 'do you think you ought to? You've had three and it's only nine o'clock.'

'Oh, Petey!' cried Honey reproachfully. 'The Sacheverals always carry their liquor like gentlemen and ladies!'

'All right,' sighed Petey. 'Wait till the waitress comes around this way again.'

'And speakin' of crazy people,' said Honey, 'they let that little Morrison girl come right back to Birnham House. Now I call that right silly. She might murder us all in our beds, for all we know.'

'Oh,' said Petey knowingly, 'that's the one they had the piece about in the *Messenger* – about did she murder Kevin Boyle.'

'Well,' said Honey doubtfully, 'they said she couldn't have because I saw her in Birnham on the day of the murder between five and six or something, but how do they ever figure it out about a thing like that? I mean, maybe she did it some other time, or something.' Honey's smoky eyelashes were hanging low over her halcyon eyes. 'Oh, Petey!' she mumbled, yawning as frankly as a kitten. 'I'm *so* sleepy. That ole Alexayunduh better hurry up!' She rested her flower head on her rosy palm.

'Maybe they – had some sort of other evidence,' said Petey distractedly. 'Listen, Honey, don't go to sleep – don't you want some coffee or something?'

'Don't want – nothin' – but – a – little old – Alexayunduh,' murmured Honey, drooping lower over the table.

'Listen, Honey!' cried Petey desperately. 'let's dance – come on – I'll put some real jive on the box!'

But Honey was out like a light, her Botticelli countenance flushed, her cheek pillowed on her hand.

'Wake up! Wake up!' cried Petey frantically. 'Honey, you can't –' and then, as the waitress came down between the tables, he tried to look as if he were interested only in his few drops of beer. When she was out of sight again, he raised his honest whiskerless countenance to the ceiling and whispered to nobody in particular, 'Gee, what are you supposed to do when your girl passes out?'